Praise for M

'Ian Simpson is a real f..... *Murder on Page One* is a beautifully crafted, gripping piece of crime fiction that holds the attention from page one until the very end.'

Alexander McCall Smith

'This well-crafted, pacey, humorous whodunit from ex-judge Ian Simpson is an highly enjoyable read.'

Lovereading

'An enjoyable, witty page-turner brought to life by the well-drawn, believable characters.'

Journal of the Law Society of Scotland

'The twists and turns keep pace with the rising body count in what is a highly enjoyable piece of crime fiction. A follow-up encounter with Inspector No would be most welcome.'

University of Edinburgh Journal

And for *Murder on the Second Tee*:

'An entertaining police procedural and full of well-drawn characters ... recommended.'

Eurocrime

'Great fun ... as a great, non-challenging accompaniment to a long flight or a holiday read it is perfect.'

Book Talk Bournemouth

'A superb read, following on the success of his first book, *Murder on Page One* ...The author weaves together two strong story lines ... (he) clearly has fun exposing and developing the bankers' characters. St Andrews is defined to a tee. ... This is a rollicking read.'

Journal of the Law Society of Scotland

'Definitely a series to watch out for from a new talent on the crime writing scene.'

Crime Fiction Lover

'An engrossing mystery'

The Herald

MURDER

IN

COURT THREE

Matador
9 Priory Business Park
Wistow Road
Kibworth Beauchamp
Leicester LE8 0RX, UK
Tel: (+44) 116 279 2299
Fax: (+44) 116 279 2277
Email: books@troubador.co.uk
Web: www.troubador.co.uk/matador

ISBN 978 1784622 138

British Library Cataloguing in Publication Data.
A catalogue record for this book is available from the British Library.

Typeset in 12pt Minion Pro by Troubador Publishing Ltd, Leicester, UK
Matador is an imprint of Troubador Publishing Ltd

Printed and bound in the UK by TJ International, Padstow, Cornwall

MURDER

IN

COURT THREE

IAN SIMPSON

For Rosie, Matilda, Harry and Verity

What man was ever content with one crime?

Juvenal, Satires xiii

The characters you will meet (and those associated with them):

The Police

Deputy Chief Constable Stanley Davidson
Detective Chief Inspector Maclean, Edinburgh
Detective Inspector Flick Fortune, Cupar
Detective Inspector Fergus Maxwell, her husband, Dundee
Chief Superintendent Graeme Traynor, Edinburgh
Lynda Traynor, his wife
Detective Sergeant Lance Wallace, Cupar
Detective Constable Billy di Falco, Cupar
Detective Constable 'Spider' Gilsland, Cupar
Detective Sergeant Bagawath Chandavarkar, 'Baggo', Serious Fraud Office
Constable Alex McKellar, St Andrews
Detective Inspector Bryan Hepburn, Coatbridge
Detective Sergeant Kelly, Glasgow
Sergeant Smith, Glasgow

The Lawyers

Lord Hutton, a judge
The Dean of the Faculty of Advocates
Kenneth Cuthbert QC
Jen Cuthbert, his wife
Rob Bertram, Advocate
Molly Bertram, his wife
Percy Oliphant, Advocate
John Logan, Advocate

The Fraud Trial

Lord Tulloch, the judge
Farquhar Knox QC, crown counsel
Eloise Knox, his wife
Ranald Knox, his son
Reginald Buchan, his brother-in-law
Mark Radcliffe QC, substitute crown counsel
Melanie Arbuthnot, Advocate, crown junior counsel
Lachlan Smail, a farmer
Nicola Smail, his wife
John and Ellie Primrose, his friends
Gideon Maltravers, a planner
Joe Thomson, a builder
John Burns, a timeshare salesman

The Others

Ex-Detective Inspector Noel Osborne
Pete Bothwell, a journalist
Tam Walker, a forger
Mona McBride, his girlfriend
Father Neil, a priest
Johnny Dolan, a waiter
Gary Thomson, a waiter
Brenda Lenaghan, an artist
Lord and Lady Craigdiller, the chief Archer and his wife
Dr MacGregor, a pathologist

1

'… and you will be hanged by the neck until you are dead.' Speaking quietly, Farquhar Knox QC glared through sepulchral darkness towards the empty dock which, over the years, had held many of Scotland's most notorious criminals. For a moment he wished he had sat as a judge when trials were short and sentences could be for ever. How times had changed. He leaned back in the high-backed leather chair, well-padded for today's softer judges, and checked his fly zip. It was nearly time to go.

He heard a creak to his right and swung round, prepared to bully an intruder into going away. But the blustering tirade died on his lips as the sharp point of an arrow pierced his dinner shirt, entered his torso below the ribs and was pushed up until it penetrated his heart.

A few gurgles were the last sounds Farquhar Knox made. His own day of judgement had arrived.

2

'This is a nightmare,' Stanley Davidson stated. Scotland's Deputy Chief Constable in charge of Crime and Operational Support swivelled his chair away from his desk and looked out at the lawns of Tulliallan Castle, where the country's senior police officers were based. The sun shone on grass that was green and carefully striped by the mower. The trees were in leaf and still had the yellow tinge of new growth. It was Sunday morning and Davidson had missed his tee time on a day perfect for golf. But that was not the cause of his nightmare.

He turned to the two officers, one from Edinburgh the other from Fife, on the other side of the desk. 'So after a glittering function at Parliament House on Friday night, with half the great and the good present, an eminent QC who is prosecuting a high-profile trial is found dead in the judge's chair of Court Three. He has an arrow in his heart and we are told he probably had sex minutes before he died. The arrow was one used by the Royal Company of Archers and now there are rumours that he was having an affair with the wife of the Divisional Commander responsible for the inquiry. Have I missed out anything?'

Detective Inspector Flick Fortune said nothing. The shock on receiving the phone call informing her of

Farquhar Knox's murder had given way to anxiety. He had been prosecuting the big fraud trial in which she was the senior investigating officer. The effect on the trial might be drastic. The later call the previous evening, from the DCC himself, summoning her to this emergency meeting, had perplexed her. She was a Fife officer and the murder had taken place in Edinburgh. Now she was beginning to understand, and she was apprehensive. Instinctively, she put her hand on her swollen stomach. Her baby kicked out in the womb, as if to protest.

'Well, there's the press, sir.' Chief Inspector Maclean from Edinburgh had a lantern jaw and a lugubrious manner. 'They're still obsessed by the fraud and the missing four point five million pounds, but it won't be long till they realise there are other lines of inquiry. Involving sex,' he added mournfully.

'What is the evidence that Knox had sex just before he was killed?' Davidson asked.

Maclean cleared his throat. 'There were stains on his clothes, the front of his shirt and his boxers.'

'And what about Mrs Traynor's involvement?'

'She was seen conversing with the deceased in a confidential manner after dinner. A number of witnesses noticed them. Kenneth Cuthbert QC, a friend of the deceased's admitted there were rumours of an affair between them. When pressed, Mr Cuthbert conceded the deceased had a reputation as a ladies' man.' He paused, looked down and cleared his throat again. 'There have been rumours circulating about Mrs Traynor and men, sir.'

'I know that.' Davidson said sharply. He knew those rumours were true. The woman was a liability to her long-suffering husband, Chief Superintendent Graeme Traynor, and the further he climbed the more embarrassing she had become. Six months earlier, she had seduced then harassed a good-looking young detective sergeant before he put in an urgent request for a transfer. Her behaviour had been a matter of official concern before this situation arose. When he had been appointed Deputy Chief Constable, Davidson had been particularly thankful his wife was quiet and supportive in company, a rock for the family at home.

'Do we know the time of death?' he asked.

Maclean said, 'The body was found about three on Saturday morning by a security guard and he had been dead for some hours, sir. Knox was observed talking to Mrs Traynor shortly before ten, and we think that is the last time he was seen alive. There was an archery competition which finished about twenty past ten and all the bows and arrows were stored in a room not far from Court Three immediately after that. The murder could have taken place from, say, ten twenty-five onwards. We'll have a clearer picture after the post mortem, sir.'

'How advanced is your inquiry?'

'We've managed to interview some of the people present, but it was a while before we realised there was a, well, a problem. And it's impossible to focus inquiries on our own Divisional Commander and his wife and remain discreet. The crime scene has been thoroughly gone over but when I heard about the complication I got Dr

MacGregor from Dundee to do the post mortem. It'll be taking place now.'

'Is there a Mrs Knox?'

'Yes, sir, quite a grand lady, I gather. When the function ended at half past twelve she left with the Cuthberts. She was angry with her husband and assumed he had gone off without her. It wouldn't have been the first time, apparently.'

'And you are unable to exclude Graeme Traynor as a suspect?'

Maclean shook his head. 'I wish I could, sir. After the meal everyone seemed to mill about. I haven't spoken to the Chief Superintendent. Or his wife. I thought it best not to.'

'You're probably right.' Davidson grimaced. It was as bad as he had feared. 'Do you have any suspects at all apart from the Traynors and Mrs Knox?'

'Not really, sir, except if you count two of the accused Mr Knox was prosecuting who were at the function.' Flick sighed and shifted in her seat. Nearly six weeks from her delivery date, she was uncomfortable for much of the time and looking forward to winding down during her last two weeks before going on maternity leave. A rugby fan, this conversation made her feel like a full-back waiting to catch a high ball with the opposing scrum thundering towards her.

Maclean referred to a note. 'Lachlan Smail and Gideon Maltravers were there. So was Mrs Smail.'

'What exactly was the occasion?' Flick asked, feeling the need to become involved in the discussion.

'Very grand,' Maclean said. 'The Faculty of Advocates and The Royal Company of Archers had a celebration to mark their long, shared history. It was held in Parliament Hall, drinks then dinner. After dinner the tables were cleared and there was an archery contest, Advocates against Archers, down the length of the hall with a bullseye target at one end. The Archers won. The bows and arrows were stowed in the judges' retiring room shortly after ten-twenty and a band started. There was dancing till it ended at half past midnight.'

'How did Smail and Maltravers come to be there?' she asked.

'I believe Smail is an Archer and Maltravers was on the table of a QC who does a lot of planning work.'

Davidson asked, 'How has the trial been going?' He looked at Flick. 'And remind me what it's all about.'

'Well, sir, the fourth week starts tomorrow. It's in the High Court building across the road from Parliament House. Knox seemed quite happy with the way the evidence has come out. You probably know it was an elaborate fraud, well thought-out with good technical knowledge, graphics, artist's impressions and so on. The accused persuaded the Scotgrow Enterprise Loan Fund to advance them four point five million pounds for a golf course near St Andrews designed by Jack Nicklaus.' She paused, conscious of her South of England accent, then grinned. 'Only I doubt if there was ever going to be a golf course and for sure Jack Nicklaus had never heard of it. The accused told the Loan Fund that to get the detailed plans Nicklaus had prepared, they needed to lodge two million in a Cayman Islands account before Christmas. Once they had the plans they could submit a planning application early in the New Year. The Loan Fund had been criticised for not lending enough to new enterprises, so, for political reasons, they paid the whole four point five million to the fraudsters before Christmas. All the money was sent to the Caymans and just disappeared. We have a case against Smail, who owns the land, Maltravers, a planning consultant, and a builder called Thomson. They are all out on bail. The brains behind it, Burns, has been in custody since his arrest in January. We've been watching the trial in the hope of getting some idea where the money might be, but nothing's come up. Our best guess is that Burns has salted it away for when he gets out.'

'There's been a lot of press interest,' Maclean said. 'They're gunning for the Loan Fund managers and the Scottish Government are watching closely as it's public money that's missing.'

Davidson leaned on his desk and looked hard at Maclean. 'Do you have any instinct about this murder? Do you think it was some Black Widow killing her lover, a jealous partner, or something else, perhaps something to do with the fraud?'

Maclean scratched his jaw. 'I can't say I do, sir.'

A concerned look on his face, Davidson looked at Flick. 'I'd forgotten you were pregnant. When do you go on maternity leave?'

'In a fortnight's time, sir.'

He grimaced. 'Do you have a good team?'

'Yes, sir. Small but very good.'

Davidson leaned back in his chair and turned again to the window, staring out but seeing nothing. After some thought, he faced the officers. 'It is impossible for Edinburgh officers to continue to investigate this murder given the position of their Divisional Commander. I am going to place Inspector Fortune in charge of the inquiry, using Fife personnel.'

A knot formed in her stomach. She wanted to scream, refuse to accept the assignment. Her life was about to change. For the next year or so she was going to be a mother first, a detective inspector second. She saw the DCC searching her face for a reaction. She closed her eyes. 'Alright, sir,' she heard herself say. She felt a hard kick in her womb.

The DCC continued, 'The press will be told that we believe the murder could be connected to the fraud trial, and that an officer familiar with that is in the best position to identify the killer. And we will stick to that story. Every effort is to be made to keep Chief Superintendent Traynor's name out of the press, including the internet. Any officer found leaking details will be prosecuted. Please let that be known. Any questions?'

Flick said, 'I have one or two, sir, but they don't concern my Edinburgh colleague.'

She swapped contact details with Maclean, who promised to e-mail everything he had to her. As the door closed behind him, Davidson looked at her and smiled.

'I can see that this may be the last thing you want to land in your lap right now, but the reputation of the force is at stake, and if there was anyone else who could credibly take this on I would have given it to them.'

There was a kindly expression on his face. She remembered he was a family man himself. Feeling tears were not far away, she swallowed and managed a grin.

'You must give this absolute priority,' he said earnestly. 'I'll shift officers from other Divisions if you need cover in Fife. I don't want any Edinburgh input into the inquiry apart from what's already been done. And I rely on you to be thorough. If Graeme Traynor murdered Knox, you must get evidence to convict him. If it was someone else, and I hope it was, their QC will doubtless try to say you never properly investigated Traynor. You must be able to demonstrate that you left no stone unturned to see if he murdered his wife's lover, if Knox was his wife's lover. Right?'

'Right, sir.'

'Hopefully you will discover it was not Lynda Traynor that Knox had sex with before he was killed, but it's common knowledge that she led her husband a merry dance. I have never been close to him, and what I know I've heard from others, but I can give you this file which sheds some light on her behaviour and their marriage.' He removed a thin, brown folder from a drawer and slid it across his large, highly polished desk. 'It'll be a good starting point. As you will realise, it's very sensitive. It was not stored electronically in case it was shared inappropriately. I rely on you to be as discreet as possible, though that will not be easy.'

Flick picked up the file and opened it. It contained a few sheets of A4 paper covered in typescript with scrawled marginal notes.

Davidson continued, 'I think your Incident Room should be in Cupar. It's near St Andrews so it will look as if we think the murder is connected to the fraud. You'll have your own computers there and it'll keep you away from Edinburgh.'

'Right, sir.'

'Can you think of any reason connected to the fraud why someone should want to kill Knox?'

She shook her head. 'Honestly, no. Do you think this will end the trial, sir?'

He snorted. 'With lawyers you can never tell.' Flick knew he was himself a qualified solicitor, and was interested to hear disgust in his voice. He smiled at her. 'I've heard a lot of good things about you, Inspector, including that you're a rugby fan. I wouldn't be throwing you this hospital pass if I didn't think you could cope. But keep me informed of developments. If there's anything I can do to help, anything, let me know.'

She had heard that before from senior officers who had ducked below the parapet as soon as the going got tough. She looked in the DCC's eyes and thought she recognised sincerity. 'Right, sir. There is one thing. An officer from the Serious Fraud Office helped our original investigation. An old colleague of mine from our days in Wimbledon. He knows all about money laundering and stuff like that. I'm sure he'd be a huge help in our inquiry, particularly with the tight deadline. He's actually in Scotland as Knox wanted him around to comment on Burns's evidence. Knox was cross-examining Burns on Friday afternoon and was due to continue tomorrow morning.'

'I'll make the call to the SFO tomorrow. What's his name?'

'Detective Sergeant Bagawath Chandavarkar. His family come from Mumbai,' she added, seeing Davidson's raised eyebrows.

After spelling the name for him, Flick left the Deputy Chief Constable. She had not met him before and he struck her as being intelligent and practical. When he had been appointed, there had been mutterings that he did things too much by the book and would not tolerate what some termed 'old-fashioned methods'. If that was true, he was absolutely her idea of what a senior police officer should be like.

Tulliallan is on the west border of Fife. As she drove east to her home in St Andrews, Flick adjusted her mental vision of the next few weeks and planned how she should start this challenging and high-profile inquiry. But why, oh why, had it come at this particular time in her life? She wondered what Fergus would say. And her dad. She dreaded telling him when she phoned him that evening.

As she approached St Andrews, on her left were the flat fields where the Jack Nicklaus Diamond Links were to have been laid out. Cows and sheep grazed contentedly on new grass and pigs snuffled about on bare earth beside the sludgy mudbanks of the Eden Estuary. The bank of a railway line, disused since the 1960s, created a weal across the otherwise featureless ground supposed to become 'one of the greatest finishing stretches in the world'. The fraudsters had produced inspired paintings of how the finished project would look, a metamorphosis of heroic proportions. A song title from the musical *Barnum* came to her, *'There's a Sucker Born Every Minute'* and she wished she could remember the words.

3

There was no reply to her shouted greeting when Flick returned to her grey, sandstone house on the west of St Andrews but an aroma of roasting meat filled the hall. Her husband Fergus Maxwell, a detective inspector with the Dundee police, inspired by what she thought of as gastronomic pornography on the television, had become enthusiastic about cooking. He had discovered that a shoulder of lamb, slowly roasted at a low heat, required the same cooking time as he took for a round of golf and a pint, so was perfect for a Sunday morning. The rissoles he made from the leftovers were easily warmed up after a midweek evening game. Feeling bloated, Flick would have liked something lighter, particularly in warm weather, but she didn't want to curb his enthusiasm. She made herself coffee and sat at the kitchen table, noting that the only part of the voluminous Sunday newspaper that bore signs of having been read was the sports section.

Curious about the contents of the file, she had been tempted to stop the car and read it on her way home. Sipping her de-caf coffee with the usual pang of regret that it was not the real stuff, she opened the folder. It contained two reports, both relating to Lynda Traynor's extra-marital activities. She wondered initially if a male partner of a senior officer would be investigated as thoroughly, but it did not take long to see that Mrs Traynor was a very loose cannon who had given no thought to her husband's career as she indulged herself.

The first report went back four years. An undercover officer had spotted her alone in a South Edinburgh pub under surveillance by the drugs squad. Worse, she had been greeted by the owner and went through the back with him, reappearing after half an hour, her face flushed. There had been half a dozen similar liaisons observed before the superintendent who had compiled the report spoke with Graeme Traynor. He had taken the news calmly, more concerned by the identity of her lover than surprised by her infidelity. The pub meetings had stopped and when the raid came there was no sign of Mrs Traynor. Her lover had been convicted and was one third of the way through a ten year sentence. In theory at least, Flick thought, as few were made to serve anything like the time handed down by the courts. A marginal note in red biro read: 'Strongly warned to prevent wife from gaining confidential or operational information. W.W.' Flick recognised the initials of the then Chief Constable of the now defunct Lothian and Borders force.

More recently Detective Sergeant Malloy had requested a transfer from Edinburgh. He had chatted and flirted with Mrs Traynor at a police function then accepted her invitation to meet her in a hotel in Peebles. He had described the sex as 'awesome', something that Superintendent MacKay of Inverness, the writer of the second report, recorded with presbyterian disapproval.

Malloy had begun to think with his brain and worked out that making a cuckold of his Divisional Commander was not a great career move. Lynda had not taken rejection lying down and had pestered him with phone calls and texts until he had felt compelled to speak to a senior officer. MacKay had been brought in and had spoken with Traynor, who had not appeared to be particularly hurt, more concerned that the affair should not become widely known. The sergeant was now working in Glasgow having been lectured by MacKay to abstain from adultery and other immoral behaviour. 'Mrs T sexually insatiable. Keep an eye on her as potential embarrassment to police. GT to go no further.' The less biblical marginal note was not initialled, but it spelled the end of Traynor's upward mobility.

Who needs a tabloid Sunday newspaper if you can read a file like this, Flick thought. She could not understand Lynda Traynor. If she was fed up with her husband, why didn't she simply leave him? It was almost as if she had selected lovers who would embarrass him. And his reactions had been restrained. Too much so, perhaps. Flick could see an affair with Knox as being the last straw. Traynor having had a few drinks and seeing his wife go to meet a lover might well have felt murderous. He had to be a suspect. Flick realised that she had already formed a strong dislike of Mrs Traynor. Apart from anything else she was responsible for the later stages of her pregnancy being thrown into confusion.

She phoned her team individually, calling a meeting that evening at six in the Cupar office and apologising for spoiling a rare summer Sunday with good weather. She rang Chandavarkar's mobile, and left a terse reply to his pre-recorded 'Hello, caller, say what you want to say and I may get back to you', the sing-song in his voice more exaggerated than normal. Then she found Dr MacGregor's mobile number.

'Inspector Fortune! Are you keeping me under observation? How did you know I had just entered your jurisdiction?' The pathologist's plummy voice came down the line.

'Are you driving, Doctor? I trust you're hands-free?'

'Even if I weren't, my reply would not incriminate me as you failed to caution me.'

'You weren't a suspect at that stage, so if you had admitted it you'd be convicted.'

'Are you desperate to get your numbers up for the dreaded statistics, or is there a real point to this call?'

'Have you done the PM on Farquhar Knox?'

'Yes, so I'm driving home with my scalpels in time to carve the Sunday roast and I've just crossed the Forth Bridge.'

'It'll surprise you to know that I'm in charge of the inquiry.'

'Nothing surprises me about this. It was strange they didn't use an Edinburgh pathologist and I've been sent away with the bloody arrow I removed from Mr Knox's abdomen and a plethora of samples to analyse in Dundee. Why?'

Flick hesitated. The fewer who knew about the Traynors the better, but she wanted MacGregor's full cooperation and Lynda Traynor's DNA might be an important factor. 'Had Knox had sex just before he died?' she asked.

'Yes.'

'Well, we have reason to believe that the woman in question may have been Lynda Traynor, the wife of the Edinburgh Divisional Commander.'

There was a silence. 'Ah, I see,' MacGregor said.

'We are trying to keep this quiet, and the line is that I am taking on the inquiry because I was the lead officer in the fraud trial Knox was prosecuting when he died. Please be as discreet as possible. The longer the press remain in the dark the better.'

'I shall try not to give the game away.'

'What can you tell me?'

'The cause of death was an arrow through the heart. It entered below the rib cage to the left of the front midline and went up and in till it reached the right ventricle. The deceased was probably seated when he died and unless the killer lay on the floor at his feet and shot upwards, which I believe would have been very difficult, the arrow was pushed in manually, and that would have taken some strength, although a strong woman could have done it. The arrow was sharp.'

'Would the killer be likely to have blood on them?'

'Not necessarily. Perhaps on their hands or wrists. Any suspect should certainly have their cuffs examined. The bleeding that killed him was internal.'

'What about time of death?'

'About half past ten, give or take half an hour. I deduce

that from the stomach contents. He had eaten and drunk about an hour and a half before he died and was nearly three times the UK limit for drink-driving. Stains on his underwear and shirt and substances found on his private parts indicate recent sexual activity. I hope I might be able to extract some DNA from the samples I have taken.' He paused. 'You know, it was strange seeing him on the slab. I never much cared for Farquhar Knox. He always seemed unnecessarily arrogant and aggressive. He was very bright. I've quite often felt the sharp end of his tongue in court, but I got no satisfaction using my scalpel on him.'

'From what I gathered during the fraud trial he could be pretty awkward, though I personally never had a problem with him. In court I bet you gave as good as you got,' she added.

'I tried, Inspector. His weakness was pomposity, which is best pricked with a little humour. Even in murder trials.'

'Well, thank you, Doctor. I'll be in touch.' Although she was trying to develop it, she knew her sense of humour was too weak to use as a weapon.

'As usual, the written report will take a day or two, but I'll let you know if I find anything of interest.'

Going back to the file, Flick tried to imagine life in the Traynor household. The brief biographical details in MacKay's report revealed that she was thirty-five, eleven years younger than her husband. They had been married for fourteen years and had one son, now fourteen. She did not work. What might drive her to such shamelessness? The folder contained no gossip, only details of two affairs that impacted on her husband's job. Flick was sure there would have been others. Was Traynor impotent, or gay, or a wife-beater? Perhaps he was just profoundly boring. Flick patted her stomach thoughtfully, impatient for Fergus to return. Conflicting emotions made her edgy.

* * *

'An arsehole.' Fergus delivered his terse obituary of Farquhar Knox as he finished his plate of lamb. 'It's because of men like him that they have all these lawyer jokes.' He took a swig of Chianti. 'What do you call a smiling, courteous person at a law conference? The caterer. What do lawyers use for birth control? Their personalities.'

Flick grinned. 'Doctor MacGregor said he was arrogant and aggressive and could be pompous.'

'Could be? Pompous might have been his middle name. He was utterly ruthless. When he was defending he went out of his way to attack the police. To listen to him we were all lying scumbags, though I've heard he switched like a weather vane and really stuck up for us in court when he was representing the crown. But even when he was prosecuting quite a few found him difficult to work with. And he wasn't nice to little people. I heard him give one of the High Court attendants an awful bollocking because he hadn't told him his taxi was waiting.'

'Do you know Traynor?'

'Not well, but I suspect few do. I've met him a handful of times at conferences and meetings. He doesn't say much. He's got a reputation for being very organised and a good strategic thinker. Runs a tight ship. That's why he's Divisional Commander. Hard to see him suddenly stabbing Knox with an arrow, but I suppose everyone has their breaking point.'

'Othello killed Desdemona, leaving Iago to try to kill Cassio,' Flick mused.

'If Traynor was going to kill anyone, I'd expect it to be his wife. But all the same, he's got to be a suspect.' He finished his wine and looked closely at Flick. 'You will be able to do this, won't you, darling?'

'Of course,' she replied sharply. 'And if I have to delay maternity leave by a day or two, I will.' She drained her water glass and began to load the dishwasher.

He got up to help her. 'I'll be glad when you've stopped work. You're obviously uncomfortable. Has our wee rugby player been busy again?'

'Yes, but I'm fine, I keep telling you. And anyway, she's a ballet dancer.'

'It'll be nice when we're both on leave. Just the two of us and him or her. And the Open on the telly,' he added.

'And my career going into reverse,' she countered.

'It'll pick up. Don't worry.'

'How do you know? You can't tell. All I know is I've fought every inch of the way to be accepted, first as a woman, then up here as an Englishwoman, and I've finally got there. I know my team believe in me, I'm in charge of a difficult and important case and I have to go off and have a baby. It's so unfair. If it was you having the baby you wouldn't mind because you haven't had to struggle to get where you are and you don't really care if you don't rise any higher. Just so long as you have good meals, a few glasses of wine and of course, your bloody golf.' Aware she had raised her voice, she glared at him.

'You sound as if you don't want the baby.'

'How dare you say that,' she practically screamed. Shaking, she stormed out of the room, slamming the door behind her.

In the privacy of their bedroom she lay on the bed and wept. They had both wanted a baby, he more than she, but as she experienced a new human growing inside her she had felt her femininity being affirmed in a way she had not anticipated. Now the safe delivery of the child that was kicking and squirming inside her was the most important thing in her life bar nothing. But her career still mattered. A lot. As her dad always said, life was never meant to be fair. She closed her eyes, took deep breaths and calmed herself. The memory of Fergus's stricken face as she left the kitchen made her feel bad. And a little bit better, too.

Soon her brain was buzzing. The Farquhar Knox she remembered was shrewd and quick and treated her with respect. He had judged her by her competence, not her gender. He had been brutal in tearing a strip off DC Billy di Falco over the non-availability of a witness, so much so that she had quietly pointed out to him later that he was doing her job for her. 'Just keep your whip ready for the next time,' he had replied with a smirk. That had been the only suggestive remark he had made to her, but there had been something masterful and sexy about him and she could imagine him relishing the challenge of having sex with another man's wife on the bench of the High Court.

Outside the mower started. It made an angry noise with lots of revs and abrupt, jerky turns. After half an hour it stopped. Flick got up and tidied herself, ready to go out. She went downstairs, made two mugs of tea and carried them outside. Fergus was scratching at the rose border with a hoe but came over and joined her on the bench which caught the afternoon and evening sun. They sat in silence for a while.

'I am alright, Fergus, and I know what I'm doing,' she said quietly.

'I'm sorry I said that thing about not wanting the baby, but you can't blame me for worrying.' He put a hand on her knee.

'I know, but please stop fussing. I can't bear it.'

'Okay, okay. It's a difficult time, and I know how important your career is to you.'

'But no more important than the baby. Or you. I'm looking forward to being a mum. Really. And look what we've got compared with, say, the Traynors.'

'Absolutely.'

'I really value your comments on my cases, you know. But please keep the Traynor thing quiet.'

'Of course, but who's fussing now?'

She grinned, got up and kissed his forehead. 'I'm off to Cupar. See you later.' She picked up the mugs and went inside.

'Love you,' Fergus whispered as she turned her back.

4

Flick's office was cool and quiet. The team would arrive in less than three hours and she wanted to feel in control by then. She booted up her computer and found two zip files from Maclean. She opened the first one and started reading.

There were more than four hundred people who, in theory, might have killed Knox. With a handful of no-shows, there were nearly three hundred people at the function, which was called Advocates and Archers. There were more than a hundred waiters, chefs, security people and attendants. The Edinburgh police had been busy and Flick found lists containing the names of all those entitled to be in the building, with addresses and phone numbers for many. Thirty tables, each seating ten, had been placed on the floor of Parliament Hall. The contact details of advocates and archers were in the dossier, but only the names of those invited as guests. The fifty waiting staff had been divided into teams of five, each team looking after three tables. The catering company had provided full details of all of them, plus the twenty-five chefs who had put the food on the plates. The security staff and attendants were also fully documented. Brief statements had been obtained from twenty-nine people. A number of them would need to be seen again. Once informed of what had happened, Mrs Knox was reported as being 'inconsolable' and her brother had refused to allow the police to ask any meaningful questions.

The second file contained photographs of the scene. Flick was impressed by how grand the building looked, even in crime scene photographs. Parliament Hall had a particular majesty with its dark wooden rafters, highly-polished and lighter-coloured floor and huge stained-glass window at the South end. Great lawyers of the past, commemorated in stone or oils, observed whatever goings-on the twenty-first century brought in front of their haughty stares.

Flick sat back, thinking. Then she busied herself making arrangements and printing excerpts from the files which she assembled into six folders. She knew that her willingness to undertake menial tasks generated respect from her team. She wondered if Chandavarkar had got her message and hoped she had not made it too peremptory. After all, she was not his line manager. It was the irritating tone of his recorded message that had made her speak more sharply than she had meant. She liked him and respected his abilities, but his cheeky, puerile attempts at humour were so annoying.

Detective Sergeant Lance Wallace was the first to arrive in the incident room. The reassuring way he sat still, waiting to be told what was happening, boosted her confidence. 'Dour' was an adjective she had heard applied to him, but as far as she was concerned he was strong, silent and reliable. She gave him the short version of why they were being brought in. He showed no reaction other than a frown of concentration as he thought through the implications. Five minutes after six the odd couple, as they were known, entered together. Well-tanned and debonair, Detective Constable Billy di Falco looked cool and casual. His great friend, Detective Constable 'Spider' Gilsland, was a casualty of the warm weather. His crumpled shirt was stained at the front by chocolate ice cream and under the arms by sweat, while his baggy khaki shorts revealed the knobbliest knees Flick could remember seeing. At least he had sprayed himself generously with after-shave, although his bright red face suggested he should have used more sun cream.

Ignoring their tale of car keys in the wrong trousers, she handed round the folders she had assembled, leaving one for her and two more on her desk. She had not copied the file on Lynda Traynor but began by explaining its contents and why they had been given the case.

'This is the crime we are dealing with,' she said as she stuck a photograph at the top of the whiteboard. It showed a man in a dinner jacket lolling in a red leather chair. On the wall at his right shoulder part of a coat of arms was visible. The man had dark, wavy hair, thinning at the front, a sharp nose and a double chin. His mouth gaped in an expression of astonishment and blank eyes seemed to stare straight ahead. His hands had gone to his stomach, from which the end of an arrow protruded, its feathers plainly visible. Flick stood back to let them all see then stuck up another three photographs giving views of the court and the corridor outside.

'This is going to be a big job,' she said, 'and Graeme Traynor must never appear on the whiteboard, though we have to investigate him thoroughly.'

'We are always thorough, Inspector, ma'am.' Detective Sergeant Bagawath Chandavarkar, known to everyone except Flick as 'Baggo', burst in. He was wearing the sort of multi-coloured trousers favoured by golfers and some comedians. His broad grin showed off his white teeth against his lower face, which was dark brown and unprotected by his golf cap. His sallow forehead made him look slightly ridiculous. 'I regret missing the start of your briefing, but I have just gone round Carnoustie in ninety-four. I got your message when I had finished and rushed here post-haste. It is conveniently near my route back to Edinburgh.'

While the others chuckled, Flick smiled. 'Well pick up a folder and see what we've got,' she said then gave him the very short version of why they were involved. As the chairs were taken, he sat on the edge of a desk, grimacing as he studied the pictures of a man he had come to know and respect, if not like.

Flick continued with the briefing, summarising what MacGregor had told her. 'I think the most likely scenario is that Knox took advantage of the archery contest to go off to Court Three to have sex. That would be some time between ten and ten-twenty. He did have sex, if the rumours are right, with Lynda Traynor. Then someone who had picked up one of the arrows from the judges' retiring room where they had been stowed after the shooting, stabbed him. The archery finished about twenty past ten, and all the bows and arrows were placed in the retiring room, which is in the judges' corridor, immediately afterwards, so the murder took place between twenty past ten and eleven. We have to account for the movements of any suspect during that frame. As I said, it's not going to be easy, particularly if we must be discreet about the Traynor angle.'

'Would it not have been possible for someone to take an arrow while the archery was still going on?' di Falco asked.

'Not according to a Captain Carstairs, who refereed the shooting and was responsible for the safekeeping of the equipment. Edinburgh were quick to get a statement from him,' Flick replied.

'I take it that, whoever she may be, the lady who had sex with Mr Knox is a suspect,' Baggo said. Glancing at Flick with a twinkle in his eye, he added, 'The great writer, Kipling, had a point when he wrote, "the female of the species is more deadly than the male," Inspector, ma'am.'

She wasn't going to rise to this. Looking blankly at him, she said, 'Absolutely.'

'I see the Traynors were on the top table,' Wallace said.

Flick said, 'Yes. There are no statements from any of the top table people, and we have no information about the Smails or Maltravers. Although privately we see the Traynors as real suspects, we have to show significant interest in the accused in the fraud, and their trial. Lance, I would like you to be in court tomorrow morning to see what happens and then interview Mr and Mrs Smail and Maltravers. They'll probably bring in their lawyers, but as it's a separate inquiry and they're not suspects yet, there's no reason for them not to help us.'

'And if they refuse?' Wallace asked.

She shrugged. 'Best not push it till we have to, I think. We don't want to risk compromising the trial.'

She continued, 'After them, you should move on to some of the others, beginning with the people on the same tables as Smail and Maltravers. There are a lot to get round and we have to be seen to be concentrating on that angle so you'd better take someone with you. I think McKellar would be the man. He's not going to be overawed by important people, and he can read a situation well. For this inquiry he should be out of uniform. Will you arrange that?'

'Yes, boss,' Wallace said, picking up the last folder and trying not to show his surprise at the inspector choosing McKellar to help. When she had first arrived in Fife, the experienced, old-school constable had not concealed his lack of regard for the young Englishwoman. He had become more respectful over the months but the sly digs had not stopped completely, and the inspector knew that.

'I also will be in court tomorrow morning,' Baggo said. 'The main accused, Burns, is still giving evidence and I have been told to be there for eight sharp to brief the QC who will take over from Knox. I stay in court and listen to what is said and I pass notes to the crown lawyers. Once these duties have ended I will be able to help Lancelot.' He grinned at Wallace, knowing he hated his full first name, reputedly selected by his parents because he had been conceived after they had seen the show *Camelot*.

'Thank you, Bagawath,' Wallace muttered, shaking his head.

Flick sighed. For some reason the two very different sergeants got on well, finding humour where it was never meant to be found. She turned to Gilsland. 'Spider, I want you to go to Parliament House, getting there for half past eight, well before the courts sit. The security people will be expecting you. I want you to take photos of the place; the hall, the courtroom, the corridors, the kitchens. I gather it's a rabbit warren so please map all the passages, stairs and cupboards so we can see how someone might have gone from the hall to the courtroom and back, picking up the arrow en route. Identify possible hiding places too. Then, still at Parliament House, I want you to check the CCTV of the night. The Edinburgh police have set that up, but from what they say I'm not hopeful. Bring the tapes back here. There may be discrepancies between what people say and what the camera shows.'

'What about me, boss?' di Falco asked.

'You, Billy, will be coming with me. Your main job will be to charm the grieving widow into talking properly to us. Then we'll move on to the top table, including Chief Superintendent Traynor and his wife, though I think we should leave them till last. It'll be an early start as our first call of the day will be Fettes, the Edinburgh HQ, at half past eight to pick up productions. I've made sure there will be three pool cars available in the morning. Any questions?'

There were none. Making arrangements or just chatting, they drifted out. Baggo was the last to leave.

'Er, Bagawath,' Flick said, 'thank you for coming tonight. I hope you didn't mind the brief message, but I've asked for your help in this.'

He shrugged. 'No problem, Inspector, ma'am. I am very much enjoying my stay here in Scotland. As you know, I have taken up golf and I have made good use of the long evenings. My ambition is to play the Old Course at St Andrews and this inquiry may give me time to do that.'

Flick looked doubtful. 'It looks like a case of sexual jealousy, but if it's not and the murder really is linked in some way to the trial and the fraud, you're the man to get to the bottom of it.'

'And, following separate lines of inquiry, we should between us reach the truth?'

'Exactly. We have a fortnight before I go on maternity leave, and I would dearly love this to be wrapped up before then.'

'Please look after yourself, Inspector, ma'am. You must take care for the baby's sake.'

She saw genuine concern on his face and choked back the defiant retort she would have made to Fergus. She said, 'I will. Please don't worry. Oh, there is one more thing; you should call me Flick when it's just the two of us. We've known each other for a while.' She moved in her seat and felt herself blush.

'On the condition that you call me Baggo, and not just when it's only us. I know you don't like the name, but I am happy with it and everyone uses it.' Once she had told him that she thought the nickname was undignified. He had put that down to her political correctness, and considered it ridiculous. But he had a lot of time for her. She was good and loyal and brave and competent. It was just a shame about the political correctness and lack of humour.

'Fine, er, Baggo.' Seeing his broad grin, she answered it with a smile.

'That is much better, Flick. But try to miss out the "er" before the Baggo or people will think I'm called Erbaggo, and that would never do.'

As he left he saw she was still smiling. Still a bit uptight, but the iron knickers tendency was waning. She would not have used first names so freely, even in January during the investigation. He had been up for the previous week, first giving evidence then advising crown counsel, and had not seen much of her. She had definitely changed, and for the better. Was it marriage, pregnancy, or getting away from Inspector No that had relaxed her? He thought back to the tension in the Wimbledon CID room as the slobbish, unprincipled Inspector Noel Osborne had bullied and made fun of the bright, determined Sergeant Fortune, who had great integrity but seldom cracked a smile.

5

'I'm relying on you to charm her, duke's daughter or not,' Flick told Billy di Falco as he put on the dashboard the POLICE OFFICIAL BUSINESS sign Maclean had thoughtfully given them when they collected the productions at Fettes.

They were in a street unusually bumpy even for Edinburgh, paved with rectangular dark cobbles. Substantial stone townhouses with tall windows and black cast iron railings formed a classical Georgian terrace which ran down a slope with views across the Forth to Fife. The doors of India Street were all immaculate and many bore brass plates, the word ADVOCATE printed under the owner's name.

Flick now felt more positive about the inquiry. The previous day's row had cleared the air with Fergus. Later, as usual on Sundays, she had phoned her dad and he had been typically proud and supportive, not voicing the fears she knew would keep him awake. She resolved to phone him more often until the baby was born and wished he lived closer so that she might keep an eye on him. A widower in his late sixties, he continued to live in the family home in Maidenhead. They worried about each other.

But that was life and you just had to get on with it. With di Falco driving, she had used the journey time to phone the people she wanted to see. She had also looked up some of them, as well as Farquhar Knox, in *Who's Who* online. She learned that Knox had been a QC for five years. Educated at Stirling High School and Edinburgh University, he had married Lady Eloise Charlotte Buchan, third daughter of the Duke of Lochgilphead. They had one son, aged fourteen. Knox had been a member of the New Club and The Honourable Company of Edinburgh Golfers.

'I think that's Muirfield,' di Falco said.

That did not surprise her. She disapproved of single-sex clubs, and Knox had been a chauvinist. She had expected his origins to have been grander. He spoke with barely a trace of a Scottish accent and she assumed that he had attended an expensive public school. He had clearly married several social notches above himself. As she heaved herself out of the car and negotiated the deep, sloping gutter, unchanged over the centuries, Flick told herself that the duke's daughter they were about to see was an ordinary woman, just like her.

A man with tousled fair hair wearing slacks and a checked shirt opened the door as Flick debated whether to ring twice. He identified himself as Reginald Buchan, Mrs Knox's brother. With an air of reluctance, he led them through an imposing hallway presided over by a glass-eyed stag's head mounted on the wall facing the stairs and into a spacious drawing room at the back of the building. Looking down his nose, he told the detectives he would find out if Mrs Knox could see them.

'We'll have to speak to her sooner or later,' Flick said, sitting uninvited in an upright chair with her back to the window.

The room had a high ceiling with an intricate cornice. The wall facing the window was curved, forming a perfect bow. The furniture was either well-preserved antique or repro. A flame-effect gas fire sat in the substantial fireplace while on the mantelpiece various invitations with italic printing were propped behind pieces of cranberry glass. While they waited, di Falco prowled round, inspecting the silver-framed photos. Many were black and white, featuring a grim-looking stone mansion surrounded by pine trees with different people posing in front of it. There was a coloured photo of Knox looking pleased with himself beside a dead stag and another of him, equally self-satisfied, wearing a QC's full-bottomed wig. In pride of place on a long bookcase filled with hardback books stood a photo larger than the rest. The background was unmistakably Highland and a tweed-clad Knox posed with a woman wearing the same blue-dyed tweed. She had a thin, sharp face and shoulder-length blonde hair. In front of them stood a serious-looking boy of about thirteen with crinkly, dark hair and a triumphant expression. One hand held a rifle and the other held the antlers of another stag. The boy was half-turned towards Knox as if seeking approval, so the stag's head pointed lopsidedly towards the camera. Di Falco was appalled that the act of killing an animal could give so much pleasure and wondered if the stag's head in the hall appeared in either of the photos.

The door opened and Reginald Buchan returned, followed by the woman and boy in the photo. She stood for a moment, as if inspecting the officers then sat on a sofa well to Flick's right, forcing her to turn in her chair. The boy sat beside her and Reginald found an armchair on the other side of the room.

In the silence that followed the woman first stared at Flick's bump then ran her eye up and down di Falco. His flashing smile of encouragement was answered by a faint raising of her eyebrows. These eyes have not been crying much recently, Flick thought as she contrasted them with those of the boy, which were bloodshot and red-rimmed.

'Lady Eloise ...' Flick began.

'Mrs Knox will do, thank you,' the woman cut in. 'It's much easier.' Her lips formed a cold, superior smile.

'I'm Detective Inspector Fortune and this is Detective Constable di Falco. We are very sorry about your husband.'

'Our condolences,' di Falco said quietly.

'There are a number of questions we have to ask you, and it might be better if your brother and son were not present. I hope you don't mind.'

While Mrs Knox scowled, her brother was indignant. 'Is this necessary, Inspector? I mean, her husband's just been murdered. This whole thing is quite traumatic for her.'

Glancing meaningfully at the boy, Flick said firmly, 'It would be better for all concerned, sir.'

Mrs Knox said quietly, 'It's alright, Spare. I'll be fine.'

From her Googling Flick had learned that, after giving

birth to three daughters, the Duchess of Lochgilphead had borne two sons, the elder of whom was the heir. Reginald was the spare.

Flick thought he was going to prove awkward, but he too looked at the boy and nodded. 'Come on, Ranald,' he said kindly. He put his arm round his nephew's shoulder as they left the room. Before rising from the sofa, Ranald shot Flick a glare full of unhappy resentment.

'He worshipped his father,' Mrs Knox said quite brusquely.

Flick nodded at di Falco, who sat in the chair vacated by Buchan.

'We have to find out what happened on Friday night between ten and eleven,' di Falco said. 'Can you tell us what you did then and who you saw?'

Mrs Knox responded with a shrug. 'It's hard to remember exactly,' she said slowly, the accent clipped. 'I last saw Farquhar after dinner. He left the table then and didn't return. I never saw him again.' She paused for a moment. Her voice catching, she continued, 'I went to the Ladies then watched the archery. I stood for a time with Molly Bertram, but she saw someone she wanted to speak to and I moved about a bit. It was quite difficult to see at times. I did chat to Kenny Cuthbert. The Cuthberts and the Bertrams were in our party. After the contest was over I went outside to Parliament Square for a cigarette, or maybe two. There were a few of us. I didn't know most of them. I do remember John Logan. He's one of the bar's smokers and we've become allies.' She reached into a pocket of her linen skirt and withdrew a packet and a silver lighter. Her hand shook as she lit up.

'What was happening when you returned?' di Falco asked as Flick recoiled from the smoke, waving her hand in front of her.

'The band started. Dancing.'

'What did you do then?'

'There was a seating area in the library. I made for it but Kenny and Jen Cuthbert press-ganged me into a Dashing White Sergeant. You do it in threes and it's always the first dance of the night,' she added, seeing Flick's puzzled expression. 'Once it was over I went to the library and stayed there. Jen Cuthbert and Molly Bertram will vouch for me.'

'Can you think of anyone who might have wanted to kill your husband?' he asked.

'Several.' She gave a hollow laugh. 'Farquhar didn't go out of his way to be popular. But no. I cannot think of anyone who would have actually wanted to kill him.'

'You left with the Cuthberts, I believe, assuming your husband had gone without telling anyone?'

'Farquhar could be infuriating but he was never boring and he had a very low boredom threshold. He hated dancing and had been making fun of the Archers through dinner, humming *Robin Hood, Robin Hood* when the Captain-General, their head man, passed our table. I took it he'd drifted off to some pub.'

Di Falco's charm had worked. Flick decided it was time to get to the point. 'Examination of your husband's body has shown that he had sex minutes before he died. I have to ask if you know anything about that?'

Mrs Knox stiffened and exhaled in Flick's direction. 'I do not,' she said with emphasis.

Flick wrinkled her nose and blew at the smoke. Trying not to sound irritated, she asked, 'Have you any idea who he was with?'

'No.'

'Does the name Lynda Traynor mean anything to you?'

Mrs Knox's mouth twitched and she looked away. She inhaled deeply before stubbing out her cigarette forcefully, then fidgeting with the lace-trimmed handkerchief she had in one hand. Neither Flick nor di Falco noticed the door opening. A tall, silver-haired man wearing beige chinos and an open-necked light blue shirt strode in and stood in front of Mrs Knox. 'Eloise,' he said, 'are you alright?'

'Yes, thank you, Henry, but I think these officers were about to go.'

Flick produced her warrant. 'My colleague and I are investigating a brutal murder and we need to speak to Mrs Knox alone. We are not yet finished.'

'That's up to Mrs Knox, officer, as you well know. Would you like me to stay, Eloise?'

'Yes, please, Henry. You're very kind.'

The man sat on the sofa beside her and looked inquiringly at Flick.

'You can't just barge in like that, sir. Please don't make our job more difficult than it is.' di Falco sounded stern.

'What is your name, sir?' sensing trouble, Flick's tone remained polite.

The silver-haired man sat upright and looked coldly at her. His face was long and thin, with a disproportionately short lower jaw. He spoke grandly, with no trace of a Scottish accent. 'I am Lord Hutton. In case you didn't know, I am a High Court judge and I live next door to Mrs Knox. You are both aware that you have no right to badger this lady with detailed questions, and I'm surprised you should have troubled someone so recently widowed. I suggest you ask any questions you may have once and once only, then leave forthwith.'

Di Falco opened and closed his mouth like a fish. Flick knew the interview was going nowhere but she was not going to be browbeaten, even by a High Court judge. 'Does the name Lynda Traynor mean anything to you, Mrs Knox?' she repeated.

'It does not.' The answer came quickly.

'Did you see your husband talking to anyone in particular after dinner on Friday?'

'No.'

'Were you suspicious that he might be having an affair before he died?'

'No.'

'What were you wearing on Friday night?'

'A long, navy blue dress.'

'Was your marriage happy at the end?'

Mrs Knox's face crumbled. Hutton stood up and advanced towards Flick. 'That's quite enough, officer. Please leave now.'

There was nothing for it but to depart with such dignity as they could muster.

In the car di Falco said, 'I think you hit a raw nerve with these last questions, ma'am.'

'Definitely, but how much is she not telling us, and why?'

* * *

'I think you'd better continue the cross this morning.' Mark Radcliffe QC had a twinkle in his eye as he spoke. Melanie Arbuthnot was appalled.

'No, I … I couldn't,' she spluttered.

'There's a tradition of the crown junior taking over when the senior becomes unavailable. It happened in the Manuel trial in the 1950s. The Advocate-Depute prosecuting the case was suddenly taken ill and the judge turned to his junior, who'd been at the bar for five minutes, and told him to get on with it. It was important, too, as Manuel was a mass murderer. He was hanged,' Radcliffe added as an afterthought, winking at Baggo.

'I will help you all I can,' Baggo said earnestly. He fancied Melanie like mad and loved the way she was blushing at the wind-up. At first Radcliffe had reminded him of a mannequin in an up-market fashion display for middle-aged men, but he clearly had a sense of humour.

'I'll sit beside you, so there's no need to worry,' Radcliffe continued soothingly. By now he was grinning.

The penny dropped. 'You, you, you … beast,' she said, her relief obvious.

'To the criminal fraternity a beast is usually a sex offender,' Radcliffe pointed out. His mouth was turned down but his eyes twinkled again.

Melanie raised her eyes to heaven but said nothing.

Baggo had been impressed by Radcliffe's mastery of the prosecution brief after only a weekend's study. The three of them had spent more than an hour dissecting Knox's cross-examination of John Burns on Friday afternoon, Baggo looking for anything that might have made someone want to kill him. Knox had laboriously taken Burns through e-mails that had passed between him and his co-accused, whom he was blaming for thinking up the scam. Burns had given evidence with great confidence, but the holes in his story were obvious. While the other two were fascinated by every small point, Baggo was glad he had not become a lawyer. His boredom threshold was too low.

'Cut-throat defences seldom work,' Radcliffe mused. 'It's always good news for the crown when the different accused are at each other's throats. Burns is clutching at straws. Of course he's the one we really want to nail.'

'You'll have seen he was acquitted of a timeshare fraud in the High Court a few years ago,' Melanie volunteered. 'Not enough evidence, apparently.'

At quarter to ten Radcliffe thanked the other two for their help and went off to have a smoke then change for court. Before Melanie left, Baggo asked her if there was anything that Knox said or did on Friday that might have led to his death.

Lines of concentration creased her plump face. 'There was one e-mail he took a lot of time over. Far more than I thought necessary. Do you remember? It was from Burns to Maltravers, the planning consultant, quite early on. It gave lots of detail about the project, boring stuff like what sort of soil and grass they'd be working with. It showed Burns was driving the whole thing, but he pretended he didn't understand his own e-mail. It was pathetic, really. But that's not a reason for anyone to kill Knox.'

'I agree. Your new boss, Mr Radcliffe is a bit of a character.'

'Quite. He really had me going with that wind-up. But he's a nice man.'

Baggo nodded slowly. 'He seems very bright.'

'Yes. And he's always immaculate. He spends most of his time in the small print of contracts that are worth a fortune but as clear as mud. He was advised to prosecute for a while to develop his career, but he seems to be enjoying it. He's really fair and that makes him deadlier.'

'Knox was impressive, too.'

'Yes, but far more aggressive. You'll notice the change of style straight away.' She frowned. 'I'd better go and change, but there was something Knox said after court on Friday that I didn't understand. He'd been wiping the floor with Burns then came out of court and muttered something about us having to re-think the whole thing.'

'Did you not ask him what he meant?'

'He didn't encourage questions from his junior.'

'And you have no idea what he meant?'

'No. Now I must go and change.' As she left the room, he admired her slightly too tight skirt and generous hips. She did not wear a wedding or engagement ring. He would definitely ask her out, perhaps after court today.

He ambled along to take his seat in court, all pine

panels and artificial light. He sat just behind and to the side of the dock, where he might possibly overhear something the accused whispered, and got his notebook and biro ready. He looked round and exchanged nods with Lance Wallace, who was sitting beside a man in his forties with a craggy face. This man wore a dark suit and had the stern demeanour of a reluctant guest at a wedding or funeral. Baggo recognised him as PC McKellar, uncomfortable out of uniform but not to be messed with.

The clerk took his seat at the table in the well of the court and told the judge's macer to call the case. Flapping the wide sleeves of his black gown, the small, bald official hurried off with the cheery self-importance of a master of ceremonies.

Three men slowly rose from different areas of the public benches and sat in the dock. They neither looked at the others nor did they speak. Lachlan Smail, ruddy-faced with thinning ginger hair, stared straight ahead. To his left, Gideon Maltravers, the tallest at well over six feet with a lightly-tanned complexion, inspected his fingernails. His light blue linen suit gave an impression of style and arrogance. To his left was Joe Thomson, the eldest of the accused, whose misshapen nose, punched back into a leathery, brick-coloured face, made Baggo think of pub brawls. They were joined by a fourth, younger than the rest and handcuffed to a security officer. John Burns's dark eyes flashed round the court in a manner that was street-wise yet desperate. The officer shuffled him past the other accused to sit on the right of Smail.

As counsel took their places round the table, Baggo noted how Melanie had secured her long, brown hair in a French Roll, making the curls of her white wig stick out at the back. She sat up straight, pert and demure, her Parker ball-point ready to resume note-taking.

Baggo's increasingly erotic imaginings were cut short when the macer shouted 'court' and everyone stood for the judge's entrance. Lord Tulloch, a big, lumpy man with incongruously delicate pince-nez glasses, strode in and bowed. The lawyers bowed back then everyone sat down.

The judge, an imposing figure in his white gown adorned with red crosses, got straight to the point. 'I have not brought the jury back yet because there is something I want to say. Everyone will no doubt be aware that the Advocate-Depute prosecuting in this case, Mr Knox, died suddenly during the weekend. This is neither the time nor the place to pay tribute to a very fine lawyer. We have another experienced counsel to take his place and so the trial may proceed. When I bring the jury back, I am minded to say that Mr Knox has died during the weekend, and he has been replaced by another Advocate-Depute. They must not speculate about Mr Knox's death. Nor must they allow it to affect in any way their view of the evidence in this case. Does anyone have any submission they wish to make?'

There were mutters of 'No, my lord' from counsel. The jury were brought in, the judge addressed them, Burns resumed his place in the witness box, and Radcliffe stood up. 'Good morning, Mr Burns,' he said, a pleasant smile on his face.

As Melanie had said, Radcliffe was nicer than Knox, and much more polite, but Baggo found him even more boring. Cross-examination was a bit like cricket, he thought, only with an important difference: the questioner kept on bowling at the witness, but no matter how often the batsman was caught out, he never moved from the crease.

It was not long before his thoughts drifted back to Melanie.

6

'Now we're off to the Grange. The Dean of the Faculty of Advocates is expecting us,' Flick told di Falco as he reversed the car out of the India Street gutter, causing a van coming down the hill to swerve. 'Do you know your way round Edinburgh?'

'Not very well, ma'am,' he admitted.

'I don't think that matters. The council kept changing the road lay-out for the tram works. Apparently the public money that's been lost through the Nicklaus golf course fraud is dwarfed by the cost of these trams, which no one wanted.'

After an interminable wait at temporary traffic lights and an inspired change of lanes which caused a lorry driver to wave his fist, they reached a quiet road, again cobbled, with large grey stone houses set back from the street behind front gardens full of rhododendrons, azaleas and camellias.

Flick was undecided about how much information she should give the Dean. As di Falco put the Police card back on the dashboard she took a deep breath.

A clump of lily-of-the-valley was flowering beside the front step. Flick inhaled its clean scent as the heavy door opened. A tall lady wearing a maroon skirt and a red blouse smiled at them. She carried no fat and held herself upright. Her brown hair was in a short bob and her pale skin had no make-up. She had applied some dark red lipstick and Flick could see hair on her upper lip. 'Good morning, officers,' she said.

Di Falco produced his warrant. 'Good morning, ma'am. Is your husb …'

Flick cut in quickly. 'Dean of Faculty, thank you for seeing us.'

'Not at all,' the Dean said, her eyes drawn to Flick's belly. She put her hand on di Falco's arm. 'You're not the first and you won't be the last to make that mistake. You are Detective Inspector Fortune and Detective Constable di Falco, I presume.'

As di Falco stammered his apologies, the Dean led them into a study and gestured to seats facing the massive desk in the centre of the room. As she fetched coffee and biscuits, the officers took in the shelves on three walls groaning with legal books up to shoulder height. Above the bookshelves, paintings of still life and city scenes dominated the space up to the high ceiling. Flick thought she recognised the bold colours and confident brush-strokes of Morocco. Family photographs in an assortment of frames sat on the bookcases. This time there were no dead animals. Most of the photos had been taken in cities or on sunny beaches. One showed the family, all open-mouthed on a Disney ride. The Dean's husband was a cheery-looking man, slightly shorter than his wife. They had a son and a daughter, both teenagers. Flick had to look twice to identify the happy mum, usually in jeans, her hair tousled, as the Dean.

'You will want to know what I can tell you about Mr Knox.' Coffee poured, de-caf for Flick, the Dean got straight to the point. 'The answer is not much, I'm afraid. I saw him early on Friday evening and said hello, but that was it. I can't remember seeing him after dinner.'

Flick chose her words carefully. 'We're trying to get a picture of who saw whom after dinner and during the archery contest. Can you help us about others on the top table?'

'During the archery contest I was fully engaged as a spectator. The Captain-General was with me through dinner and we watched the contest together. The same goes for the Secretary of State for Scotland. The occasion was his idea, actually. He's a member of both the Faculty of Advocates and the Royal Company of Archers. We're older than them. We started in 1532 as against their 1676, but we'd never done a combined celebration, although over the years there has been quite an overlap in membership. Last Friday went very well, but for the murder. The Archers looked particularly splendid in their dark green dress jackets.'

'I gather that the tables were cleared straight after dinner and there were no speeches?' Flick asked.

'Yes.' The Dean smiled. 'Advocates can be loquacious when speaking yet impatient when they're supposed to be listening. We didn't want to risk anyone heckling the Captain-General. I stood up, made the Loyal Toast, and declared: "Let the games begin." Shades of ancient Rome, unfortunately complete with a fatality.' She shuddered.

'When was that, roughly?'

'About twenty to ten. I had been told it would take twenty minutes to clear the tables and set up the archery butt and so it did.'

'Can you remember seeing Chief Superintendent Traynor at any time after the meal?'

The Dean's face gave nothing away. 'Personally, no, but my husband told me that during the archery he had been looking for his wife. My husband's an accountant in town. He's at work this morning.'

'And Mrs Traynor. Did you see her after dinner?'

'No, Inspector, I did not. And neither did my husband, at least not until much later. Are you prepared to say why you are interested in the Traynors?' The tone was light and she raised her eyebrows.

Flick pursed her lips. She searched the Dean's intelligent, inquisitive face and made up her mind. 'There are rumours.' She paused. The Dean was not going to help her out. 'About Mrs Traynor and Mr Knox.'

'Yes?'

Had she said too much already? 'And we need to find out if these rumours are true.'

'And that's the real reason why Fife officers are investigating this Edinburgh murder?'

It was useless denying it but she couldn't admit it. 'I couldn't comment on that.'

'But I might think it?' She smiled. Flick shrugged.

The Dean nodded. 'You have been as frank as you can be with me, so I shall return the favour. First, for all that we deal in hard evidence in our work, Parliament House is a mine of tittle-tattle, most of it unreliable. There has been talk about Farquhar Knox and Lynda Traynor over the last few weeks, and the latest story is that they went off together during the archery to have sex in Court Three. What evidence exists to support that I cannot be sure, but it is what people are saying.'

'It's an odd place to choose, surely?' Flick asked.

The Dean smiled. 'About forty years ago there was a solicitor who was wild, and completely fearless. There was a ball at Parliament House during which he was discovered having sex with a friend's wife on the bench of, I think, Court Nine. I'm ashamed to say he has had his imitators.'

'Like the mile-high club?' di Falco interjected excitedly.

'What might that be, young man?' the Dean asked severely, then smiled as he started to babble. When she saw the glare that Flick aimed at him, she shook with silent laughter.

Flick wanted to get back to the point. She asked, 'So this rumour about Mr Knox and Mrs Traynor having sex in Court Three will be widely-known, ma'am?'

'It's the talk o' the steamie, as we say.' Her mild Scots burr broadened before reverting to normal. 'We were out to dinner on Saturday and heard all about it. What we were told was that one of the bar's great gossips, Percy Oliphant, effectively spied on them going along the darkened corridor and sneaking into Court Three while the archery was on. Now that's hearsay, and it may well have been distorted in the re-telling.'

'We should speak to Mr Oliphant,' Flick said.

The Dean opened the laptop on her desk and pressed some keys. 'I'll give you his contact details,' she said. 'It's in everyone's interests that this is cleared up as soon as possible. I would be grateful if you would take what I am saying on a Chatham House basis?'

'Certainly,' Flick replied. Di Falco looked bemused.

'Percy Oliphant is one of our more exotic birds, Inspector. He is one of the few who continue to wear pin stripes and black jacket, usually with a colourful tie and a bowler hat. His natural habitat is licensed premises. Here.' She pushed a slip of paper across the desk. Flick noted the bold, clear handwriting.

'Did your husband see Mrs Traynor later in the evening, ma'am?' di Falco asked.

'Yes, he did. She was with the Chief Superintendent about half past eleven. They left together, but my husband says they appeared to be barely speaking. He told me that during the archery, when Traynor asked if he'd seen his wife, he didn't appear unduly anxious or upset. You may want to question my husband but I anticipated this interview and took care to find out exactly what he could say.'

'Thank you,' Flick said. 'I'm afraid it probably will be necessary to get a statement, but there's no rush. Did your husband say what Mrs Traynor was wearing?'

'A long, black dress.' She smiled. 'Actually, he said she was "a stunner". I'll leave you to work out what that might mean.'

Wishing di Falco would not giggle sycophantically,

Flick took a note. 'Do you know Mrs Knox?' she asked as an after-thought.

'Eloise? Yes, of course, but not well.'

'Did you, or perhaps your husband, see her during or soon after the archery?'

'I'm afraid I can't help you there, Inspector. I asked my husband that question and he didn't remember seeing her either.'

Their business concluded, the officers left, Flick having taken advantage of the Dean's offer to use her loo. As di Falco walked ahead to the car, the Dean took Flick's arm. 'Well done for taking this on,' she said quietly. 'Just remember that murders are ten-a-penny but your children are special. You must look after yourself. And your baby.' As if to emphasise the point the baby delivered a mighty kick to Flick's womb.

* * *

The next person on their schedule was the Captain-General of the Archers, Lord Craigdiller. He lived at Craigdiller Hall, some distance down the A7 then through a Sat-Nav-testing maze of minor roads. The verges and hedgerows were thick with new growth and the heavy scent of oil seed rape was in the air. Eventually they found a drive snaking into trees. The paint on a sign had peeled but the Sat-Nav insisted they had arrived.

'He looks like the gardener but I bet it's His Lordship,' di Falco said as, bumping along the pot-holed surface, they approached an elderly man in dungarees using a stick to poke at a large heap of rotting tree-stumps. He stopped half on the verge beside the man and asked if they were on the Craigdiller Hall drive.

The man straightened and glared through the open window. 'Mebbe, but whit's yer business?' he growled. Flick barely understood him.

Politely, di Falco explained.

'Richt oan,' the man said and resumed his poking.

They rounded a bend and the hall stood proud and grand before them on a rise, surrounded by mossy lawns. As they drew near, the thin gravel, poor pointing and tired paintwork told their own story. On one side of the house a marquee jutted out. The dark stains on the dirty white panels suggested semi-permanence. This was probably a venue for weddings, Flick thought. She wondered if the old man beside the drive really was the laird, as the Scots would call him.

The doorbell at least functioned well. Its strident ring summoned what sounded like a pack of dogs barking and scratching at the heavy door. A posh male voice shouted 'Quiet' and the noise became a whimper. The door opened and the officers were greeted by a middle-aged man wearing tweed plus-fours, two black Labradors sitting at his feet. This was Lord Craigdiller, who welcomed them with the matter-of-fact joviality he probably used for paying guests at a shoot.

The dogs took their cue from their master and they sniffed and licked at the officers all the way into the drawing room. While di Falco stood, Flick perched on the edge of a finely-crafted chair that did not look as if it had been re-upholstered since the days of Bonnie Prince Charlie. She faced the laird and his wife across the great stone fireplace where the ashes of a wood fire remained. After some general questions she asked about the Traynors.

Tweedy, un-made-up and with hair looking as if it had been cut by a hedge-trimmer, Lady Craigdiller spoke with a cut-glass accent and did not mince her words.

'That man Traynor was the most awful bore. He had been put beside me at dinner and all he could talk about was the deployment of police personnel in Edinburgh.'

Thanks to a table plan provided by Maclean, Flick had known that Chief Superintendent Traynor had sat between Lady Craigdiller and the wife of the Lord Provost while his wife had Lord Craigdiller and the Secretary of State as her companions. She nodded sympathetically, hoping to encourage indiscretion.

'I had expected some cracking stories, true-life Rebus stuff you know, but he was just a blasted pen-pusher. Are all senior policemen like that?'

While di Falco shrugged and pulled a face, Flick said, 'He's noted for his organisational skills.'

Lady Craigdiller snorted. 'He could hold his drink, though. I'll say that for him.'

'Did he have a lot to drink?' Flick asked.

'He hoovered up a bottle of nice Beaune without any effort. But he was just as tedious after as before. As far as I was concerned, it was a dire evening. On my other side was the Dean's husband. An accountant. Actually, he wasn't too bad. At least he listened to me.'

Seeing the glazed expression on her husband's face, Flick detected a dig. 'Did you see anything of Mr or Mrs Traynor after dinner?' she asked.

'Yes, Inspector, I did,' Lady Craigdiller sounded triumphant. 'As soon as the meal was over, she got up. I saw her talking very earnestly to a dark-haired man, glancing round as she did so. Their heads were jolly close together, I can tell you. Her husband lost the thread of whatever he was trying to say to me and stared at them. He wasn't at all happy. The man she was talking to, could it have been that fellow, Knox, who was killed?'

'Quite possibly,' Flick said. 'Did you see them after that?'

'No. The tables were cleared, then there was the archery contest. After that I'd done my duty and spent the rest of the time with friends. Don't tell me you think Traynor bumped off his wife's lover? He's gone up in my estimation if he did.'

'Can you tell us any more than that, Lord Craigdiller?' Flick asked, ignoring his wife's last remark.

''Fraid not. I was luckier than my wife at dinner, as I had the Dean on one side and Mrs Traynor on the other. A vivacious gal. Cut quite a figure with a long, black dress slit up one thigh. Fitted her like a sheath.' His wife coughed. 'I remember her getting up right after the meal, but I had my back to where people were mingling.'

'After the archery contest, can you describe exactly what happened to the arrows?'

'They were pulled out of the butt and collected by our secretary, Captain Carstairs. He placed them in quivers and the quivers were put, with the bows, in a room reserved for judges, apparently not far from where that poor chap was murdered. It was along some dark corridor and we were assured that the things would be safe.'

'And what time were they placed there?'

'About ten-thirty. Possibly a bit before that.'

'Could anyone have seen them being put there?'

'If they had been passing the end of the corridor.'

'And all the arrows were put there?'

'Yes.'

'Do you know Mrs Knox?'

'Oh yes. We said hello briefly when we arrived. But I don't remember seeing her after the archery. Do you, dear?' he asked his wife.

'No. Poor Eloise. Still …'

Flick did not ask her to elaborate. She rose and said they would be on their way. The Craigdillers would have none of it. 'We're proud of our hospitality in the Borders,' he said firmly. 'You must stay for lunch.'

They sat at one end of a huge mahogany table overseen by previous generations of Craigdillers, gilt-framed and severe, many wearing dark green jackets, the uniform of the Royal Company of Archers. Their host explained proudly that he was not the first in the family to be Captain-General. Over pea soup, home-baked bread and local cheese, di Falco sang for his lunch with a convoluted tale of a retired teacher in St Andrews who went round his neighbourhood at dead of night vandalising cars he considered badly parked. When caught at two in the morning with a bag of new potatoes to shove up exhaust pipes he had replied, 'They're for chips.'

His tongue loosened by claret, Lord Craigdiller started talking about the dead man. 'He didn't like me, you know. I passed near him a couple of times and he started to hum that silly Robin Hood tune. He had wanted to be an Archer, you know. I think he blamed me for not getting in, but I had very little to do with it. It was his own, frankly objectionable, personality that was the problem. He'd wormed his way into the New Club and Muirfield, but we were a bridge too far. Our members are elected, but not all candidates are accepted.'

'It's strange that he should have gone at all on Friday night,' Flick said.

'Probably thought it would look funny if he didn't. We are very discreet about those we turn away. If they talk about it, that's their business, but we don't broadcast it.'

He moved on to describe the Archers' history which had evolved into a purely ceremonial role as the Queen's bodyguard in Scotland. They still took a pride in their archery. Chuckling, he recounted how, in 1818, they out-shot a visiting party of American Indians, only to be loftily informed that the Indians had long since converted to firearms.

'I'm glad we stayed for lunch,' di Falco said as they waved goodbye.

'Very useful,' Flick agreed, getting out her mobile. 'Now I'm going to track down this Percy Oliphant.'

7

When the court rose for lunch Baggo struggled to his feet, his bum as numb as his brain. For the first hour, Radcliffe had picked more holes in Burns's defence without disturbing his self-assurance. When Radcliffe had finished, Burns aimed a supercilious grin at the jury. Baggo readily imagined him as an unscrupulous timeshare salesman, exaggerating and lying with brazen persistence. He hoped the jury would see through him, but if you told a big lie well enough and often enough … The rest of the morning had been taken up with defence witnesses who confirmed that certain uncontroversial parts of Burns's story were true. Mere window-dressing, but would it fool some members of the jury?

Baggo had planned to test the water with Melanie, but she went off in earnest discussion with Radcliffe. Outside in the foyer, Wallace and McKellar approached Lachlan Smail, who immediately called out to his solicitor. The four men moved to a corner where they began an animated discussion. Watching keenly, her brow furrowed, a tall, elegant woman of about forty stood a short distance away.

'Mrs Nicola Smail, I think?' Baggo gave her his broadest smile.

'Yes?' she responded coldly.

'I am Detective Sergeant Chandavarkar and I would like to ask you some questions.'

She frowned. 'I know who you are. You gave evidence against my husband last week.'

'The questions I have relate to the murder of Mr Knox.'

'Why should I help you?' She spoke sharply with a mere suggestion of a Scottish accent.

'I cannot think of a good reason why you should not help our inquiry, ma'am.'

She looked at him appraisingly then glanced in her husband's direction. He raised his voice and snapped at his solicitor. The words 'get it over with' carried across the foyer. She said to Baggo, 'Very well. What do you want to know?'

'Could we go somewhere more private?'

'I want to stay here and keep an eye on what is happening with my husband.'

Baggo decided not to argue. 'As you please. I know you were at the function on Friday night. Did you see Mr Knox at any stage?'

'I saw him after the meal. He was talking to a striking-looking woman in a long black dress. I don't remember seeing either of them after that.'

'What were you wearing that night?'

Her eyebrows shot up but she replied casually, pushing her blonde hair back from her face. 'I also wore a long, black dress. And, should you want to examine it, I haven't had it cleaned since Friday.'

'What were you doing during the archery?'

'Watching, with my husband.'

'And afterwards?'

She screwed up her face. 'I believe I went to the Ladies. Yes, I did. With Ellie Primrose. And then I chatted to some friends. When the dancing started I did a Dashing White Sergeant with my husband and Ellie Primrose.'

'When did the dancing start?'

'I really don't know. Perhaps twenty minutes after the archery finished.'

'What did your husband do immediately before the dancing?'

She glanced in his direction again. Their eyes locked for a moment. She smiled, he nodded to her and she nodded back. Addressing Baggo, her eyes wide open, she said, 'I have no idea. I don't tag him, you know.'

'I am glad to hear it.' He smiled. She responded with a slight curl of her upper lip. 'And after the Dashing Sergeant?' he asked pleasantly.

'There was a Duke of Perth and Hamilton House. I did the Duke of Perth with my husband and Hamilton House with John Primrose.' Although she volunteered this extra information, her tone of voice and posture remained hostile.

'Did you ever leave the area where the party was? Did you explore any corridors?'

'Definitely not.'

'It's unusual for an accused person to be at the same social function as someone who is prosecuting them during the trial. Why did you go to this one?'

She looked him in the eye. 'Not only is my husband presumed innocent. He is innocent. He is a member of the Royal Company of Archers and he is absolutely right to hold his head up and go about as if nothing has happened. I think I've answered your questions, and now, if you'll excuse me.' Abruptly, she went over to stand beside her husband who was talking to Wallace and McKellar. The solicitor hovered nearby, glowering.

Baggo moved closer.

Smail was saying, '... so I stayed at the table talking to John Primrose till they came to clear it. I finished my wine, went for a pee, chatted to one or two people, then watched the archery with my wife.' He talked in a curious, staccato way. Baggo thought he belonged on a parade ground or in kennels.

'What did you do after that?' Wallace asked.

'I believe I bought a drink. Yes. And one for John Primrose. It was a bit of a scrum. Not enough people serving.'

'And then?'

'I drank it, of course.'

'With?'

'John Primrose.' He spoke as if the question was stupid. He moved towards Wallace so their faces were inches apart. 'This nonsense,' he paused to gesture towards the courtroom door, 'has shown me who my friends are, Sergeant. John Primrose has been an absolute brick.' He continued to invade Wallace's space as if defying him to contradict him. 'When the dancing started my wife got us up for the Dashing White Sergeant.' She reached for his hand.

Wallace asked, 'Did you leave the dancing area at any time after that, Mr Smail?'

'Of course I did, when we went home. I went for a pee later on and I bought some more drinks. The rest of the time we were dancing or sitting on one of these odd benches they have down the sides of the hall.'

'Did you see or hear anything that might help us find out who killed Mr Knox?'

'No, and I probably wouldn't tell you if I had.'

Baggo saw his wife squeeze his hand and frown at him. He shook her off and she suppressed a twitch that was almost a recoil.

Smail barked, 'Come on, Nicola. We're off for lunch. I've had enough of these damn fool questions.' He turned on his heel and strode towards the exit, his wife following. Head down, a bulky file under one arm, the solicitor slunk after them like a sheep-dog trying to control unruly sheep.

'Smail's pretty forceful,' Wallace said.

'And he has a temper,' McKellar growled. 'In St Andrews he has a reputation for lifting his hands. But no one speaks up against him so his record's clean.' The St Andrews bobby shifted from foot to foot, still uncomfortable in civilian clothes.

'But lunch is a good idea,' Wallace said. 'Coming, Baggo?'

'Thank you but no. I am staying in an excellent B and B run by a retired chef. He serves the best breakfast in Edinburgh and I do not want to burst out of my trousers.'

'No one would want that to happen,' Wallace laughed and he led McKellar out of the building.

The B and B in the Newington area of town was run by a retired chef who believed in sending out his guests well fed in the morning, but Baggo's priority was to speak to Melanie on her return to court. He found a seat in the foyer and checked his mobile. He found a text from his boss in London confirming his assignment to the murder inquiry and instructing him to make an arrest and get back as soon as possible.

'Melanie!' he exclaimed as, in wig and gown, she approached from an unexpected angle.

'What is it?' she sounded distracted.

'Do you fancy meeting for a drink tonight?'

'What?' She paused, looking perplexed. 'Well, yes, I could, I suppose. I'll be at the Canny Man's at nine. Must fly.' Her gown swishing behind her, she hurried into court.

'Great, see you there,' he enthused as the door swung behind her.

He decided that he might as well wait inside the courtroom and resumed his unpadded seat near the dock. He took out his notebook and pretended to study it. At counsel's table, Melanie was busy with genuine work. Her lips pursed, one hand turning a page then playing with a curl of her wig just above her ear. Her pen poised then suddenly active, she was a picture of concentration. His anticipation of the evening grew as he watched her. He brought out his mobile and Googled the Canny Man's. It turned out to be an unusual pub in Morningside, like Newington on the south side of the city. Interesting. What would she drink? Wine, probably. Or would she be one of those girls who like to play men at their own game and drink pints? He had developed a taste for heavy Scottish beer. He found himself licking his lips.

When court resumed, it was the turn of Lachlan Smail to give evidence on his own behalf. His counsel was a man with a large gut, a loud voice and strangled vowels. Smail kept his answers short, always a good idea, but not if it gave an impression of aggressive snappiness. From the expressions on their faces, many of the jury did not take to Smail.

Smail himself appeared oblivious to the impression he created. His chin jutting out, he insisted that Burns had duped him. He believed Jack Nicklaus was truly involved in building a first-class golf course on his land. He had, he said, been furious when told that Nicklaus had never been on the farm and that the pictures of him had been superimposed on images of empty fields. Baggo did not believe a word of it and wondered how Smail would fare in prison.

When court rose, Baggo went to meet Radcliffe and Melanie for a post mortem. In the foyer he heard Maltravers refuse to speak to Wallace and McKellar. 'I still have a planning practice to run,' he protested.

There was nothing for Baggo to contribute to counsel's discussion and Radcliffe agreed that over the following days he should concentrate on the murder. After swapping mobile numbers he left them. 'See you later,' he whispered to Melanie. She rewarded him with a conspiratorial smile.

The sun was shining on the Royal Mile when he emerged into daylight. He pulled on a long-visored golf cap. A Brahmin, brought up to avoid the sun, he could not understand all the fair-skinned native Brits who exposed as much as they could, turning themselves into lobsters in what seemed to Baggo to be a reversal of evolution.

He checked his mobile and found a message from Flick.

* * *

'We're early, but that shouldn't matter,' Flick said to di Falco as he pulled back the door of The Verdict pub, a short distance from Parliament House, where they were due to meet Percy Oliphant. A thin, stooped young man with acne partially hidden by uneven facial hair barged past them, causing Flick to grab di Falco's arm.

'Excuse me!' she shouted at his back as he ran up the street. 'Don't worry, Billy,' she told di Falco, who was set to chase him.

It took a moment for their eyes to adjust to the subdued light inside the pub, which was presided over by a sour-looking man leaning idly on the bar. Round the walls were murals depicting famous criminals. They were boldly painted in garish colours and stopped just short of grotesque, the names inscribed underneath in elaborate calligraphy.

It was early for after-work drinkers and only a few lunch time patrons remained. A noisy group of students occupied a corner, one of them insisting that the first question had been unfair. Flick had a sudden flash-back to similar post-exam sessions from her days at Bristol. At the far end of the bar two men in ill-fitting suits talked confidentially. Both aimed shifty glances at Flick. She recognised the type and knew what verdict she would give them.

Identifying Oliphant was easy. Dressed in a black jacket with a tie that looked as if someone had vomited paella over it, he sat alone in a booth, a half-empty glass of what looked like gin and tonic in front of him.

'Inspector Fortune, I presume.' He spoke in plummy tones, slightly slurred, and stared at Flick's bump.

With some difficulty Flick eased herself onto the bench opposite, noting that the plastic cover was warm and a half-pint glass remained on the table, some beer undrunk. Di Falco sat beside Oliphant, hemming him in and looking with distaste at the dandruff sprinkled generously over his shoulders.

'I settled my case this morning, on excellent terms, I might say. My client was most grateful, and after a celebration lunch, the rest of today must be a *dies non*.' He looked for a reaction from Flick but got none. 'I suppose you want to see me about Night?'

'Night?' she asked.

A superior smile creased his pale, pudgy face. '*Nox, noctis* – night. Latin, you know. A play on words. Knox's bar nickname was Night, and by Jove he lived up to it.' His fingers caressed his glass. They were soft, small fingers with long nails. A woman's fingers.

'I want to know what you can tell me about Friday evening. I believe you were there at the function?'

'I was.'

'I believe you saw Mr Knox after dinner?'

He shifted in his seat. 'I did.'

'And?'

'And so?'

Flick leaned across the table and spoke quietly. 'You have been gossiping about seeing him with someone. If that is not true, you must tell us now. If it is true, it is your duty to give us all the information you can. I shouldn't need to remind you that you are an officer of court. We can do this at a police office, you know.'

His dark eyes narrowed and he exhaled audibly, the alcoholic fumes making Flick wrinkle her nose. She could tell he was quite drunk. His reluctance to cooperate and his insufferable air of intellectual superiority showed him to be one of those lawyers who instinctively dislike the police, just as some dogs loathe cats. She had come across the type before and had no time for them. It was the police who found the bodies, tackled the mad and the bad and kept society safe, while the lawyers …

'I do not need to be lectured, Inspector,' he said. 'I required you to focus your queries on what you want to know about.' Having tried to save face he took a deep breath. 'Mr Knox had a reputation with the ladies. Recently there have been stories that he was having an affair with the wife of the Edinburgh Divisional Commander. When the Traynors were invited to join the top table last Friday, some of us were curious to see her. It was easy to tell her from the other women at that table.' His lips stretched into a lecherous grin. 'After dinner, I saw her talking confidentially with Mr Knox. She wore a particularly seductive black dress with a slit up one thigh. When the bows and arrows came out I stayed at the back of the crowd and kept an eye open. I suspected they might try something scandalous. I spotted Mr Knox, on his own, going down the main corridor leading to Court Three. I was distracted and when I looked again he had disappeared. There were no lights on once you got further down the corridor. Next thing I saw was Mrs Traynor following Mr Knox. I couldn't see well because of the lack of light, but she disappeared about where the judge's door of Court Three is. That was it. Mr Knox must have bribed the security staff because all courtroom doors are supposed to be locked.'

'Can you be certain it was Mrs Traynor?'

'I believe so, yes.'

'Did you see her face?'

'Not actually in the corridor, but I'm sure it was her with her black dress and blonde hair. Who else would it be?'

Flick ignored the question. 'What did you do then?'

'I went back to the archery for a bit and found Rory McIntyre. He'd been fascinated by Knox and Mrs Traynor, and I told him what I'd seen.'

'Where were you when you told him?'

'In the hall, where the archery was.'

'Might you have been overheard?'

'There were a lot of people nearby.'

'Was Chief Superintendent Traynor among them?'

'I honestly don't know. He might have been.'

'Lachlan Smail?'

'Don't know him.'

'He was in Archers' uniform.'

'There were a lot dressed like that. One or two could have heard me, I suppose.'

'Gideon Maltravers?'

'The planning consultant? I don't remember seeing him close by, but he might have been.'

'Mrs Nicola Smail?'

He shrugged. 'I don't know the lady.'

'Did you see either Mr Knox or Mrs Traynor later?'

'Not Mr Knox. I saw Mrs Traynor making her way towards the Ladies before the dancing started. I remember noticing that her face was flushed.' He raised his eyebrows.

'How long after you believe you saw her enter the judge's door was that?'

'Twenty minutes, half an hour. I really couldn't be sure.'

'How much had you had to drink at that stage, sir?'

Anger flashed in his dark eyes. 'It had been a good evening, Inspector. I have no idea exactly how much I'd had, but I was well able to recognise what I saw and remember it.'

'Did you tell anyone else apart from Mr McIntyre at that time?'

'Well, yes, I did. It was pretty hot stuff.'

'And you could have been overheard?'

He shrugged. 'Of course. So is the Chief Superintendent your prime suspect?'

'We don't have a prime suspect. We think the murder may have been linked to the trial Mr Knox was prosecuting.' Flick hated to tell Oliphant anything, but the DCC's instructions to divert attention from Traynor had been clear. 'Please do not discuss this inquiry further, sir. It is unhelpful if too much information is made public.'

'From henceforth my lips shall be sealed, Inspector. But the circumstances give rise to the question, *quis custodiet ipsos custodes*?'

Flick stood up less elegantly than she would have liked and looked down on him. 'Any complaints should be addressed to the Scottish Police Authority. We've come a long way since Juvenal's day, you know.' She paused long enough to enjoy the look of astonishment that she should know the author of the quote before marching out into the fresh air.

'Has he not got the most punchable face, boss?' di Falco asked.

'I wouldn't stop at his face,' she muttered.

Appalled by what she had just said, and the look of delight on di Falco's face, she left a message on Baggo's voicemail asking him to interview the Lord Provost after court and a similar message on Wallace's asking him to see the Secretary of State for Scotland.

'We're off to talk to the scarlet woman,' she told di Falco.

* * *

The Traynors lived on a private road in the affluent suburb of Colinton. The police pool car, its springs knackered, bumped along the uneven surface before pulling into a well-raked gravel driveway in front of a pristine-looking two-storey snowcemmed house with red pantiles. Neatly-clipped boxwoods sat in terracotta pots on either side of a front door studded with black metal bolts designed to hint at a historical pedigree but were shiny enough to have been recently taken off a shelf at B and Q. Bordering the gravel, the sharply-edged lawn completed the impression of order and pride. This could be 'Craigperfect', the lovely home of the MacPerfect family, all of whom, naturally, lived ideal lives.

'This place must have cost a packet,' Flick said as Di Falco parked beside the sole discordant note, a grimy white Polo slewed at an angle to the house and carrying battle scars on its front wing.

Flick pressed the bell button and winced at the twee chimes that announced their arrival. After a minute she rang again. 'I wonder if she's round the back,' she said. Di Falco went to see and Flick stepped back to check the windows.

'Can I help you?' It was a woman's voice with the lilt of the west coast. Her tone was not welcoming. Wearing a crumpled and faded cotton dress with fancy-looking sunglasses pushed up to sit on her shoulder-length blonde hair, her appearance and posture were too casual for her to be the lady of this house. Her smooth, lightly-tanned skin glistened with sun cream. When asked however, she agreed that she was Mrs Lynda Traynor.

When Flick told her the nature of her inquiry the woman's face darkened. With evident reluctance, she led the way through a wood-panelled hall into a sitting room facing the back of the house, the slap of her flip-flops on the polished floor expressing her irritation. She gasped with surprise when she saw di Falco peering through a window, but pointed him towards the French door with an expression of semi-amused disdain, as if Inspector Clouseau had come calling. Without offering refreshment or inviting them to sit, she reclined on the sofa, nonchalantly pushing a cushion to the floor. It was a strange, arrogant gesture, one that dissociated her from her immaculate surroundings. Flick's dislike for her intensified.

'Well?' said Lynda Traynor.

Flick sat on an upright chair facing her. With almond-shaped eyes, a prominent nose and full lips, Lynda Traynor was not classically beautiful, but she had an hour-glass figure and a confidence about the way she carried herself that explained why men were attracted. Di Falco was having difficulty taking his eyes off her legs, which she had angled to give a hint of an intimate view. Flick frowned at him but he paid no heed.

'As I said, we're here to see you about the murder of Farquhar Knox,' Flick said. 'And we thought we should do it while your husband was not here.'

'Stop right there,' Lynda Traynor snapped. 'Have you read my file?' Seeing Flick's look of astonishment, she carried on quickly. 'Yes. I can see you have.' She turned to stare at di Falco. 'But you haven't, though you'll have heard what it says. I'm a "loose cannon", am I not? Correct? Well, I live my life in my way and have every right to do so. I'm not going to help you. And don't try that "we'll do it down at the station" routine, because it won't wash. Now excuse me but I have an appointment with a sun lounger.'

Flick did not move. 'Mrs Traynor, we have reason to believe you had sex with Mr Knox just before he was killed. Is that the case?'

'That is a very impertinent question.'

'As I just said, this is a murder inquiry. We have witnesses who saw you talking to him in a confidential manner and one who saw you heading for Court Three, which you probably entered using the judge's door. There is also evidence that soon afterwards you went to the Ladies, looking flushed. Scientific evidence has been obtained and it would be conclusive if your DNA were to be found among the stains that will be examined. If we need to, we will easily get a warrant to obtain a sample from you. It really would be in your best interests to cooperate. I should also say that we are Fife officers. Your husband will not have access to this inquiry.'

As Flick spoke, her tone measured, Lynda Traynor's expression changed from defiant to thoughtful. For some time she did not speak then sat up straight and spoke directly. 'That is all very interesting, but the ifs and probablys tell me you don't have evidence to back your theories. I'm not going to say more because my private life is none of your damn business. But I did not kill Farquhar Knox and I do not believe my husband did, either. I saw nothing suspicious and I have no idea who did kill him.'

'What were you wearing that night?'

'A long dress. It was black.'

'And figure-hugging?'

'Yes. With a slit up one side.' She did not conceal her impatience.

'And how did you wear your hair?'

'As it is now.'

Flick could see how she would have caught the eye of most men at the function. 'What did you do between the end of the meal and the start of the dancing?'

'This and that. I talked to some people. Probably went to the Ladies.'

'Did you talk to Farquhar Knox?'

'I believe I did. Just after dinner. Then we both went to speak to other people.'

'Did you see him after that?'

Mrs Traynor screwed up her face as if in thought. 'I really can't remember,' she said.

'When did you next see your husband after dinner?' Flick asked.

'The dancing had started. They were doing that silly one where they go round the floor in threes.'

'How was he?'

'Fine. A bit drunk maybe.'

'Did he seem angry?'

She thought for a moment then said quietly, 'He said that if he saw that cunt Knox he'd punch his lights out. I coaxed him into the library. He had bought a bottle of wine and I sat with him in a far corner. We left a bit early. I kept a look-out for Farquhar but didn't see him.'

'Did you and your husband argue that night?'

'Yes. If you must know, he kept saying I'd crossed a boundary.' There was no hint of guilt in the way she spoke.

'So he believed you'd had sex with Mr Knox?'

'He must have. I actually denied it.'

'So he was with you from the time of the dance they do in threes, the something Sergeant I think they call it?'

'Dashing White Sergeant, boss,' di Falco interjected as Mrs Traynor nodded.

'Can you think of anyone who might have wanted Mr Knox dead?'

'No. And my husband cares too much about his career to commit a crime of passion. It wouldn't be his thing.' Her voice dripped with contempt.

'And have you subsequently told him that you did have sex with Mr Knox?'

'No. Don't be silly, Inspector. I wasn't born yesterday.'

'Are you prepared to give us a sample of your DNA? The fewer times we have to call the better, I would have thought. Fingerprints, too, for elimination purposes.'

'Come back once you have a warrant. If you manage to get one. Now if that is all …'

As di Falco made to move, Flick sat still. She longed to dent the confidence of this spoiled, self-centred creature. She leaned forward and stared silently until Mrs Traynor met her gaze. 'I do intend to find out who killed Mr Knox, no matter how long it takes. Until I do, the shadow of suspicion will be on you and, more importantly, your husband. The longer that shadow exists, the worse the damage to your husband's career, which has already suffered because of you. You probably don't care much about that, but the less he has to lose, the less we bother about the impact of our inquiries on you. If you had sex with Mr Knox in Court Three and left him alive, it would be in everyone's interests if you told us what you can. Please reconsider.'

Mrs Traynor began to shake her head before Flick had finished. 'You're all so predictable. Now get out.' She rose and led the way to the front door.

As the door slammed shut, the officers made their way to the car, Flick trying to conceal her fury.

'I wonder what the atmosphere in that house is like. Do they have children, boss?' di Falco asked as they exited the driveway.

'One, a boy born four months after the wedding. He'll be fourteen now.'

'There wasn't much evidence of him around the house. I didn't even see a photograph.'

'I saw in the file that he's at some fancy boarding school. Her family has money.'

'I wonder what their sex life is like.'

Flick glanced at him, wrinkled her nose then smiled. 'Non-existent or bizarre, I would have thought. Better not go there.'

8

The spell of good weather continued to make Edinburgh untypically warm. 'Too hot' was a phrase on many citizens' lips. It made Baggo think nostalgically of Mumbai. Only Edinburgh was far less crowded than either Mumbai or London. He appreciated the space. As he headed for the Canny Man's along grey streets strewn with short-lived blossom he felt alive and stimulated. This was a city he had imagined as being permanently cold, lashed by winds off the North Sea. In the balmy evening air it lived up to its claim to be the Athens of the North. The weather had taken him by surprise. That week he had bought long-sleeved summer shirts and trousers and wished he had a Fedora or Panama hat so he could strut about like a gentleman. He pulled the visor of his golf cap down. The lower part of his face was still regrettably brown after the golf.

But this was a stimulating investigation. He had enjoyed meeting the Lord Provost. The physically unimposing, soft-spoken little man, well into his sixties, had beamed when Baggo had told him how much he was enjoying his stay. But he had not been able to help the investigation. On Friday he had not sat next to either of the Traynors and remembered nothing of their movements, while his wife, who had sat next to Graeme Traynor and discussed roses with him, had forgotten her distance glasses and observed nothing.

'Sorry!' a man shouted from behind a hedge as Baggo caught the spray of a misdirected garden hose.

'Do not worry,' Baggo replied, hoping the stain down one leg of his cream chinos would dry before he reached the pub.

Cutting his pace, he replayed the phone conversation with Flick as she drove back to Fife. After describing her own day, she had told him about Wallace and McKellar's interview with the Secretary of State, a man with a reputation for womanising. A political advisor and two civil servants present, he had denied any recollection of the Traynors on Friday night, despite being seated between Lynda Traynor and the Lord Provost's wife. 'If he'd been an ordinary punter they'd have jogged his memory at a police station,' Flick had commented. The politician's wife had been no more helpful.

'Are you going to question the Chief Superintendent?' Baggo had asked.

'Not yet. Spider Gilsland hasn't found anything helpful on the CCTV but I want to have a good look at it. Also, I got Knox's laptop and mobile from Fettes and I'll give them to Spider when I get to Cupar. Dr MacGregor took the arrow out at the PM and the lab has had it since this morning. I'm still waiting to hear if there are any fingerprints on it. The Edinburgh SOCOs took some prints from the court and I have them with me. We won't get any comparisons till tomorrow. We don't have enough to arrest Traynor, but if I interview him I'd have to treat him as a suspect. He'd have to be suspended and the news would spread like wildfire. I'm going to talk to the DCC before I take that step.'

They agreed that there was no point in Baggo attending the briefing in Cupar the next morning. He would stay in Edinburgh and continue his inquiries there.

It was just after nine when Baggo found the door of the Canny Man's. A brass plate beside it forbade credit cards, cameras, mobile phones and backpackers. It did not look like his sort of place. He was relieved he had taken out cash recently. As neither policemen nor Indians were banned, he shoved his cap in his pocket, checked his phone was on silent and pushed open the swing doors. The interior was beyond quirky. A profusion of clocks, jugs, stuffed birds and animals, old photographs and paintings decorated the place. A mannequin in a faded sequin dress was suspended from the ceiling above copper-topped tables. Beside a row of Champagne magnums the gantry held a stupendous collection of spirit bottles, mostly whisky, a mirror at the back making it appear even more extensive.

'Hi, there!' As Baggo peered round Melanie broke away from one of the younger groups of drinkers and gave him a chaste kiss on the cheek. She wore jeans and a tee shirt with a low neckline.

'This is Baggo,' she said to her group. 'What do you want to drink, Baggo?' she asked.

'A pint, please, real ale if they have it,'

'And a pint of real ale,' she shouted to a man at the bar. 'Good timing, mate!'

None of the group asked what he did. Articulate, quick-witted and sparky, they continued their conversation. They all seemed to be lawyers. When they began to talk about the murder Baggo learned nothing he did not know, but it was clear that the police were barely ahead of common gossip.

After half an hour, muttering something about the Appeal Court, a woman got up to go. The rest drifted out after her, refusing Baggo's offer of a drink. When only he and Melanie were left, she moved to an alcove with room for two only and asked for a pint of IPA.

'Well?' she asked, sipping the rich, brown beer appreciatively, 'tell me about yourself.'

So he did. She listened intently as he described his childhood in Mumbai, his move to England as a teenager and some of the difficulties he had encountered, despite his father being an eminent urologist.

'Why a policeman?' she asked.

'I loved cop shows and detective stories.' He looked round the walls of the alcove which, papered with sheet music and varnished, had turned a yellow-brown colour. 'I read all the Rebus books and expected Edinburgh to be gritty and cold. But it is warm and civilised.'

'Not all the time,' she countered. 'Let me get you one, then I must go.'

'What about you?' he asked when she returned.

'Very boring, I'm afraid. I was brought up in Morningside, went to school here, George Watson's, then

Edinburgh University and followed my dad into the law. I still live in Morningside and my folks are five minutes away.' She pulled a face.

'You are very lucky. It is good to be comfortable in a place, and I do not find you at all boring.'

Her face lit up. 'Comfortable is good if it's not boring. And Edinburgh has lots of culture and history.'

'You are right there. So your father was a lawyer?'

'Dad was at the bar. He always wants to know what firms are instructing me, and gets quite pissed off if the firms that used to instruct him thirty years ago don't send work to me. Now he's a sheriff in Airdrie. Sheriffs are judges, you know. I hope he'll retire soon and go off and play lots of golf, but he says he still wants the buzz of work. Mum says she won't know what to do with him if he's around all day. Sorry, I'm gabbling.'

Baggo reached across the table and put a hand on hers. 'You gabble beautifully,' he said then added, 'Sorry, that's pure Bollywood.' They both laughed and she blushed a little.

'So how's the inquiry going?' she asked.

'Frankly, we're not much ahead of the gossip, but please keep that under your hat. I expect we will get a breakthrough soon. Patient work generally pays off.' He wished he meant what he said. 'We are going round all those at the function on Friday night. It is a huge task.'

'Well I saw nothing that would help.'

'But you were not there.' He had checked the lists, looking for her name.

'Oh yes I was. Angie Jack, the first woman to leave this

evening, had a migraine. I was at a loose end and took her ticket.'

She grinned sheepishly. 'I got truly smashed. The next morning I was calling God on the big, white phone. Not good. So you can write "too pissed to notice" opposite my name on your spread-sheet.'

Baggo looked into her twinkling eyes. There was an electricity between them which he was sure she also felt.

She drained her glass. 'Time to go,' she said.

Outside, the long Scottish summer twilight had faded and the streetlamps were lit. They were heading in the same direction. After about a quarter of a mile Melanie turned down a wide street and Baggo walked her to the outer door of her tenement, hovering as she found her keys.

'See you tomorrow,' she said quickly then turned the lock and slipped inside. The heavy door swung back and gave a loud click as it shut.

As he walked back to Newington, initial disappointment gave way to quiet optimism. 'Patient work generally pays off,' he repeated to himself.

9

'A lot of serious assaults are committed by people who wouldn't say boo to a goose,' Fergus said as he stirred the scrambled eggs. 'They take it so long then explode.' He pulled several rashers of bacon from the grill, arranged them on plates and served the eggs. 'Eat up,' he commanded.

Flick smiled wanly. Her appetite was poor and the quantity of food on her plate was putting her off. 'You mean Traynor suddenly had enough?'

'Could be.'

'I need something more to go on. There isn't the evidence to arrest him at the moment and he's too smart to incriminate himself if I ever do get to interview him.'

'What about Mrs Knox? She seemed a bit ...' the phone interrupted him. He answered then passed over the receiver. 'The DCC,' he mouthed.

Flick's greeting was cut short. 'Have you seen *Good News* this morning?' the DCC's voice was an octave higher than the last time they had spoken.

'No, sir.'

'It's all blown open. Knox and Mrs Traynor, how he died, the lot. They're saying Traynor should be suspended and even offering a reward, twenty thousand pounds, for anyone who brings them evidence that directly results in a conviction. They say they'll pass everything they get to us immediately, meaning as soon as they've used it as a scoop. They practically accuse us of protecting our own and looking to pin the murder on someone connected to the fraud trial. They've even hired some retired cop from London to advise their readers about what should be happening. Some buffoon called Osborne. He seems to know you.'

Flick's heart sank. Inspector Noel Osborne, known as Inspector No, had been the bane of her life when she had been his sergeant in Wimbledon. Lucky not to have ended up in jail beside the criminals he had framed, and even luckier to have retired with an intact pension, he had gone to Spain but had not sunk quietly into Rioja-sodden Andalucian obscurity. He neglected no opportunity to make money or boast about cleaning up the East End and now he was about to make Flick's life even more difficult.

'What does he say?' Flick asked shakily.

'Let's see. Yes. "My protégé is a good girl, no doubt, but it's as obvious as the nose on your face: you can't hatch babies and catch villains at one and the same time. I had no pregnant women on my team when I cleaned up the East End." Inspector Fortune, you don't need me to tell you how bad this is. I want to know where they got their information, how the inquiry is going and what you plan to do next. Work on that and come to see me at noon today. Right?'

'Right, sir.'

'And Inspector, not one word to the press without my say-so.'

'Right, sir.' The DCC had already ended the call.

Good News was a comparatively new morning paper dedicated, it boasted, to delivering positive news and campaigning journalism. After an encouraging start, circulation figures had declined and it was trying to regain public interest with publicity stunts. Good news was now only a title.

Unable to eat more than a few mouthfuls, Flick emptied her plate onto Fergus's and told him what had happened. As she spoke, her voice caught. Fergus put his arm round her and led her into the sitting room where they sat hugging each other on the sofa. At length Flick got up to wash her face in the cloakroom. As she stared at her red-eyed reflection her anger grew. She stormed back into the kitchen. 'I'll give him protégé,' she fumed. She cast her mind back to her visit to The Verdict and the thin young man with acne who had barged past her. Then she phoned Baggo.

* * *

His bacon and eggs finished, Baggo was savouring home-made marmalade on brown toast when Flick called. The other residents had not yet appeared for breakfast so he was comfortable speaking on his mobile. He listened carefully, said little and arranged to meet di Falco in Dublin Street as soon after nine as his colleague could make it from Fife. Then he buttered another slice of toast and poured more coffee.

An hour and a half later the two officers were standing at a corner, waiting. In front of them sat an elderly Jaguar, its age concealed by a personalised number plate. A call to the police national computer had confirmed that the car was registered to Percy Oliphant. It was carelessly parked in a residents' bay so that it protruded some six inches onto a double yellow line. Remembering what Flick had said about Oliphant's drinking the previous day, Baggo asked himself if he should call the traffic cops.

Before he had made up his mind, at twenty past nine Oliphant stepped out of his doorway and started to walk up the hill towards Parliament House. Baggo and di Falco blocked his path. After giving their names and showing their warrants Baggo said he wanted a word.

'I'm in a hurry,' Oliphant said in a superior tone, the stale alcohol on his breath only partially masked by a pungent after-shave.

Baggo moved closer, sniffing ostentatiously. Di Falco stood beside him.

'We believe you have been speaking to the press, Mr Oliphant?'

'Journalists should not reveal their sources.'

'Some do, eventually. I repeat, we believe you have been speaking to the press.'

'What if I have been?'

'Oh, it is a free country, no doubt, but you did tell my colleague Inspector Fortune that your lips would be sealed, and from what Mr Pete Bothwell wrote in *Good News* this morning it would appear that you may not have kept your promise.'

With a supercilious smile that made di Falco clench his fist, Oliphant replied smoothly, 'I never said anything about texting. And it's not a crime to embarrass the police. Actually, it's rather good sport.'

Baggo kept a poker face. 'But it is a crime to obstruct or hinder the police in the execution of their duty, and publishing details of a case, making assumptions on the basis of inadequate evidence, can often obstruct or hinder us.' Oliphant raised his eyebrows but did not respond. 'So this is a warning: do not give details of the Knox murder case to the press. Should you do so again and if it does hamper the investigation, we will charge you. I hope you understand.'

Oliphant curled his lip. 'Are you finished?'

Baggo and di Falco stood aside. 'I mean it,' Baggo said as the advocate strode off to court.

'I didn't know the journalist had named him as the source,' di Falco said.

'He didn't. The inspector worked it out. But there's no harm in sowing a little distrust there. Lawyers are not the only ones who can play games with words.'

'Do you think he got the message?'

'I believe so. Now we should try to catch Mr Maltravers before he goes into court.'

They had not gone far when they saw a traffic warden. 'There's a Jaguar with a personalised number partly on a double yellow line in Dublin Street,' Baggo told her.

'That was mean, but I like it,' di Falco said.

'My old boss, Inspector No, would have gone much further. If he knew the man had been drinking, he would have pointed out the parking problem to him, but only after he had called the traffic cops and had them waiting round a corner. As soon as the man started to re-park his car No would buzz the traffic cops who would breathalyse and arrest another drunk driver. We would have caught Oliphant with that trick this morning.'

'You thought about it, didn't you, Sarge?'

'Of course I did, but I am just a kitten.'

Di Falco gave him a funny look. He didn't know that Baggo had been afraid that Melanie might hear of it, and strongly disapprove.

* * *

Gideon Maltravers was standing outside the court building in the Lawnmarket, his mobile clamped to his ear. Baggo and di Falco waited until he had ended his call before approaching him. Tall, saturnine and stylishly dressed in a beige suit, the planning consultant was not pleased to see them. 'I'm trying to run my practice,' he snapped.

'You will have to speak to us eventually,' Baggo told him. 'This will not take long and then we should be able to leave you in peace.'

'According to the press, you'll try and pin a murder on me.'

'That is nonsense, Mr Maltravers, and I am sure you know it. Of course, when someone is reluctant to speak to us we ask ourselves why? I am sorry to bother you, and I know things must be very difficult for you at the moment, but we simply want to know about your movements last Friday between dinner finishing and eleven pm.'

Baggo's conciliatory tone worked. 'Well I suppose that's easy. I sat at the table till we were told to move. Then I went outside for a smoke. Then I went for a pee. Then I watched the archery. I hate dancing and fortunately most of the people at Hamish Harris's table did too so we found a quiet corner of the library where we settled with a couple of good bottles.'

'Did you go straight to the library after the archery?'

'We mingled for a bit, something I wasn't keen on. I had seen Knox earlier and didn't fancy having to meet him. Hamish was at the bar buying the wine and that took some time. Perhaps I did have another cigarette. Yes, I believe I did. Actually I think I had two.'

'Please think carefully. We will check what you say against the CCTV and it should be easy to pick you out because of your height.'

'And I was one of the very few in a white tuxedo. Of course the waiters wore white as well. One or two of them sneaked out for a fag. Nicotine addiction is a great leveller. Yes, I definitely did go for a couple more fags before the dancing started. I remember giving one of the waiters a light and I asked him if the band was ready. He said no and I had another one.' His face twitched and Baggo saw the strain he was under. 'This is a bugger, you know,' he spat out suddenly. 'I didn't want to go on Friday, but it was good of Hamish to stand by me. You know, all evening I could feel people's eyes following me as if I was a leper.'

'And after your cigarettes, what did you do?'

'As I said, I met up with the rest of Hamish's table. They were waiting for me, actually. Hamish had got the wine and we made a bee-line for the library before anyone asked us to dance.'

'Did you go with anyone?' Baggo asked.

He snorted. 'No. I don't have anyone at the moment. When this blew up I did, but ...' His voice tailed off.

'One more question: what was Mr Knox doing when you saw him?'

'Talking to someone. It was just before the archery. He spotted me, registered surprise then stared right through me. I didn't catch anything that was said.'

'Anything else?' Baggo asked his colleague. Di Falco shook his head and Baggo thanked Maltravers for his time.

'It is no joke facing trial in the High Court,' Baggo mused. 'To us putting people on trial is a process, part of the job, but for the individual concerned it is life-changing. Guilty or innocent.' He glanced towards Maltravers who was back on his phone, fitting in another call before his trial resumed.

* * *

'There used to be a brothel a few doors along,' Molly Bertram informed Baggo and di Falco. 'It was quite famous and when an American aircraft carrier docked in Leith the queue ran along the street and round the corner. They had to bus in extra girls from Glasgow.'

They were sitting in the front room of the Bertrams' ground floor and basement flat in Danube Street. Down the hill from the more exclusive India Street, it was dark and cobbled and oozed middle class respectability.

Warming to her theme, and responding to the officers' grins rather than her husband's half-hearted frown, she went on to describe how the madam frequently appeared before the courts and used these occasions for free publicity, titillating journalists with quotes about how busy she always was the week the General Assembly of the Church of Scotland met.

Molly and Rab Bertram were in their early thirties, Baggo judged. They were friendly and she was definitely vivacious. Both casually dressed, she was at pains to explain her husband's unshaven face, tee shirt, khaki shorts and sandals. 'Rab had a big case which settled at the last minute so he's staying at home to catch up on his written work.'

He pulled a face. 'Pleadings, opinions and so forth – great fun.' He picked up a child's plastic telephone and began to fiddle with the buttons.

'I believe on Friday you were at the same table as the late Mr Knox?' Baggo asked.

Instantly serious, he replied, 'Yes. He was my devil-master, meaning I was his pupil. The Cuthberts organised the table.'

'What can you tell us about Mr Knox?'

'Generally?' He looked at the ceiling as if for guidance. 'He was very clever, very intuitive, in court anyway. He had a lot of energy, didn't suffer fools. Praise from him really meant something. He had an eye for the ladies, but I suspect you know that.'

'Not just an eye,' Molly interjected.

'How would you describe their marriage?' di Falco asked.

'They clung to it, but not to each other, I think,' Molly said.

'How well did you know Mrs Knox?'

'Not well,' they said in unison.

Di Falco carried on, 'Did either of you see Mrs Knox during the archery?'

Rab shook his head. Molly said, 'Yes. We chatted about shooting. Or rather she did.'

'Did you see someone else and go and talk to them?'

She laughed. 'Is that what she told you? She's the world's worst for looking over your shoulder when you're speaking to her. She may tell you she likes to be called Mrs Knox, but she needs you to know she's really a Lady. For some reason that evening she was quite dismissive about bows and arrows and went on about properly lethal firearms. Ironic, really. Anyway, after she'd told me what a brilliant shot her son was, she spotted someone more important and moved on.'

'Do you know if she's very friendly with a judge, Lord Hutton?' di Falco asked.

Rab clapped his hands gleefully. 'That would be a cracker! Of course, 'Orrible 'Utton's her neighbour. I haven't heard anything about that. Have you, darling?'

She shook her head. 'But it would fit. She's a dreadful snob and loves a handle. Tell them about the basement. Go on.'

He appeared genuinely cross. 'It's not relevant.'

'In which case they'll forget it. But it's good background.'

'Background is always helpful,' Baggo said encouragingly.

'Well when I was devilling, Eloise liked me to go down the steps to the basement door when I visited the house. She and Farquhar could tell it was me as the basement bell sounded different from the main door bell, but really she didn't want a scruff coming to her front door. Unless I'm dressed for work I don't really bother.'

'I am the same,' Baggo said. He went on to ask the important question, 'Did either of you see Mr or Mrs Knox between the end of the archery and the start of the dancing?'

They looked at each other thoughtfully then in unison said 'No.'

'Did either of you see Mr Knox with a woman in a long, black dress?'

Rab replied, 'We both saw him with a lady we believe is Mrs Traynor. They were talking earnestly immediately after dinner. Then you saw Mrs T in the Ladies, didn't you, darling?'

'Yes. This woman in a long, sexy, black dress came in as I was about to leave. She had blonde hair, which was a bit dishevelled and she was flushed, but trying to act cool. She started talking about the band taking an age, which was nonsense. I thought at first she might have been drunk, but she didn't smell of drink. That would have been between half past ten and quarter to eleven, but of course I wasn't watching the clock.'

'Tell them what you said to me, Molly,' Rab said.

She coloured slightly. 'I said to Rab, "If that's Mrs Traynor, I bet she's just shagged Night." Sometimes we called Farquhar Night.'

'So we've heard,' di Falco said. 'How did Eloise Knox behave during the rest of the evening?'

Molly said, 'She did the Dashing White Sergeant with the Cuthberts then spent almost all the time in the library with me and Jen Cuthbert. You could tell she was furious with Farquhar, but she didn't go searching for him. She kept asking Rab if he'd seen his devil-master.'

'As if I was responsible for him in some way. I looked about for him but it became pretty clear he'd done a bunk. He sometimes did, you know. Eventually Kenny and Jen took her home.'

'Did you see the Traynors later on?' Baggo asked.

Rab said, 'I spotted them at the far end of the library when I was trying to find Farquhar. At least it was Traynor plus the woman in the black dress we'd seen earlier. It was just the two of them and a bottle of wine. They didn't look happy. A bit before midnight they passed near us, on their way out, I suspect.'

Molly cut in, 'They looked as if they'd been arguing and Eloise glared at her.'

Baggo asked, 'Can you think of any woman other than Mrs Traynor with whom Mr Knox might have gone to Court Three to have sex?'

They both shook their heads.

Baggo asked, 'Do you remember anything, however

trivial, that Mr Knox said during the evening about the fraud trial?'

Molly shook her head. 'And I was beside him at dinner. He always seemed to arrange that. He was going on about the Archers. Actually he was very funny. He could be, you know, if he was in the mood.'

'Was he in a good mood during the meal?'

'Oh yes, no doubt anticipating his tryst with Mrs Traynor. It was a bit embarrassing when he sang the Robin Hood song when the head Archer passed the table. Funny too, though.' She giggled.

Rab said, 'He did say something to me before the meal when we were having drinks. He said during the trial he was in he'd been re-visiting – that was the word he used – the sort of grass you could grow in different types of soil. Six years ago, before he took silk, I was devilling to him and he was involved in a massive planning inquiry about a golf course near Montrose, Culrathie it was called. There was lots of evidence about grasses and soil types and we had to become quite knowledgeable about them – birds' nesting habits and so on. That's one of the odd things about the bar, you occasionally have to learn an awful lot about stuff you'd never expect to know about.

'It's odd you should mention Henry Hutton. He was our senior in that inquiry. There's nothing like a big planning inquiry for boosting your income at the bar. One night Hutton got pissed and told us he intended to paper his study with twenty-pound notes after that one.'

'That is interesting,' Baggo said as di Falco took a note.

There was nothing else. The officers thanked the

Bertrams and left. As they drove away, passing drab net curtains and colourful window boxes, di Falco said, 'I wonder which house was the brothel?'

* * *

Kenny and Jen Cuthbert lived in the Murrayfield area of the city, an easy walk to the rugby stadium. Their house was like many: part of a grey stone terrace three storeys high with a small front garden, which was trim and colourful. Baggo and di Falco had to wait before the bell was answered. Locks clicked then an anxious-looking woman opened the heavy front door a fraction.

Baggo put on his warmest smile. 'Mrs Cuthbert?' She nodded. 'Detective Sergeant Chandavarkar and Detective Constable di Falco. May we come in, please?'

Mrs Cuthbert almost sniffed their warrants as she examined them. She peered up and down the street then stood aside for them. 'You'll guess why I'm nervous,' she said.

'May we sit down and discuss this?' Baggo said, wondering what had scared this middle-aged, middle-class woman who was married to a QC.

She took care to lock the door then, scurrying like a mouse, led them into a sitting room which was north-facing and dark. It had a high ceiling, an attractive cornice and a dado rail. The sofa on which both officers sat although comfortable, was not new and covered in chintz whose colours clashed with the rich red of the large Oriental rug covering half of the polished wooden floor.

An eclectic collection of paintings, most done in oil or acrylic, made Baggo think of a badly curated art gallery.

'We are here to investigate the murder of Farquhar Knox,' he said. 'But please tell us why you are nervous.'

'The threats, of course.' She pursed her lips. She was a small, wiry woman, barely five feet tall, with short, jet-black hair and dark, wandering eyes. Her irregular eyebrows looked as if they had been painted on during a mild earthquake. Her blue trousers were tailored but the matching blouse looked a size too big.

'Please tell us,' he said gently.

'You know my husband is defending Harry Nugent?'

Puzzled, Baggo smiled vaguely. Di Falco cut in, 'Yes, of course, in Glasgow. The assisted suicide case.'

Mrs Cuthbert clearly expected Baggo to be aware of this. He nodded gravely and hoped di Falco would keep going.

The younger man paused then took the hint. 'What about the threats?' he asked.

'It's these damned right-to-lifers,' she said with sudden vehemence. 'My husband's been getting letters. There were two last week and I wanted him to report it then but he didn't. And there was one yesterday. It was the worst and it had been posted after the murder, so I insisted. You probably know my husband's tall and dark-haired, like Farquhar Knox. Do you think they meant to murder him and killed Farquhar by mistake?' Her face crumpled as she held back tears.

'We don't know yet,' di Falco said, 'but do you have the letters?'

'My husband took them to Glasgow to show the police there.'

'When was Knox's identity revealed publicly?' Baggo asked di Falco.

'Mid-day or early afternoon on Saturday, I think, but the internet will have got it earlier.'

'We were phoned with the news on Saturday during breakfast,' Mrs Cuthbert said. 'News travels round the bar like wildfire.'

'We'll certainly look into this,' Baggo said. 'We'll take fingerprints from you and your husband for elimination purposes. You can find prints on paper and that would be excellent evidence.'

'He didn't open the third letter till he returned home last night. He was all set to laugh the whole thing off. But I'm left here alone and it's not funny.' Her voice caught again. After a couple of deep breaths she stared at the floor and spoke slowly at first, increasing in speed and decibels as she warmed to her theme. 'Bar wives have a reputation of being status-conscious and unfriendly. But we have to keep the show on the road; appear well-off when there's no money; cover up drunkenness; nurse a sick child when your husband's every waking hour is spent on his practice; boost confidence after a mauling in court; keep his feet on the ground after a triumph. What is it Kipling said about triumph and disaster? It should be carved on every bar wife's heart. Oh, and you must be stoical if your family is threatened.' After that bitter, hysterical outburst, she glared at the officers.

Taken aback, Baggo murmured, 'That must be

difficult for you.' In a business-like tone he said, 'We will look into it, but could I ask you to think back to Friday night?'

She nodded, calmer after letting out her pent-up resentment.

'Was there anything that happened during the dinner that might have a bearing on Mr Knox's murder?'

She took more deep breaths then shook her head. 'Kenny sat near him, so that might explain how they got mixed up.'

'And after dinner what happened?'

'Farquhar got up. He'd adopted the detached expression he often put on when he was bored. Eloise and I chatted for a bit before they cleared the tables. I don't remember seeing either her or Farquhar till Kenny and I did a Dashing White Sergeant with Eloise, which was after the archery. Molly Bertram and I spent most of the rest of the evening in the library with Eloise. We all got up to dance a couple of times, I think. I certainly did. I don't remember if Eloise did, actually. The men, Kenny and Rab Bertram I mean, milled about, mostly near the bar. It became pretty clear that Farquhar had done a bunk and I could tell Eloise was furious, though she didn't let it show too much. We took her home and Kenny saw her into the house. Of course Farquhar wasn't there, but we assumed it was just another of his dalliances.'

'Did he have many of these?' Baggo asked.

Her face clouded. 'He was a rat. I shouldn't speak ill of the dead, but he was. We all knew about that poor policeman's tarty wife.' She clamped her mouth shut.

'Did Mrs Knox know about her?' di Falco asked.

'She must have. But she kept their problems behind closed doors. I think I am as close to her as anyone connected with the bar and she doesn't confide in me.'

'Was their marriage reasonably happy overall, do you think?' Baggo asked.

'How many bar marriages are good ones?' she responded. 'They put up with each other. He had cash and she had class so some would say it was a marriage made in heaven.'

'Can you think of anyone in particular who might want your husband dead?' She shook her head. 'Or Farquhar Knox?'

'No.'

Baggo thanked her. When di Falco took her fingerprints, her fears and distress returned. Leaving her rocking to and fro on an upright chair, the two officers saw themselves out. As they walked down the path they heard a key being turned.

In the car, Baggo asked about the case Cuthbert was in.

'It's a big one. Harry Nugent's wife had some dreadful disease. She was in pain and could hardly move. She wanted to be put out of her misery, and said so to many people. Nugent is a lawyer. In Scotland the law's not the same as in England. Apparently it's not a crime in Scots Law to commit suicide, so Nugent says it can't be criminal to help someone do something that's legal.

'What he did was acquire the poison they use in Switzerland, mix it with water and present it to his wife in a glass with a straw. She could have done none of these things herself. He held the glass while she sucked it down quickly and she died. The whole thing was filmed and before she took the poison she repeated that she wanted to die. Nugent's been charged with culpable homicide, equivalent to manslaughter in England. The defence is that he was just assisting a suicide and that should not be criminal.

'That's what the case is about and I heard they've made up a special court with extra judges in the middle of the trial to decide it. A lot of people hold strong views one way or the other, but the pro-life lobby has been really vocal. They've been demonstrating outside the court. It wouldn't surprise me if one of their extremists tried to scare Nugent's lawyer.'

Baggo had not bothered with the news while he had been in Scotland. He was impressed by the way di Falco described the case. 'Do you find the law interesting, Billy?' he asked.

'Not really. When they realised I would not become a priest, my parents wanted me to train as a lawyer. But I couldn't be bothered with the small print and arguments in which you go round and round in circles. I did social sciences at uni.'

'What made you join the police?'

'Because I believe the best helping hand you can give some people is a kick up the arse. The police welcome graduates and I always wanted to be doing good in some way.' He shrugged with embarrassment then blurted out, 'I know about Nugent's case because it has caused a lot of arguments at home.'

Baggo did not ask further. He thought for a bit. He had spoken with Melanie before court started and she had told him that Smail's character witnesses, the Primroses, were due to give evidence in the afternoon. He wanted to hear what they had to say. And he wanted to see Melanie. 'I'll take a bus to the court and see what's happening there. We're on the right side of town for the M8. Would you take the car to the High Court in Glasgow and see what Mr Cuthbert has to say? You should manage to see him during the lunch break. Try to get his fingerprints.'

10

'Well?' The DCC's face was grim as Flick faced him across his desk.

'We're doing all we can, sir. And we are building a picture of what happened. It's a bit like a jigsaw ...'

'I know about jigsaws. I used that analogy when I wasn't making much progress with a case.' He smiled. 'Come on, what do you know?'

'Detective Constable Gilsland learned that Knox arranged for the judge's door of Court Three to be unlocked from dinner time onwards. He gave a security guard fifty pounds to unlock it then lock it up once the function was over. When the guard did this about three, he checked the court and found the body. The guard has been dismissed, but the point is that Knox had this planned, apart obviously from his murder. We still believe it was Mrs Traynor Knox had sex with, but she won't admit it, and the evidence is a bit dodgy, the main witness being an alcoholic advocate who viewed the woman at some distance, from the rear and in poor light. Mrs Traynor was wearing a long, black dress and had her blonde hair down to her shoulders. But Mrs Knox has shoulder-length, blonde hair and wore a navy blue dress that would have looked like black in the dark. There seem to have been a few women in black, including the wife of one of the fraud accused, Nicola Smail, and she too has blonde hair. There is other evidence pointing towards Lynda Traynor, but it's far from conclusive. If the lab can find DNA in the stains on Knox's clothes we should get a warrant to obtain samples from Mrs Traynor at least. She does admit that the Chief Superintendent was angry with Knox later on in the evening, and threatened to assault him. He must have overheard or been told gossip about his wife.

'Now one of the obvious suspects, Mrs Knox, has given us an account of what she was doing during the relevant time, which is from during the archery to the first twenty minutes of the dancing, and today Detective Sergeant Chandavarkar is checking the witnesses she named. So far they back her up. It seems their marriage wasn't happy but they stuck together. She's quite posh, by the way, the daughter of a duke, and the judge who lives next door, Lord Hutton, is very protective of her. We have tried to track Chief Superintendent Traynor's movements but we don't know much except that after spending time in the library with his wife, they left early.

'I had hoped that CCTV would help, but it doesn't cover the court door or the corridor leading to it. There is a camera which shows the main concourse beside Parliament Hall but all you see is people coming and going, and you can't make out where they are heading when they go out of the picture. The arrow has been tested for fingerprints with a negative result. It was pushed in, not shot in according to Dr MacGregor.'

'And the fraud angle?'

'Getting nowhere, so far. Both Smail and Maltravers can account for their movements. Smail's witnesses should be checked today and I was able to identify Maltravers on the CCTV covering the area outside where smokers congregate. He was wearing a white tuxedo and you can see him giving a waiter a light. Incidentally, I think I can identify Mrs Knox having a cigarette there very soon after the archery finished, as she claims. Gilsland has been examining the dead man's mobile and laptop but has found nothing except ambiguous evidence which could point to an affair with Mrs Traynor. What should I do about the Chief Superintendent, sir? If I interviewed him he would be bound to want a lawyer then say nothing. I don't have enough to arrest him.'

'Wait till you're good and ready. I am going to have to suspend him, but I shall do so only because of the unfortunate publicity which for now makes his position untenable. I won't even get away with calling it leave.'

'His wife says that night he was drunk and went on about her crossing a boundary.'

'Apparently her family has money. That may have something to do with his stoical forbearance. But do you know how *Good News* got their information?'

She recounted her meeting with Oliphant and what Baggo had told her in a lengthy call before she had left for Tulliallan.

The DCC nodded. 'Well carry on as if nothing has happened. I like the way you're approaching this and let's hope you get a breakthrough soon. I'll give a press conference this afternoon supporting you and telling the public to come to us if they have information. If the press try to speak to you, say nothing and refer them to me.'

Flick sighed with relief. 'I'm sorry, sir,' she said.

'You've nothing to be sorry about. If it takes time to identify Knox's killer, so be it. If there's anyone who can hatch babies and catch villains at the same time it's you, Inspector. Now, will you join me in a bowl of soup before you go?'

* * *

Pete Bothwell stood in the arrivals hall of Edinburgh Airport watching for passengers from the Malaga flight. He did not have a board on which to write a name, but he thought he would be able to identify the retired London cop who was going to advise *Good News* about the Knox murder inquiry. That morning, with a string of expletives, his editor had told him how important for the paper the project was. Ex-Detective Inspector Osborne would continue to comment on what the police appeared to be doing, advise how they might do better, then hand them the evidence to identify and convict the killer, after the paper had used it as a scoop. The twenty thousand pounds reward would be bound to loosen someone's tongue, and to get it they would have to come to the paper first. Not quite in the Watergate class, but a massive journalistic coup that would draw readers and advertisers like a magnet.

The plane had landed but it was taking an age for the

passengers to come through immigration and customs. Bothwell had shaved that morning and his face itched. He scratched it and felt something burst. Trying to be unobtrusive, he dabbed the spot with a tissue. So far, it had not been a good day. He was still furious at that puffed-up prig, Oliphant, who had phoned to accuse him of revealing his source. He had replied that, as Fortune had seen him leaving The Verdict after speaking to Oliphant, she did not have to be Miss Bloody Marple to work out where he had got his information.

At last the Malaga passengers began to come through the doors and Bothwell paid close attention. He had spoken to Osborne on the phone and thought he sounded a bit like the cockney comedian, Jim Davidson. He pictured him as looking like the man who had played Inspector Wexford on TV - tall, ruggedly handsome and with a face that inspired respect and obedience.

The passengers were a mixed bag. All were sun-tanned but many seemed tired. Bothwell paid close attention to men over fifty travelling on their own. A corpulent, red-faced, cross-looking man, his yellow shirt half in, half out of his trousers passed in front of him pulling a suitcase just small enough to be cabin baggage. His shirt had a large, dark stain down the front and he was covered in glitter. He left a strong smell of alcohol in his wake. Close behind was a dapper little man dressed in coordinating shades of green with a mincing walk. The only other over-fifty male on his own would probably not see eighty again. He tottered along using a walking stick, a determined expression on his face.

After checking at the luggage carousel, Bothwell concluded that the detective must have missed his flight and went to the Jet 2 desk in the departures hall to inquire. The corpulent man with the glitter was there, pointing his finger at the girl behind the desk. As Bothwell approached he could hear what the man was saying: 'I told that man to control his kids and the stewardess with the fat arse …'

'Flight attendant,' the girl interrupted.

'The flight attendant with the fat arse told me to calm down …' It was the same cockney voice as he had heard on the phone. 'I do want to make an issue of it. I was in the aisle seat minding my own business and that family ruined my flight. First there was the girl always running about till she knocked me so I spilled my wine. Instead of giving her a smack her father told me it was my own fault. Then when he was getting stuff from the overhead locker he spilled a tub of kiddies' glitter over me. On purpose. Your stewardesses did nothing. How often do I have to tell you?'

Bothwell's heart sank. He had not imagined the retired detective would be anything like this. The idea for the project had been his but the editor was set to claim credit. If it worked. Otherwise it would be back to being his idea and his job was hanging on a shoogly nail. He decided not to intervene and stood back till the confrontation was over.

His face purple, Osborne left the Jet 2 desk ten minutes later. Putting on a welcoming smile, Bothwell stuck out a hand to introduce himself. Osborne acknowledged him with a grunt and let him take his case.

Bothwell led the way to the car park and opened the passenger door of his Fiat.

'Not much of a car,' Osborne said, then lit a cigarette.

'Did you get my e-mail with all the details of the case?' Bothwell asked as he opened the window.

'Yeh.'

'What did you make of it?'

Silence.

'Do you have your computer with you?'

'Yeh.'

'I've stuck an envelope full of up-to-date cuttings into the front pocket of your case.'

Silence.

'The editor wants a piece for tomorrow. We should talk about it when we reach the hotel.'

Silence.

Despite the open window, a combination of smoke, alcohol fumes and BO caught the back of Bothwell's throat. His day was getting worse by the minute.

The G and V Hotel, formerly the Hotel Missoni, is ideally situated for the courts. It is also a byword for style. Bothwell had thought it would suit the great detective perfectly, but now he felt awkward leading Osborne to reception past the porters in their distinctive uniforms of black shirt, blue tartan kilt and rough, ankle-length socks.

'We have a wee room for you,' the receptionist stated in an East European accent, flashing a broad synthetic smile.

'A wee room? I'm not sleeping in a broom cupboard.' Osborne glared at her.

'There are no brooms in it but we have bonnie and braw rooms available,' she replied, consulting a computer. 'The muckle rooms are all taken. I'm so sorry.'

'How big is a wee room?' Bothwell asked nervously. The tariff he had been quoted was not wee.

'In most hotels they would call it standard room, but as we are in Scotland …'

'Where they don't speak fucking English,' Osborne finished her sentence for her. 'All right. Stop farting about. I'll take it.' He grabbed the pen she offered him and filled in a short form.

'Pavel will take your case. I hope you enjoy your holiday,' the receptionist trilled.

'I'm here to bloody work,' he replied.

Making a quick deduction from the glitter, the receptionist tried to recover. 'I'm so sorry I didn't recognise you. Which theatre will you be in? Or is it film this time?'

Osborne stared at her as if she were mad. 'I'm not a fucking actor,' he growled. 'Now give me my fucking room key so I can get rid of this rubbish.' He brushed some glitter to the floor.

The receptionist handed over the key card without a word.

Bothwell smiled apologetically at her and shrugged. 'When can we meet to discuss the case?' he called after Osborne, who was following Pavel's swinging kilt to the lifts.

'Tomorrow at ten. Meet me here,' he replied then turned round. 'By the way, what's your name again?'

'Pete Bothwell.'

Osborne looked at the journalist's acne-cursed face.

'I'll call you Pizza,' he said. Cracking his first smile since landing in Scotland, he entered a lift.

'What about tomorrow's piece?' Bothwell asked, scrabbling at the closing doors.

'Make it up,' was all he heard before the doors slid shut.

* * *

Noel Osborne, Inspector No to most who had come across him, was an alcoholic. He knew that and for some years had alternated between disapproving sobriety and uninhibited excess. Recently, encouraged by Maria, his housekeeper and occasional bedmate, he had been drinking in what he fancied was moderation. At first this restraint kept his intake down to one bottle of Rioja per day, but life being what it is, one had become two. He told himself that as he usually consumed bottles which were only twelve point five per cent proof he was more disciplined than those who drank more robust wines.

The knowledge that he was on expenses had dented his self-denial, and there was no one to withhold the sexual favours with which Maria tantalised him. There had been Rioja in Malaga before take-off, three small bottles of strong Argentinian red (and another that had ended up down his shirt) during the flight and now he surveyed the mini-bar in his room. A half bottle of Chianti had his name on it.

Lying back on the comfortable bed, his mood improved with every slurp of wine. He just wished the curtains did not have that zig-zag pattern that made him feel drunker than he was. He closed his eyes …

He came to with a start. That stupid glass had overturned and this time it was his trousers that caught the spilled wine. Fortunately, not too much. He poured more from the bottle and thought about what he should tell Pizza to put in his newspaper. He looked forward to having a good dig at Flick bloody Fortune, whose Goody Two-Shoes attitude to police work had got on his wick when she had been his sergeant back in Wimbledon. The trouble was, while he might advocate 'old-fashioned methods' he could never publicly reveal what these had been.

The Chianti bottle was dead. There was beer in the mini-bar and he knew he needed food. He dialled room service and ordered the hottest curry the kitchen could make.

* * *

'They haven't got a bloody clue.'

'It's ludicrous to think the accused in the fraud might have thought they could stop the trial by killing Night. Their counsel didn't even try to argue for a desertion.'

'I'm all for encouraging women in the police, but to put a vastly pregnant woman in charge of a big investigation is plain bonkers.'

'I feel sorry for her, actually.'

'Do you reckon some high-up misogynist has handed her a poisoned chalice?'

'That would be the polis we know and love.'

Along the bar of The Verdict from a group of gossipy male advocates, Baggo finished his salami toastie, drained his glass and slipped out, he hoped unrecognised. Unfortunately he could not disagree with most of what he had overheard. He checked his phone and found a text message from di Falco asking him to call.

'I've pulled over on the hard shoulder,' di Falco told him when he answered. 'Cuthbert was as forthcoming as a clam at first, "I've already given a statement," and so on, but when I mentioned the letters he took me somewhere quiet and was all fake smiles and chumminess. He hadn't reported the letters to the Glasgow police, said he was going to after finishing his lunch. I don't think he took them at all seriously. Anyway he handed them to me. The envelopes are white and cheap. Cuthbert's name and address are individually typed in capitals on adhesive labels. All have a Glasgow postmark, the most recent being Saturday, with first-class stamps.

'The messages are all typed in capitals on single sheets of ordinary A4, neatly folded. The first one says: DEATH COMES TO US ALL IN GOD'S TIME. YOURS COULD BE SOON. The second says: WIN YOUR CASE AND DEATH WILL BEAT YOU. The third reads: NO MERCY FOR MERCY MURDERERS OR THEIR LAWYERS.'

'Not at all nice, but I've seen worse on Twitter,' Baggo said. 'Might someone have killed Knox mistaking him for Cuthbert? How similar were they?'

'Both quite tall and dark, but Cuthbert's much pudgier, if you know what I mean. You'd be unlikely to mistake one for the other, though you might in poor light. Of course they weren't wearing wigs on Friday night.'

'What did he have to say about the murder?'

'Well, like a lot of people he knew about Knox's affair with Mrs T. He'd spotted them together in Perth a few weeks ago, so he may have been one of the first to be aware of it. He said that on Friday Knox was clearly impatient for dinner to end and as soon as it did he made a bee-line for Mrs T and they had a short but serious-looking conversation. A bit later Mrs Knox came up to Cuthbert and asked if he had seen her husband. He said he prevaricated and she twigged what was going on. "He's off with that whore, isn't he?" she asked him. He replied that he didn't know what she was talking about. She said something about bloody men sticking together then stood behind the people watching the archery, looking furious. When it was over she made for the door. Cuthbert thought she might have been going home but she was back, much calmer, for the first dance, which she did with the Cuthberts. It's apparently one you do in threes. She spent most of the rest of the evening in the library and was still angry when the Cuthberts took her home.'

'Did he say anything about the Knox marriage?'

'He said it wasn't great but they both seemed to find reasons for staying together. He said Mrs Knox was a cool customer and that if she had wanted rid of her husband she would almost certainly have favoured divorce over homicide.'

'Did he expand on that?'

'No. Oh, incidentally, Knox had been due to play something called a dinner match at Muirfield on the Saturday and one of his opponents had said he was just the sort of chap to get himself killed rather than lose.'

'And Cuthbert told you that?'

'Yes. He was there. He didn't let the murder stand in the way of his golf. I think it was his way of saying he didn't like Knox himself.'

'Where are you at the moment?'

'On the motorway, nearly out of Glasgow.'

'Why don't you go back to the court and have a look round? Keep an eye on the spectators. If there is anything in Mrs Cuthbert's theory, we'll look pretty stupid if we've ignored it.'

'What do I look for?'

'Goodness knows, but you'll recognise it when you see it.'

* * *

The old High Court building in Glasgow is a classical, confident structure fronted by a Doric portico in the Greek style. As more court time was needed to try serious crime, an extension was built at the back. This clean, modern edifice now dwarfs the original but the courtrooms with most atmosphere are the North and South Courts in the old building. Di Falco felt this as soon as he took his seat in the public gallery of the North Court and looked round. He admired the solid wooden furniture, stained dark brown and dignified. It was easy to imagine previous generations of judges presiding from the imposing bench, passing death sentences on men in the dock now occupied by a person whose only crime had been to help ease a loved one out of a miserable existence. It was a topsy-turvy world.

Unusually, there were three judges crowded on a bench meant for one. This was obviously the important hearing to decide if assisting suicide was a crime in Scotland. The prosecutor was on his feet, giving the court a detailed account of how suicide had been regarded through the ages, and not just in Scotland. On the other side of the large semi-circular table, Cuthbert sat, his head back as if in thought, leaning forward to take the occasional note. The jury box was empty. The jurors would return to court once the issue had been decided. The accused, Nugent, sat still in the dock, small and white-haired with bowed shoulders, a picture of defeat and misery. But di Falco's mother would not be sympathetic. The Nugents were Catholics and the case had caused ructions in the church and in the di Falco family. Billy loved his mother but he had little time for the doctrines of the church she held so dear. To him, the dock of the High Court should be reserved for bad people and Harry Nugent was not bad.

A few journalists occupied the front seats. Behind them sat a number of spectators. Some appeared to be middle-class intellectuals, men and women who were concentrating on proceedings, one or two taking notes. They were scattered round the public benches. In front of di Falco and to his right, a group of about a dozen sat together. They were dressed mainly in black, most were male and all appeared to be under forty. There was an aggressive intensity to their body language, but not all of them concentrated on what was being said. Some stared ahead blankly and one young man's lips moved as he read a book on his lap, di Falco guessed the Bible. There was a blue plaster of the type used in commercial kitchens on his left index finger.

Di Falco tried to follow the argument but his attention wandered and he kept an eye on the group. If there was a zealot threatening Cuthbert he or she might well be among these people.

The afternoon passed slowly. By the time the judge chairing the court asked the prosecutor if it would be a convenient time to adjourn, di Falco had decided to follow the group. As luck would have it, he had dressed in dark clothes so he would fit in.

His gut feeling that these might be fanatics was supported when the police overseeing the public gallery told them to wait until the court had been cleared. When di Falco said he was with them, the constable raised his eyebrows then moved on. The members of the group turned, their stares suspicious and unwelcoming.

After leaving time for the other spectators to get clear of the courthouse, the policeman allowed them to leave through the doorway that took them out to the street. Di Falco brought up the rear. It was a fine, sunlit afternoon and even the city air smelled good. As he breathed in, one of the group, a man in his thirties with a face scrubbed till it shone and not a hair out of place, approached. He wore a dog collar. A cheesy smile showed off sparkling teeth but did not hide cold eyes.

'Father Neil,' he said, extending his hand.

'Billy,' di Falco said, shaking it warmly.

'Did I hear you tell the policeman you were with us?' There was a hint of Southern Irish lilt in his voice.

'Yes. I think suicide is a very great sin.'

'Well spoken, Billy. We too believe that our lives are in God's hands and it is a grave sin to shorten it. If Nugent gets away with what he has done, many will feel encouraged to do the same.'

'The sin of Ahitophel and Saul,' di Falco responded, briefly thankful for the intensity of his religious education.

Father Neil's lips smiled and this time his eyes did too. 'Each morning we demonstrate outside the courthouse. Our blessed Marjorie takes away our placards and stores them for us so that we can go into court, where we listen and pray for wisdom and righteousness. When the lawyers finish we have been in the habit of going somewhere to pray and reflect on the day. Would you join us?'

'I'd be happy to.'

They walked up towards Glasgow Cross then turned right into the Gallowgate. On the way, Father Neil gently but insistently probed into di Falco's life. He gave his true surname and said he worked as a waiter at the Old Course Hotel in St Andrews. A devout Catholic, he felt so strongly about assisted suicide that he needed to go to the court on his day off and pray for the correct decision. He knew he was making it up as he went along and cursed himself for not preparing a better story. He would have to contact a girl he knew at the hotel to back him up if they checked.

At length they arrived at a church hall to which Neil had the key. The atmosphere inside was chilly and damp. They climbed a stone stairway with a shaky bannister then trooped into a small, drab room on the first floor that needed cleaning and dusting. Half a dozen placards condemning suicide had been put in one corner. Wooden chairs, some obviously unstable, were arranged in a semicircle. Father Neil stood in the centre and the rest sat down. The last to claim a chair, di Falco lowered himself gingerly onto the only one left. It was rickety with a cracked seat but it held.

'We should welcome Billy to our group,' Father Neil began, his voice strong and melodic. 'He has come all the way from St Andrews to pray with us for the correct decision.' The others muttered hellos and two managed to smile at di Falco, who grinned back and said 'thank you'.

'Yesterday I mentioned undeserved suffering, and that goes to the heart of what this case is about. Nugent did not want his wife, whom he loved very much, to suffer. She was a good woman and did not deserve to die a painful and difficult death. The answer to that lies in the nature of life itself. Our lives are not our own to shorten as we choose. God has put us on earth for His purpose and for the length of time that He decrees. A player who decides to leave the pitch when he is tired is no use to his team. It is not up to him to decide when his match ends. From start to finish, our whole lives belong to God. It is as simple as that. *Vita Dei. Vita Dei. Vita Dei.* And we remember the words of Saint Faustina, "If the angels were capable of envy they would envy us for two things: one is the receiving of Holy Communion, and the other is suffering." Suffering is part and parcel of being a Christian. God gave Mrs Nugent the opportunity to share in Christ's burden of suffering and her husband took that from her.'

His acolytes had doubtless heard all this or stuff very like it before but that did not diminish the enthusiasm with which they lapped it up. Di Falco took his cue and nodded forcefully. A lengthy prayer followed and the service was ended by another repetition of '*Vita Dei*'.

Tea and biscuits were available in a larger, adjoining room. As di Falco sipped the industrial strength brew from a chipped mug he sought out the man with the finger plaster.

'You're in catering too?' he asked, glancing at the finger.

'Yes. But I serve the Lord in other ways. Where do you work?' The accent was Glaswegian, the tone serious.

'The Old Course Hotel in St Andrews. What about you?'

'Here and there. Where the Lord leads me.'

Di Falco nodded then glanced again at the finger. 'That looks nasty. A burn?'

The man flexed his hand. Di Falco observed that his knuckles were red and calloused, a fighter's knuckles. 'I forgot to put white gloves on before serving hot plates at one of these big dinners.'

'Interesting people there?'

'Interesting to themselves, no doubt, but sinners, most of them.'

'And they do not know the danger of Godlessness.'

'One was taken during the night. A lawyer. Murdered. The papers are full of it. An adulterer.' He spat out the last word.

'I've read about it. Did you see him before he was killed?'

'Yes. He was at the same table as that evil man, Cuthbert. Looked like him, too.' The young man might have been twenty-five. He had a sharp, bony face and protruding eyes. His mouth twitched when he spoke.

Di Falco hoped his interest didn't show. 'Do you live in Edinburgh?' he asked as casually as he could.

'No' likely. I stay in Glasgow. They run minibuses to these big dinners.'

'By the way, I'm Billy.' Di Falco stuck his hand out.

The answering handshake was peremptory as if the acolyte was thinking of other things. 'Johnny.' His right shoulder twitched up. 'Don't you get angry at the sinners you have to serve?' The aggression in his voice was almost palpable.

Di Falco nodded. 'But Jesus washed sinners' feet. I just have to give them food and wine.'

'Father Neil tells me that. But I see evil winning everywhere. I want to fight back. That's why I joined *Vita Dei*.'

'I see why.'

'We have to …'

'Now Johnny, Billy doesn't want to be troubled with too much on his first time with us.' Father Neil took di Falco's arm and led him aside. 'I'll have to be going myself and I'd be happy to walk with you to the train station, or did you come by bus?'

'Train,' he said, thinking quickly.

'Excellent.' Putting down his mug, the priest turned to his followers. 'Thank you all for your presence today. I hope to see as many of you as possible tomorrow. Our visible stand against the devil's work is pleasing to Our Lord. Bless you all, and particularly dear Marjorie for the most welcome tea and biscuits. *Vita Dei!*' He aimed a smile at a hefty, untidy woman with a shock of curly red hair. Di Falco had not seen her at court and guessed she must be the caretaker.

Out on the street, di Falco asked, 'You kept repeating *Vita Dei*. Is that what you call this group?'

'Yes. It's Latin for God's Life, as you probably realise. It seemed right to focus on the issue we're concerned with.' He set off at a brisk pace. 'Which station?'

'Queen Street.' Di Falco hoped the priest was not going to see him onto the train. He had left the car with the police business notice on the dashboard in a metered bay beside Glasgow Green.

'I'm going that way, as it happens. Tell me, how is the church in St Andrews?'

Di Falco's parents lived in St Andrews and his mother was a devout parishioner of St James Church on The

Scores. Although he had not darkened the door for a couple of years he was able to respond to Neil's questions with enough verifiable information to pass the obvious test.

'An intense young man, Johnny,' he said, when Neil paused.

'Yes, but his heart is in exactly the right place.'

'Is it difficult to restrain followers who are thinking of acting unwisely?'

'That's a police question,' Neil commented sharply. 'What concern is it of yours?'

'I just want to know what I'd be getting into if I joined you.'

'You would be welcomed into a dedicated, God-fearing body. Is there any organisation which does not number individual law-breakers in its membership?'

'You have me there,' di Falco said. They had crossed George Square and were outside Queen Street Station. 'It's been good meeting you, Father. I hope I might see you again, but it is difficult to take days off during the summer. Is there a number at which I could contact you?'

Handing over a card, Neil squeezed his hand. 'I hope you will continue to support us, Billy. Good men are like gold. God bless.' He waved his hand and disappeared into the rush hour crowd.

Di Falco bought a coffee at the station buffet. It took away some of the taste of the tea and he checked his mobile which had been off for the afternoon. He waited for quarter of an hour before leaving the station to pick up the car.

11

When the fraud trial resumed after lunch, Lachlan Smail was being cross-examined by Radcliffe. It made Baggo think of a dog-fight between an elegant Afghan Hound and a yappy Terrier, with the Afghan winning easily. His concentration soon went and he felt like dancing. What excited him wasn't the fact that Melanie had agreed to meet him again that night, it was the way her face had lit up when he had asked her.

Shortly after three, Radcliffe sat down. Smail's counsel made a valiant attempt to repair the damage before his client, looking quite pleased with himself, returned to the silent refuge of the dock. Nicola Smail gave him a smile of encouragement, but during his aggressive performance in the witness box she had looked glum.

The next witness was John Primrose. Well over six feet, trim, tanned and patrician, he had known Lachlan Smail since boyhood. Smail was loyal, courageous and, above all, honest. At school he had always owned up when he had done wrong, even if it meant certain punishment.

When it was Radcliffe's turn he asked, 'Do you never wonder, Mr Primrose, whether, after all these punishments, Mr Smail might have decided to stop owning up, guilty or not?'

'Not him,' Primrose countered, ignoring the grinning faces in the jury box.

When court rose, Baggo approached Primrose, whose wife, a mousy, thin woman in beige looked up at him adoringly. With the air of someone doing a favour rather than his civic duty, Primrose confirmed most of what Lachlan Smail had said about his movements after the archery, as his wife did for Nicola Smail. However, there were times between the end of the archery and the start of the dancing during which either could have killed Knox, if they had moved quickly.

There seemed nothing more to be learned from the Primroses. Baggo thanked them and went to meet another John, Mrs Knox's smoking friend, John Logan.

The meeting point was a consulting room a couple of hundred metres down the Royal Mile from Parliament House. Logan was a thin, embittered man with frayed shirtcuffs and dandruff liberally sprayed over the shoulders of a suit shiny with wear. There was no doubting his smoking credentials. Nicotine-stained fingers, not allowed to hold a cigarette in that room, drummed the table in frustration and Baggo recoiled from the stale tobacco on his breath. The papers in front of him were dog-eared and grubby, and Baggo suspected their purpose was to create the illusion of a busy practice. After a diatribe against the nanny state and health fascism, Logan confirmed that as soon as the archery had ended he had gone outside for a cigarette and had been joined by Eloise

Knox. He could not remember how long she had stayed there, but she had seemed tense and cross. She had cheered up slightly when they compiled a list of those they would have liked to have used as human targets for the archery. 'I could easily shoot Farquhar tonight,' had been the last thing she had said before going inside. 'But she laughed as she said it,' Logan added, not entirely convincingly.

Baggo thought this cynical man might have a new insight into the case but although he was happy to talk, he merely added some scathing observations about the deceased's social climbing. Baggo took his leave despairing about ever finding someone who had genuinely liked Knox.

* * *

Pete Bothwell stared miserably at the computer screen in front of him. It was empty. He had less than an hour to produce the piece demanded by his editor and he had no idea what to write. He had heard of 'writer's block', an affliction that had plagued previous generations with their blank sheets of A4 and these curious typewriters with their rollers and ink and keys that thumped the letters against the paper. Nowadays, with computers and the material available on the internet, there was always something to fill the space. But not today.

When Osborne had called him Pizza it had added disrespect to disappointment and awakened unhappy memories of school, where he had been known as Face, short for Pizza-face. This train of thought had continued when he attended the Tulliallan press conference. He had been the only journalist made to stand, the last to have his question answered and the only person escorted to see the DCC immediately afterwards. In the privacy of his office, the DCC had torn a strip off him. He had prejudiced the investigation by reporting facts that had not been established; he had adversely and unfairly affected the career of an excellent officer who had been suspended only because of the scandalous article in *Good News*; he had ridiculed a female officer because she was pregnant. 'You're not experienced in crime reporting, are you?' the DCC had asked. 'Not very,' was the reply. 'Well understand two things,' the DCC had said, his face red, his eyes staring, 'one, we can make life very difficult for those who hinder us, and two, any information about this crime that comes to you or your paper MUST be shared with us before it is published.' It had been like a long-ago visit to the head teacher after he had head-butted another boy, breaking his nose. And that had been nothing like the trouble he was in at home after handing his parents the letter informing them of his suspension.

It had been similar that afternoon. His head still spinning when he returned to the office, his editor had lambasted him for the lack of anything worthwhile to report on the Knox murder. 'What does Osborne say? We're paying enough to have him here.' 'Why has no one come forward with information to claim the twenty K reward?' His stuttering replies had fuelled the unpredictable man's anger and he had been told to write a fucking sensational piece which would set the fucking cat among the fucking pigeons within an hour. Bothwell was uncomfortably aware that the paper was losing money and only his editor's goodwill stood between him and the dole queue.

There was only one thing for it. He checked the number, phoned the G and V and asked to be put through to Mr Osborne's room.

At first he thought there would be no answer, but after a while he heard a slurred 'hello'.

'Mr Osborne, it's Pete Bothwell. I really need some input from you for tomorrow's paper. My editor's breathing down my neck and I have to have something from you as we've paid for you to come over here and it was my idea. Please, please help me or I'll lose my job.' His voice caught and he was close to tears.

A long pause made Bothwell's heart sink. Surely his day couldn't continue to get worse? But he had succeeded in bringing home the urgency of the situation. Through the alcohol Osborne realised he had to sing for his supper or this carnival would soon be over.

''Ang on, Pizza, 'ang on. No need to make a drama out of a bleeding crisis. I've 'ad more bosses chewing my arse than I've 'ad 'ot dinners and I'm still 'ere. Now tell me, what are the police up to?'

'They say they're pursuing a number of lines of inquiry, and Traynor's been suspended, they say because of my article in today's paper. They seem to have been questioning a lot of the people who were at the big function.'

'In other words, they know fuck all, and Felicity Fortune isn't about to use her delicate little hands to dig up the dirt. When I cleaned up the East End, I didn't do it with the Human Rights Act, if you know what I mean. I got my hands dirty. You've got to crack eggs to make an omelette, Pizza. And there's Felicity Fortune, looking like the side of a house, no doubt, sitting on the eggs and hoping one will hatch.'

'What should she be doing?'

'What she should be doing, Pizza, is she should be finding criminals. There's bound to be a few at that party with a record, and she should start with them. Even if one of them didn't kill whotsisname, one of them will know something. Criminals do, you know. They're aware. And you can persuade them to talk. If you know what you're doing, that is. Felicity should get her pretty arse off her fucking eggs, roll up her sleeves and make a fucking omelette.'

'I thought she was your protégé?'

'I taught her all I could, Pizza. But it's guts what makes a copper, not the ability to recite the fucking Human Rights Act backwards while standing on your head. Get my drift?'

It wasn't just the slurred speech that told Bothwell that Osborne was drunk. He wondered how much of this he could use. Fortunately he was recording the call so no one could claim he had made it up. 'I think so,' he said doubtfully. 'Thank you very ...' Before he could finish, Osborne had rung off.

It took a moment for Bothwell to work out that he was more frightened of his editor than the DCC. His fingers danced across the keyboard and his computer screen filled up.

12

'That newspaper is out of line,' Baggo said, his mouth full of bacon and egg. Anxious to leave early for the briefing Flick had called for nine am in Cupar, he had been ambushed on his way out by the owner of the guesthouse, who had risen early to cook breakfast especially for him. Now the man sat opposite. Thrilled at having a real detective staying, he had read out Bothwell's piece in *Good News* and was curious to learn more.

'We are not sitting on our backsides waiting for eggs to hatch,' Baggo told him, wiping a dribble of yolk from his chin. 'These days police work is very technical. We have to wait for results to come back from the lab. We have to look at hours of CCTV footage. The man who gave the paper these quotes is a dinosaur. I know, because I worked with him.'

'But he says Detective Inspector Fortune was his protégé.'

Baggo drained his coffee cup. 'In his dreams. They were chalk and cheese. And still are. Now, please excuse me. I must be off.' Seeing the look of disappointment on the man's face, he added, 'Thank you for a wonderful breakfast. It will give me the energy to be busy all day, getting my hands dirty as necessary.'

As he steered his way through traffic towards the bypass, he thought about some of the things he'd like to do to Mr Pete Bothwell. Then his thoughts turned once more to Melanie. Last night had been a successful date, revealing shared interests and political views and a common sense of humour. He had walked her home, his arm round her waist, but at her door she had pecked him on the cheek and quickly scuttled into her block of flats, the outer door locking behind her. Mentally undressing her, he wondered why she was not more physical. He didn't think she was the frigid type, he was sure she wasn't gay, so had she had a bad experience? Was she just taking things slowly, or might she have taken fright at the thought of dating an Indian? A horn-blast behind him brought his attention back to the road. He continued his journey, a bit of him hoping the inquiry would not be over too soon.

The bypass behind him, Baggo made good time against the flow of commuter traffic crawling into Edinburgh from Fife. Crossing the road bridge built in the nineteen sixties, he looked to his right at the dark red railway bridge. Its steel cantilevers, three quarters of a century older but structurally sounder than their younger companion, were one of the iconic sights of Scotland. He wound down his window and breathed deeply. It was another glorious morning, perfect for a drive through the rich agricultural land in which the old market town of Cupar sat.

When Baggo sailed into the Incident Room, a cheery good-morning on his lips, he quickly sensed the atmosphere of gloomy embarrassment. There was no banter. The detectives were sitting at computers, staring at screens, appearing busy. Wallace caught Baggo's eye, frowned and shook his head. 'She hadn't seen it till now,' he hissed, nodding at the copy of *Good News* lying on an otherwise empty desk. 'Waterworks,' he added. On the wall beside the desk the whiteboard bore witness to a busy, if unproductive, inquiry. Along the top were photos of Knox as he was found, his wife, Lynda Traynor with a blank space beside her, Smail and his wife and Maltravers. Green writing noted evidence while questions were in red. There was more red than green.

It was five past nine before Flick appeared, eyes blood-shot and make-up smudged. She gave the slightest nod towards Baggo then clapped her hands for attention. Everyone turned respectfully towards her, even McKellar. Before she opened her mouth Wallace stood.

He spoke steadily and without emotion. 'I believe I speak for everyone, ma'am, when I say that article is a disgrace and we will find a way of making Mr Bothwell suffer for it. Mr Osborne, too. You're a damned good boss and there's nothing wrong with the way you're leading this inquiry. We'll get whoever killed Mr Knox, even if it takes a while.' As he sat down, some stamped their feet, some clapped and Baggo said 'Hear, hear'.

Taken aback, Flick looked confused and Baggo wondered if she was going to cry again. Instead she took a deep breath. 'Thank you,' she whispered, looking round the room. 'Thank you. That means a lot. Now, Detective Sergeant Wallace, you have been collating information. I want every one of us to be up to speed on all branches of the inquiry. Please tell us what you have learned.'

Wallace went over to the whiteboard and began a painstaking summary of what they knew. It came down to very little. The CCTV was of poor quality and the cameras were not helpfully placed. It did not give any of the suspects a foolproof alibi, and neither did the statements that had been taken. A few fingerprints belonging to neither Knox nor the security staff had been found on a wooden bookcase on the bench, but Wallace was reluctant to fingerprint the judges who had sat there before the murder unless it was clearly necessary. 'It is,' Flick said. 'Please organise that today.' The judges' retiring room, where the bows and arrows had been stowed, had also been used to store candelabras and other items belonging to the caterers. A succession of waiters had come and gone from there, but there was no evidence that any of the suspects had been there. The lab had confirmed that the stains on Knox's clothes contained vaginal fluid and they could compare DNA. Once they had something to compare it with.

'Well, get a warrant for Lynda Traynor's DNA and fingerprints,' Flick said. 'We should search the house as well.'

Wallace said, 'I believe we can assume she was the woman who had sex with Knox, at least until something else is proved, but she's only a possible killer.'

'It's hard to see any motive for her to kill Knox,' Baggo said. 'In fact, it's difficult to see how any of them have a motive, other than sexual jealousy, and both Traynor and

Mrs Knox appear to be stoical people, able to put up with their spouses' dalliances. But while we're looking at these suspects, there's something I do not understand about Lachlan Smail. Alex McKellar says that he has a temper and was lucky not to have been prosecuted yet according to Mr Primrose he is practically a saint.'

McKellar's dour face twisted. 'He's taken a stick to more than one farm worker, but he'll kiss your arse if you're a duke. Sorry, ma'am.'

Flick didn't react. McKellar continued, 'His wife has an interesting history, too. I was sure I recognised her from somewhere, and last night the penny dropped. I've checked up and I was right. She used to be Nicola Moncrieff, and in her day she was the talk of St Andrews. She was only fourteen or fifteen and at St Leonard's, the posh school in the town, but she got pregnant. Her father, who was an important businessman, took it personally and was all set to go round all the boys she saw in the school holidays. To prevent an incident I was sent to interview them. I hadn't been in the office long. Didn't recognise the hospital pass till I'd caught it.' His mouth twisted into a smile. 'All these posh boys! They talked the talk as if they were men of the world, but when they realised they could go to jail for under-age sex they made out they were virgins, which most probably were. We never did track down the father. The girl was packed off to relatives and nearly ten years later she came back. There was a rumour that she'd been in London, PA to some banker, and she'd had an affair with him. It hadn't worked. Anyway, Lachlan Smail married her. He wasn't short of admirers, so it must have been love.' He gave a cynical snort.

'What about the baby?' Baggo asked.

'The story was she'd had an abortion, but I've no idea.'

Baggo said, 'That is interesting. Now, with your permission, Inspector ma'am, you should hear about what Billy did yesterday.'

This was di Falco's cue to recount his afternoon in Glasgow with the *Vita Dei* pro-life campaigners. When he described Johnny, Spider Gilsland cut in.

'Yesterday, as instructed by Inspector Fortune, not *Good News*, I investigated the criminal records of as many of the people at the function as I could. John Aloysius Dolan, who lives in Glasgow, was one of the waiters, and he has quite a record for violence. Six months ago he got out after five years of an eight year sentence for attempted murder. He stabbed someone in the stomach. It was a sectarian thing. The victim was a Rangers fan who found himself in the wrong pub.'

'Well done!' Flick enthused. She wrote Dolan's name alongside the other suspects.

'Do you want me to follow it up, ma'am?' di Falco asked.

'Yes, and the sooner the better. I'd like you to go to Glasgow this afternoon. Make sure your Johnny is this Dolan and learn as much as you can about your *Vita Dei* friends.'

'I'll tell them I rearranged my shifts. They think I'm a waiter in the Old Course Hotel. I'll prime someone there to lie for me if that priest checks up.'

Gilsland interrupted again. 'On Friday there was another waiter with a record. Causing death by dangerous driving. He got six years and has been out nearly eighteen months. He comes from Dunfermline.' Gilsland paused for effect. 'His name is Gary Thomson, and he's the son of Joe Thomson, the builder Knox was prosecuting when he was killed.'

* * *

In the solitude of her office, Flick re-read the piece in *Good News*. It was totally poisonous and very personal. Sure, her bump was big, but Osborne's belly, full of a revolting mixture of curries, doughnuts and alcohol, would not be gone in a few weeks. She thought back to the excruciating briefing. Anger, distress and embarrassment had frozen her brain and she had said little. It had been the two sergeants, Wallace and Chandavarkar, who had made most of the running. Had she been like a fat, lame duck trying to cover too many eggs, most of which were cold? She read the article once more then folded the paper and placed it in a drawer. She would make Osborne wish he'd never questioned whether she had the guts to do the job.

She took out a spread-sheet on which she was noting names, times and activities from the end of dinner to eleven pm. Forcing herself to concentrate, she worked on identifying specific time windows during which each suspect might have taken the arrow and stabbed Knox.

She had not been doing this for long before her door burst open and a man looking like an enraged tailor's mannequin marched in and stood in the middle of the room. Behind him was a woman, taller and younger. She wore no make-up and her blonde hair was thrown forward to cover her left cheek. If recent events had deflated Flick, that was nothing to their effect on Lynda Traynor. The confident arrogance had been replaced by sullen watchfulness. Shoulders hunched, her eyes scanned the room before settling on the spread-sheet. Flick saw she was trying to read it upside-down.

Her husband put his hands on the desk and glared down at Flick. 'Detective Inspector Fortune?' he spat out.

She had seen photos of Chief Superintendent Traynor but this was the first time she had seen him in the flesh. Like his house, everything about him was immaculate. A well-pressed navy blue suit, a black and white tie so neat it might have been a clip-on, a crisp white shirt. His full head of hair, grey at the temples, had been trimmed by a skilful hairdresser. His lips, drawn back into a snarl, revealed teeth that might grace a toothpaste advert. Only a tiny scab under his jaw-line betrayed an early-morning tremor in his razor hand.

Silently, Lance Wallace entered behind the Traynors. He pushed the door back so it was barely ajar and stood uncertainly beside it.

Reassured by Wallace's presence, Flick felt surprisingly calm and confident. Despite Traynor's threatening pose, they both knew she had the upper hand. 'Chief Superintendent Traynor,' she said. 'Mrs Traynor. Please sit down.'

Breathing in short bursts, Traynor held his position as

Flick concentrated on acting unconcerned. Slowly he straightened himself then sat on the chair opposite Flick. His wife went to a chair also facing Flick but behind him and against a wall.

'I want to know what on earth you are doing, Inspector,' Traynor said, his voice full of pent-up anger.

'I am conducting a complex inquiry, Chief Superintendent.'

'My name is being bandied about in the press to the extent that I have been suspended until you can exonerate me. It is vital, not just for my sake but for the sake of the entire police force, that you get a move on and do that. Yet you haven't even had the courtesy to speak to me, let alone interview me. I want you to interview me now, check what I say, and tell the world, in particular that *Good News* rag, that I did not kill Knox.'

'I am very sorry about *Good News*, believe me. What they print has nothing to do with me or any member of my team. It was an advocate who was at the function last Friday who told them about your wife and Mr Knox, and until yesterday morning when it came out, we were committed to keeping your name out of the press while conducting a thorough and professional investigation.' A flicker of his eyes told her that the rational part of Traynor's brain accepted that. 'It would help our inquiry, sir, if your wife were to be entirely candid about what she did that evening. When I spoke to her on Monday afternoon, I'm afraid to say I found her uncooperative.'

'Inspector, my wife and I have had a discussion.' He paused. Flick glanced at Mrs Traynor, who tossed her head back. There was swelling over her left cheekbone and the surrounding skin was red. As she was not in his line of vision he did not see this and carried on in the same earnest, reasonable tone of voice. 'My wife will admit to you that she had a short affair with Knox and that she and he met in Court Three before he was killed. However when she left him he was alive. The killer struck after she was well away.'

'Is this true, Mrs Traynor?' Flick asked.

She nodded.

'I would like to take a statement from your wife now, sir, but outwith your presence.'

'But I should be with her when you speak to her.'

'Not in my book, sir. The DCC impressed on me that this matter requires to be investigated properly so as to withstand scrutiny. Please leave my office now.' She smiled at Wallace. 'Sergeant Wallace, please escort Chief Superintendent Traynor to somewhere comfortable and give him coffee or tea.'

Wallace held the door open. 'After you, sir,' he said politely. Without a word, Traynor marched out. Wallace followed him and closed the door.

Flick leaned forward. With an expression she hoped was encouraging she said, 'Well, Mrs Traynor, if you are prepared to make a statement, I should like to record it.'

Lynda Traynor shot a contemptuous glance at her and stared at a watercolour on the opposite wall. It depicted the ivy-clad All-England Club and had been presented to Flick by her colleagues when she left Wimbledon.

'I can see you dislike me, Inspector,' she said after a

pause. 'And I couldn't care less about that, but what should be private has now become very public and it matters to someone important to me that this should be cleared up as soon as possible. So I'm going to give you my side of the story. You can record it if you like.'

Five minutes later they were in an interview room with recording facilities. Di Falco had joined them and, as Flick opened her spread-sheet, he turned on the machine. Flick cautioned Mrs Traynor that she was not obliged to say anything and confirmed she did not want a solicitor present.

'I was pregnant when we got married and our son, Adam, is the only good thing that has come out of our relationship,' she began. 'We both doted on him and still do. We shouldn't have married, but my parents … had views. After a few years it was a marriage in name only and we separated. Adam went with me but saw his father regularly. Neither of us could believe how upset he got. He was only seven, but there were heart-breaking scenes every time he went from one of us to the other. He began to wet the bed. It was all horrible. Eventually we consulted a child psychiatrist who told us Adam blamed himself for us separating and that he was seriously traumatised. My husband and I are not monsters, Inspector. We both love our son. We decided to stay together for his sake until he's old enough to accept the situation. But in the meantime we would live separate lives. We are both strong characters in different ways and it has been far from easy. Last year we decided it would be best if Adam were to go to boarding school as the atmosphere in the house is sometimes toxic. This is his third term away at Glenalmond and he was beginning to get used to being there when all this came up. We got a call from his housemaster last night. Apparently he's been teased about us and is in a dreadful state. *Good News* travels, you know. We're on our way to pick him up now. Together. My husband has made it clear to me that it's in everyone's interests to wrap this up quickly. Adam's most of all. While I repeat that my business is nobody else's business, I will tell you about my affair with Farquhar Knox and why it would not cause my husband to kill him.' She had spoken in a controlled, precise way, her voice catching when describing her son's distress.

Flick could see she was now close to tears and felt less unsympathetic towards her. 'In your own time,' she said softly.

'When the marriage was breaking down my husband lost interest in sex.' She glanced at di Falco, who shifted in his chair and looked at the floor. 'I didn't, and he was not concerned if I had affairs. But he's a control freak and stubborn as they come. You'll have noticed how tidy the house is. He's totally anal about that. Anyway, he wanted to have a say in who I slept with, the important thing for him being to avoid scandal. Well, that was like a red rag to a bull and every now and again I'd pick a lover because of his potential to embarrass my husband. On Friday night he'd overheard gossip about me going to Court Three to shag Farquhar. It wasn't the shagging he objected to but the gossip. He thought people were laughing at him, and they probably were.' She looked from Flick to di

Falco who grinned nervously and checked the tape. Flick nodded then instinctively reached across the formica-topped table and briefly squeezed Lynda Traynor's hand.

'Thank you, Inspector,' she continued. 'My affair with Farquhar had been going on for a couple of months. We usually met in hotels. He was passionate, and quite inventive. When he heard my husband and I had been invited to the Advocates and Archers he got very excited and arranged to go himself. He had originally planned to give it a miss. We arranged to speak after dinner.' She shook her head. 'It's strange talking about this now he's dead. He told me to go to the Ladies and remove my knickers then, once the archery started, I was to go down a corridor he pointed out. The lighting only covered the start and I was to feel my way along the unlit bit until I found a door on the left that was ajar. I was to go in there and up a few steps. Of course I did this and found myself on the bench of this old courtroom. Farquhar was sitting in the judge's chair. Well, he had me on the bench itself. Not at all comfortable, but Farquhar was really turned on. Afterwards I tidied myself as well as I could and left. Farquhar was sitting in the judge's chair and he was very definitely alive. He said we shouldn't leave together and he'd follow me in five minutes. These were probably his last words.' Her voice caught and she paused. 'I went to the Ladies then wandered about until I bumped into my husband, who was in a foul mood. I told you how we spent the rest of the evening, Inspector.'

'Can you give a time for when you went along to Court Three?' Flick asked.

'No. The archery might have been going for five minutes or so.'

'And when did you leave the court?'

'The archery had finished. I suppose we must have spent about twenty minutes on the bench together.'

'Did you see anyone acting suspiciously as you left the court or anything that might help us find the killer?'

'Honestly, no.'

'How long was it after you left the court that you saw your husband?'

She frowned. 'Maybe ten minutes. He was buying a bottle of wine at the bar.'

'And he was angry with Mr Knox, threatening to "punch his lights out"?'

'He was more angry with me. He kept saying I'd crossed a boundary. But he was furious because he felt he was being made a fool of, not because of the sex.'

'If he had come across Knox, what do you think he would have done?'

'I really don't know, Inspector. He's a very controlled man and I think, despite the drink, he'd have done nothing.'

Flick thanked her formally and signalled to di Falco to turn off the tape. Mrs Traynor, looking drained, stared blankly at the far wall. Flick smiled at her. 'Thank you for telling us all that. It's very helpful. One thing bothers me. Did your husband use violence to persuade you to speak up?' She touched her own left cheekbone.

Mrs Traynor brushed her hair forward. 'I'm not going there, Inspector. I walked into a door, actually.'

Flick shrugged. 'Very well,' she said. 'They all say that, you know. If you should change your mind, you know where I am. Now, Detective Constable, please take Mrs Traynor somewhere she will be comfortable and give her tea or coffee. And ask Sergeant Wallace to bring the Chief Superintendent in here.'

As she got up Mrs Traynor gave Flick a curious look that seemed to combine puzzlement and gratitude.

When her husband came in and sat opposite Flick he appeared calm but was very much on his dignity. As Flick went through the standard pre-interview caution all suspects were given, he wrinkled his nose in distaste. When she finished he got straight to the point.

'I trust my wife has already informed you of the nature of our marriage. It effectively broke down many years ago but we live separate lives under the same roof for the sake of our son, Adam. He has been traumatised by the scandalous press coverage of your investigation and we are on our way to his school to reassure him.' He then launched into an account Flick could tell had been carefully thought out and rehearsed.

'Because of the nature of our marriage, I had no objection if my wife saw other men, however I asked her to be discreet. I regret to say that discretion has never been her strong point and her lack of it that evening was particularly embarrassing as we were top table guests. I was there representing the police force as Divisional Commander. After dinner I saw my wife talking with Knox, whom I recognised. I didn't see her for a while and I went to look for her. The archery contest was proceeding at the time. We did not know many people at the function personally, but I remember casually asking one of the other men at the top table if he had seen my wife. He said he had not. Then I overheard some drunk discussing my wife and Knox in the coarsest of terms. He attracted quite an audience and I could hear him say they had gone off to some courtroom. I looked round, Inspector, but I did not enter any courtroom and I did not see my wife until she approached me as I was queuing to buy another bottle of wine. We went to the far end of the library together and left early. It was not a happy night.' He stopped and looked at Flick, challenging her to ask a question.

'Did you and your wife quarrel, sir?'

'We discussed the situation and I communicated my displeasure.'

'What did she say?'

'She denied any impropriety.'

'Did you threaten to "punch Knox's lights out"?'

If the question took him by surprise, Traynor hid it well. 'Possibly.'

'How much had you had to drink at the time of the archery, sir?'

'I don't know, Inspector. All I can say is the wine was good and my glass was being topped up constantly.'

'Do you know where Court Three is, sir?'

'I do now. But not then.'

'Did you know where the arrows were stored after the contest?'

'I believe I saw them being carried off by one of the senior archers, but I don't know where they went.'

Flick said nothing then looked towards Wallace, who shook his head. She said, 'You can turn ... On second thoughts, Chief Superintendent, for how long had you known about your wife's affair with Mr Knox?'

Wallace withdrew his hand from the control of the tape. Startled, Traynor coughed into an ironed linen handkerchief. 'I ... I hadn't known about it until that night.'

'But if someone at your table were to say you seemed quite distracted when you saw your wife and Mr Knox speaking earnestly after dinner, can you explain that?'

A nervous tic beside his left eye showed that the question was a good one. 'I do not believe I reacted in that way,' he said.

Flick decided to end the interview there. Wallace turned off the tape and, as a gesture of respect for his rank, Flick stood as the Chief Superintendent left the room. But they both knew he would not be taken off the suspects' list immediately.

13

'Delivery!' Baggo shouted into the intercom beside the outer door of Gary Thomson's stair, which he had found on a steeply sloping street in Dunfermline's old town, near the Maygate. It was after ten-thirty, a time of day at which he thought a waiter might be up but not yet working. Although Joe Thomson and his wife, Myra, lived in a substantial modern house out of town past the Canmore Golf Course, Gary did not live with them.

'Okay.' The disembodied voice was accompanied by a click.

Up two flights of stairs, a scruffy young man stood in the doorway of a flat.

'Are you Gary Thomson?' Baggo asked, trying not to sound out of breath.

'Yes.' There was suspicion in the youth's voice. 'What have you got for me?'

Baggo put his foot in the door. 'Just a few questions. I'm a policeman, but there's nothing to worry about.' He shoved his warrant card under Thomson's nose. 'May I come in?'

Scowling, Thomson led the way into a sitting room in which beer cans, cigarette ends, papers and a pizza box served as ornaments. Despite the open window the air was stale and the sunshine was filtered by a greasy curtain which neither opened nor closed properly. Unaware or uncaring of the impression the room made, Thomson stood barefoot in the middle of the floor, his pose defensive.

Baggo perched on the arm of the settee. 'I am engaged in the inquiry into the death of Farquhar Knox,' he said, 'and I hope you might be able to help me.'

'So you're doing as that London polisman said, and you're going to pin it on some guy with a record?' Nearly six feet tall and slimly built, his greasy, black hair fell over his face, which was framed by a thin beard. Baggo thought he looked like a horse. A grubby tee-shirt bore the image of a woman's breasts and revealed gangly arms. His low-slung jeans appeared to defy gravity. He spoke with a strong Fife accent and avoided Baggo's gaze.

'No.' Baggo was not going to rise to that dig.

After a few moments Thomson broke the silence. 'Well why are you here, then?'

'The man who died was prosecuting your father and you were there as a waiter. So of course we're going to talk to you.'

'Okay.'

'Do you remember seeing Farquhar Knox that evening?'

'I may have seen him. I didnae know the man so I cannae help you.'

'Had you never been at your father's trial?'

'Naw.'

Baggo could not recall seeing him on the public benches. 'How do you get on with your father?' he asked.

'It's no' a secret. We dinnae get on.'

'Why not?'

There was a hard glint in Thomson's eye. 'Lots of reasons.'

'You've been out about eighteen months, I believe?'

'And I'm on licence.'

'You work as a waiter?'

'Sometimes. Like last Friday. My main job is shelf-stacking at Tesco. I'm just back from the early shift.'

'Do you know Johnny Dolan?'

Thomson pushed his hair out of his eyes and walked over to the window. 'Aye,' he said, pulling back the curtain. The extra light did not improve the room.

'From jail?'

'Aye.' Thomson stared out of the window.

'Did you see him on Friday night?'

'Aye.'

'Did you speak to him?'

Thomson turned and looked at Baggo as if he was daft. 'Naw. He's a fucking heidbanger. Half the screws were scared of him.'

'So you tried to avoid him?'

'Aye.'

'I understand he has become very religious.'

'Very Catholic, you mean. You wouldn't admit to being a bluenose near him. In jail, the word was after he'd beaten someone up he said one *Hail Mary* for every bone he'd broken. Jeez …'

Baggo had been in Scotland long enough to know that Rangers supporters were called bluenoses. 'I understand. But did you see him do anything odd or suspicious on Friday night, especially during the archery contest and, say, an hour after that?'

'Naw.'

'Did you see him go along a darkened corridor at that time?'

'Naw.'

'Did you see him go near the room where they stored the bows and arrows after the archery?'

'Aye. Most of us must have been there. We used it as a place to keep valuable things like candelabras that were ready to take away. Kingsleys, the caterers, had to bring most of the stuff themselves. After we cleared the tables we took everything downstairs. We made sure the valuable stuff was clean then carried it to that room. I think the first van came just after eleven.'

'Was there anything furtive or strange about how Dolan behaved there?'

'Naw. Not that I saw, but I wasn't watching.'

'And what did you do during the hour after dinner?'

'What the other waiters did. We had to clear the hall for the archery which was hard as naebody wanted to move. We took the stuff downstairs and packed it up then carried it up for collection. The valuable things were put in that room with the bows and arrows.'

'How many times did you visit that room?'

Thomson shrugged. 'Twice, maybe. I dunno.'

'Which tables did you serve during the meal?'

'Numbers ten, eleven and twelve.'

'Did you recognise anyone on any of them?'

'Naw. They were mostly pissed lawyers.'

'When did you leave Parliament House?'

'About eleven-fifteen. Some had to stay but they let us part-timers go once things were packed and ready to go. And before you ask, my mate drove me. I didnae breach my ban.'

'You don't live with your parents, who are in the same town. Why not save yourself some money and live at home?'

'Like I say, we don't get on.'

'Is it just you who lives here?'

'I share with a mate from school. He's at work.'

Feeling he had learned disappointingly little, Baggo thanked him and left. Looking back at the tenement from the pavement, he identified the sitting-room window and saw the greasy curtain twitch.

* * *

Flick found half a dozen missed calls on her phone, all from Fergus. She called him back and listened to a rant about *Good News*, which was nothing compared with the diatribe he then aimed at Inspector No. 'That drunken heap of horse-shit had better not stray into Dundee or I'll show him how old-fashioned methods work in Scotland,' he spluttered.

Flick found his impotent rage strangely comforting. 'I'm okay, darling, really. I'm furious about it too, but it's jolted the Traynors into coming clean about their marriage and Lynda's affair with Knox. We're finding out more all the time and we're following up everything. Even the baby feels calmer. She's dancing *Swan Lake* this morning.'

'I'm glad you can look at it that way. You're doing really well, my love. I'm so proud of you.' She could hear the emotion in his voice.

Forcing herself not to weaken as she rang off, she hoped the investigation would get the bit of luck it needed sooner rather than later.

That breakthrough came earlier than expected. Continuing to work on her spread-sheet, she was irritated when asked to take a call from Detective Inspector Hepburn of Coatbridge CID.

'We have a murder,' he told her. 'A man in his forties. Struck on the head then asphyxiated in his home. He's got a record. Forgery.' He paused theatrically. Flick said nothing, willing him to get on with it.

'In his flat we found pictures of farm land beside a river. Jack Nicklaus, the golfer, appears in many of them and he's been stuck in by some techy expert. Whoever it was, and we think it was the deceased, had a sense of humour. In one picture Nicklaus is showing some plans to pigs. There are also artist's impressions of a golf course and letters that look as if they're from Nicklaus, with his signature. They concern a proposed new course near St Andrews. I think we've found someone who was involved in your big fraud case. But we've no leads in tracing his killer.'

At her desk, Flick punched the air. One of the features of the fraud had been the expertly-produced artist's impressions of the finished project. The identity of the artist had remained a mystery. 'When was he killed?' she asked, trying to keep her voice steady.

'Yesterday evening, we believe. His lady friend found him last night.'

Flick's mind raced. 'This could be linked to the murder I'm investigating at the moment, Farquhar Knox. You know he was prosecuting the fraud. Can I come now to discuss it?'

They arranged to meet in an hour and a half. Flick phoned Baggo, who was driving out of Dunfermline on his way to see if anything useful came out at the fraud trial, and to see Melanie. He changed his plans and would meet them in Coatbridge.

Di Falco driving, Flick found Coatbridge Police Office without difficulty. A squat, ugly building, it sat beside a roundabout in the middle of a town that had seen more prosperous times. At reception they were greeted with the warm informality that the West prided itself on. Chatting happily about the weather, a young PC led them upstairs and along a drab corridor. Baggo's laugh could be heard as they approached DI Hepburn's office.

Bryan Hepburn was a muscular looking man of medium height. His welcoming smile did not detract from worldly-wise eyes. A good friend and a bad enemy was Flick's first impression. As Baggo pushed a file he had already seen over to Flick, Hepburn related what he knew.

Tam Walker had been a talented forger, but he had

over-reached himself some years earlier when he passed off one of his efforts as a Peploe. When people are asked to part with three hundred thousand pounds for a square of canvas covered in paint they are apt to be very careful indeed. It was a tribute to Tam's skill that he fooled one famous gallery owner and several art journalists before an expert hired by the would-be buyer detected something in the brush-strokes that jarred. From there it was all downhill. After an entertaining trial Tam got five years, the scale of his potential reward being uppermost in the judge's mind. After his release he had enjoyed four years of freedom during which it seemed that he had refined his skills by embracing technology. He had owned a sophisticated and expensive desk-top computer capable of doing much more than e-mails, internet and word processing.

His main companion, and occasional bed-mate, was Mona McBride, who lived across the landing. The previous day she had expected him for a drink about eight and when there was no sign of him by nine she decided to check up on him. She found his body on the floor beside the computer. Lying on his back, the cushion which had been used to smother him still covered his mouth. The African stone statue used to strike the back of his head lay blood-stained nearby. The hard drive of the computer had been removed and there was no trace of his mobile phone.

'Our SOCOs have done their job, of course, as has the photographer,' Hepburn explained. 'The items recovered have been sent to the lab in Glasgow and they have started to examine them. The post mortem will be going on now. In Glasgow, again. It was only a couple of hours ago I realised the connection with Fife.'

'Well I certainly want to be fully involved,' Flick said, examining the file. As well as photos of the body there were the letters and images Hepburn had mentioned on the phone. 'I recognise a lot of these,' she said. 'We never found out who did the art-work for the fraud. Now we know.'

Hepburn beamed. 'It suits me if you want to take over. This is one of three murders we've got right now and we're stretched. I've no time for daft turf wars. You're welcome to this one.'

'You mean I take over as senior investigating officer?' Flick was astonished. Most police officers she knew guarded their cases like a mother hen.

'Unless that's a problem. Mind, we'll probably get our balls chewed by the number-crunchers. If you know what I mean.'

Flick liked Hepburn. In a way he reminded her of Fergus. 'I know exactly what you mean. I sometimes want to stick their budgets where you won't hear the numbers crunch,' she said. Fergus had used that expression the previous week and Hepburn's informality was infectious. She saw Baggo and di Falco look amazed and resolved to startle them with more of the risqué lines she had absorbed but not used.

Hepburn said, 'We've already done door-to-door inquiries in the block of flats, with the usual result. Naebody saw nothing. It will all be on the file I'll e-mail to you. Just keep me in the loop if there's something I should know.'

It took little time to exchange e-mail addresses and arrange for the transfer of the inquiry to Fife, with the proviso that if the Nicklaus angle went cold the case would revert to Coatbridge. Pausing to pick up the dead man's computer, for whatever use it might be without the hard drive, Flick, Baggo and di Falco followed Hepburn to the crime scene.

Tam Walker had lived in a block of flats on high ground in the Whifflet area of town. The parking area was pot-holed and strewn with broken glass. Baggo's hired car and the two unmarked police cars seemed unusually obvious. The officers entered the block through a graffiti-defaced doorway. Crude images of genitalia, some accompanied by names, had been daubed on the foyer walls. High on one wall the remains of a bracket hung, parts of a smashed CCTV camera scattered below. A lift stinking of urine squeaked and shoogled its way to the third floor, where a woman in a low-cut cocktail dress waited for them. Mona McBride might have been any age between twenty-five and fifty. Laddered tights spoiled her elegant legs but it was her generous and well-supported breasts that caught the eye. Dabbing her heavily made-up face, she assured them that she and Tam had been soul-mates and that he had been a lovely man.

Hepburn had a key to the flat. He shut the heavily reinforced door in the woman's face and they heard loud sobs from the landing.

'Billy, please take a full statement from her,' Flick said,

'and concentrate on yesterday, obviously, but also what she thought he may have been doing on his computer. Had he talked much about money recently? Use your discretion. Oh, and make sure to get her key, or keys,' she added, looking at the sophisticated locks.

As soon as di Falco paid attention to her, Mona McBride stopped sobbing. Flick and Baggo exchanged glances then concentrated on the flat. Passing from a pale blue hall they came to the living room which was light and south-facing, its height giving views across nearby houses and the M8 to the green fields of South Lanarkshire. The carpet, a stronger shade of blue, was disfigured by a bloodstain beside the large but simple pine desk on which sat two computer screens, a keypad and a printer. A leather-covered sofa and two armchairs were angled towards a flat-screen television. A glass coffee table held a pile of glossy art brochures and a black stone carving in the African style, probably the pair of the weapon used to knock Tam out. Flick noted that the SOCOs had been thorough. Traces of grey fingerprint powder were everywhere.

But it was the paintings hanging on the walls that made her gasp. At first sight they were worth several millions. Above the sofa, a view of a boldly-coloured wheatfield, painted with the thick strokes of Van Gogh, was signed Vincent. On the wall opposite, a nude with large breasts and a round face carried Picasso's signature. Beside it an obscene painting of a woman, her legs splayed open, also had Picasso's name on it. 'Is that Mona McBride?' Baggo asked innocently, earning a guffaw from

Hepburn and, to his surprise, a broad grin from Flick. On the wall facing the window, two paintings of Flapper girls in the Vettriano railway poster style carried the discordant theme further. Flick examined them closely and wondered how many experts they might fool.

Next to the living room was a small bedroom which Walker had used as a studio. The smell of paint, detectable in the rest of the flat, was strongest here. The room was as shambolic as the living room had been tidy. Paints, brushes, rags and canvasses appeared to have been dropped haphazardly. A large easel stood in the middle of the chaos, the painting on it turned to the light. It was the image of a woman with a fish draped across her head.

'He couldn't stop himself,' Hepburn chuckled.

'What do you mean?' Flick asked.

'John Bellany, a very successful Scottish painter, died not so long ago. He painted a lot of women with fishes on their heads. This could have been Bellany's, you know. It would take an expert to say it's not. Perhaps Tam was needing to boost his pension.'

Another small bedroom, this time facing west, was full of photographic apparatus. The chemical smell and heavy curtains were evidence of an effective printing facility. It was in a drawer in this room that the tell-tale papers and pictures had been found.

'I'm surprised no one tried to pinch this,' Flick said.

Hepburn said, 'Tam had the sort of friends you want living here. It's amazing the number of local drug barons who have Van Goghs on their walls – Van Goghs that have never come up for sale and never will. But they look mighty impressive.'

'Could this have been an underworld hit?' Baggo asked.

Hepburn shook his head. 'Unlikely. It was well known Tam had protection and he was too smart to seriously piss off one of the big guys.'

'He had a big flat for a single man,' Flick commented.

Hepburn explained, 'When he got it he was living with a woman and five kids. She left and he kept the flat. It's not exactly the most popular place to stay in Coatbridge. Not much competition for the tenancies.'

Flick was not surprised but didn't say so. Working quickly, she and Baggo searched the flat with Hepburn's help, amassing drawings, letters and photographic equipment, anything that might prove useful. They were joined by di Falco, who had learned little new from Mona, except that the morning Tam died he'd been talking about getting some extra money. Di Falco had asked her if he had seen a newspaper that morning and she confirmed that he had. The paper had been *Good News*, she thought. She had popped in for a coffee about eleven and left half an hour later. She hadn't seen him alive again.

They locked up and left the flat together, taking the lift once more. On the ground floor they were hailed by a tiny, bent old lady wearing a shabby apron with a flower pattern.

'Tam was a good man,' she told them in a trembling voice. 'I hope ye make his killer pay.'

'Did you know him well?' Flick asked.

'Well enough,' the old lady said. 'He was good to me. Two months ago he gave me a picture of a wumman wi' a fush on her heid. He telt me I'd get three thousand pund fur it. But I like it and it's still on my wall. Imagine going aboot wi' a fush on yer heid. Daft, like. But he was a good man.'

'And I'm not going to stop her trying to get her money for that painting,' Hepburn said as they came to their cars. 'If the buyer thinks it's worth three thousand pounds it shouldn't matter who painted it.'

There in Coatbridge, Flick could see his point. Having said a cheery goodbye to Bryan Hepburn she beamed at the other two. 'Let's find somewhere for lunch.'

As she spoke, her phone rang. It was Wallace. She listened then turned to the others. 'Lance has just heard from Eloise Knox's solicitor. After a lot of humming and hawing he's admitted that she stands to receive a life insurance payout of three million pounds.' She paused. 'Unless of course it was she who killed her husband.'

14

The place they found for lunch was a drive-through McDonald's in Airdrie, a continuation of Coatbridge to the east. As they sat in Flick's pool car pretending not to enjoy their guilty pleasures, they watched police vans bearing the day's custodies coming and going from the nearby sheriff court.

They agreed that the insurance pay-out gave Eloise Knox a real motive to kill her husband instead of divorcing him. Following up on her was a priority.

After lunch they dropped di Falco at the train station so that he might go to Glasgow to see Johnny Dolan as planned. In their separate cars Flick and Baggo made for Eloise Knox's house, hoping that Lord Hutton would be kept busy on the bench until they were finished. On her hands-free, Flick asked Wallace, still pinching himself after fingerprinting half a dozen High Court judges, to stay in Edinburgh and interview the accused in the fraud trial, checking alibis for the previous evening. 'Nicola Smail as well,' she added as an after-thought.

Flick and Baggo liased in India Street, up from Eloise Knox's house. On their previous visit she had responded better to di Falco, so Flick asked Baggo to start the questioning. She would be ready to come in as good cop or even worse cop, depending on circumstances.

They had not phoned ahead and, after two loud rings of the doorbell, wondered if anyone was in. Flick was reaching for her phone when they heard the click of the inner door and a sullen Ranald opened the outer door wide enough to stick his head out.

'My mother is still very upset,' he said, his voice anglicised and defiant. From his tone he might have added 'you plebs'. He withdrew his head and made to shut the door.

Baggo was too quick for him and stuck his foot in the way. 'I sincerely regret having to trouble you but we are at an important stage in trying to find your father's murderer and we must speak with your mother.'

The boy said nothing but walked away from the door. The detectives followed him in, shutting the door behind them. Ranald went to the foot of the staircase and shouted up, 'It's the police, Mummy.' The reply, sounding more angry than upset, was 'Well show them into the drawing room then.'

A full five minutes elapsed between Ranald leaving them in the drawing room and Eloise making a theatrical entrance, complete with a lace handkerchief with which she dabbed her eyes. Unhurried, she took her seat on the sofa. Flick wondered whom she might have been phoning and how long they would have before reinforcements arrived. She nodded to Baggo, who, while inspecting the room, had been thinking the same thing.

'Mrs Knox, I regret that it is necessary to ask you this,' he began after introducing himself, 'but were you aware that your husband was having an affair with Mrs Lynda Traynor?'

Her back stiffened and she clenched her fist. 'No,' she said with a sniff.

'Yet after seeing your husband talking with Mrs Traynor after dinner on Friday, you asked a friend if he "was off with that whore". Can you explain that?'

'Just a manner of speaking.'

'And when your friend prevaricated, you made a comment about "bloody men" sticking together?'

'I don't remember saying that.'

'And when you went outside to smoke immediately after the archery, you were heard to say that you could kill your husband. Can you explain that?'

'I don't remember saying that either, but it's something lots of women say every day.'

Flick decided to intervene. 'Come on, Mrs Knox. Please don't insult our intelligence. I know this is distressing and embarrassing, but the sooner we conclude our investigation the better it will be for everyone. We know, yes, we know that your husband had been having an affair with Mrs Traynor and that they went off to Court Three to have sex immediately before he was killed. We know that when the archery was over you went out for a cigarette. We also know that you did the Dashing White Sergeant with the Cuthberts. But there is a gap of ten to fifteen minutes which you have not accounted for. You could have killed your husband during that time. Please help us. If you can establish what you were doing then, we can eliminate you as a suspect.'

'I've already told you …'

Flick cut in. 'With respect, you haven't. The last time we met you said you came in from smoking and then the dancing started. But there was a gap.'

'Maybe I went to the Ladies. I can't remember.'

'You had been to the Ladies after dinner.'

'Maybe I went again. I can't remember exactly.' Her voice caught and Flick could tell that real tears were not far away. 'All right. I knew about Lynda Traynor and I was furious, really furious, that Farquhar should make a fool of me by going off to shag her when I was being the dutiful wife. I sort of drifted about for a bit outside – it was a pleasant night – and calmed down before going back in. And, before you ask, no one can confirm that. How was I to know someone was going to stab him then?' She glared at the officers, her face full of hurt and anger.

'There's something else,' Baggo said softly. 'We know about the three million pounds insurance policy. Was that your idea?'

She looked at him steadily. 'No it was not. My husband found fidelity a challenge, as he put it. After yet another argument over one of his many affairs, he insured his own life for three million. Of course I was very grateful until he told me it was to protect himself. Because the sum was so large, if he was ever murdered I'd be the prime suspect. There would be no way the insurance company would pay out until they were sure I had nothing to do with his death. I remember his words, "With this policy, there's no way you'll ever dare to kill me." And he was right.'

'You thought about it?' Baggo asked.

A twisted smile on her face she said, 'Yes. But I only thought about it.'

'So have we finally got the truth from you?' Flick asked. 'You had your smoke, then went for a walk to calm down and then came in for the Dashing White Sergeant?'

As she nodded, Lord Hutton burst into the room. This time he wore a well-tailored dark suit and it was easy to believe he was a High Court judge. 'What is this outrage, Inspector?' he blustered. 'I thought I warned you the last time we met. Mrs Knox is a very vulnerable person. You will hear more of this matter.'

Flick gave him her sweetest smile. 'She's a lot less vulnerable than she was, Lord Hutton, now that she says she has finally told us the truth. We'll see ourselves out.' Without giving him time to come back from that, they left.

'Did you hear the doorbell then?' Baggo asked as they walked up the hill to their cars.

'No,' Flick replied.

'So does the upright judge have a key so that he can comfort the grieving widow any time he wants?'

'My thoughts entirely.'

'Did you see his jaw drop when you said about her telling the truth?'

'It practically bounced up off his tie.'

'Interesting, perhaps?' he asked.

'But he wasn't there on Friday night. I checked the list.'

'There was some late swapping of tickets. I think I'll double check he wasn't there. I know just the person to ask.'

* * *

Baggo arrived at the fraud trial in time to hear a red-faced man tell the jury that Joe Thomson was totally honest. He was overdoing it, and the raised eyebrows in the jury box told their own story.

'If he hears of one of his men doing a homer for cash he'll sack him,' the witness said belligerently.

Thomson's advocate decided not to ask any more. Baggo could see that Melanie wanted Radcliffe to cross-examine but he remained seated and the witness was discharged. That concluded all the evidence in the case and Lord Tulloch told the jury that the next day they would begin to hear speeches from the crown then the defence and he hoped the case would finish early the following week.

'See you tonight?' Baggo whispered to Melanie as she collected her papers.

'Not tonight. Mark wants to go through his speech with me.' She gave him a sad smile.

'Well can I meet you for a quick drink in half an hour? I need to ask you a couple of things.'

After arranging to meet her in The Verdict, Baggo turned his attention to the accused in the trial. They were all in the foyer talking to their lawyers. Wallace and McKellar waited nearby to check alibis for Tam Walker's murder. They agreed that Wallace should speak to both Smails, McKellar to Maltravers and Baggo to Thomson.

The builder was about to ignore him and walk away when Baggo asked if he knew Tam Walker. 'No,' he replied quickly but the flicker of his eyelids suggested otherwise.

Baggo explained that he was investigating his murder

and asked what Thomson had done from the time he left court to eight pm the previous evening.

Although he wore an expensive suit, Thomson looked like a man who had worked his way up from a poor background. His skin was coarse and bore a few scars. To Baggo it suggested whisky, fights and open air. His hands had been hardened by work. Showing neither surprise nor resentment at being questioned, Thomson said, 'I was going round my building sites, checking the work.' In a matter-of-fact way he described how the sites were spread round West Fife and West Lothian. Baggo took down details of all of them. Everyone had knocked off for the day by the time the boss arrived and no one could back up his account. 'I made some phone calls too of course,' Thomson added. 'Business calls, on my car phone.' He set his jaw, as if inviting a challenge.

'When did you last see your son, Gary?' Baggo asked.

Thomson looked startled. 'What has that got to do with anything?' he asked.

'It's a perfectly innocent question, sir,' Baggo pointed out.

'If you must know, a long time ago.'

'Months or years?'

Thomson glared at him. 'Years.'

'When did you last speak with him?'

'I've no idea. Years.'

'Did you know he was working as a waiter at the Advocates and Archers function last Friday at which Mr Knox was killed?'

Thomson scowled. 'I see. You're wondering if I put him up to killing the man prosecuting me.'

'I have to make full and thorough inquiries, sir.'

'Well understand this. That ungrateful shite would have helped any enemy of mine. So if he did kill Knox he didn't do it for me.'

There was no more to be learned from Thomson. Wallace reported that the Smails said they had left court together and driven home to Fife. No one could back this up. Only Maltravers had given names of people he had seen after court the previous day. These were business contacts and he had implored McKellar to be discreet when checking his alibi.

* * *

Melanie was waiting in a booth far from other customers when Baggo arrived at The Verdict. She had bought pints and gave him a frothy smile as he slid along the bench opposite her. For a time they chatted about the trial, then Baggo asked if she had seen Lord Hutton on Friday night.

''Orrible 'Utton? Yes, I did. I bumped into him, actually. Why?'

'I'll tell you in a bit, but how did you bump into him?'

'Remember I was pissed? Well I was on my way to the Ladies when he sort of loomed in front of me. Actually he was looking down the corridor towards Court Three.'

'When was this?'

'I think, yes it was, just after the archery had finished. I was surprised to see him on his own like that, just staring down a corridor. He had been one of the Faculty's archers, not very good but at least he hit the butt every time. Not like poor Bradshaw, who missed completely with his first shot and damaged the wall.' She giggled.

'Hutton must have been a late substitute. He wasn't on the list we were given.'

She frowned. 'He was, now you mention it. Lord McNorris was supposed to be one of our archers, but he's on circuit in Inverness and someone offered him a weekend's fishing on the Spey. So he called off. Hutton can shoot with bows and arrows and he was persuaded to take McNorris's place. McNorris is divorced and Hutton's wife spends all her time in the Borders so the numbers worked out. The only thing was, Hutton had to join Lady Pumpherston's table and they're supposed to hate each other. We were all chatting about it.'

'Are all Scottish judges Lords or Ladies?'

'All High Court judges. But it's only a courtesy title. Their children don't inherit, unless they become judges too, of course, and that's not inheritance. Well, it's not supposed to be.' She smirked.

'Flick was talking about a Lord Craigdiller. He's not a judge, is he?'

'No. He's the chief Archer, I believe. As my mum would say, he's a proper lord, blue blood in his veins and rattling about in an ancestral pile but strapped for cash.' She shrugged.

'What's Hutton like? You called him 'Orrrible 'Utton.'

Melanie winced. 'He can be really vicious, particularly if people don't stand up to him. And woe betide you if you go into his court unprepared. Apparently he's reduced quite experienced counsel to tears. He's a very sound lawyer, of course. But tell me, why all the questions about him?'

'Please keep this under your hat, as you say, but he seems to have taken a shine to his neighbour, Mrs Knox, who stands to collect three million pounds insurance money as a result of her husband's death. He is terribly protective of her and I wonder why.'

'Chivalry,' she said with a straight face, 'or lust.' She started to giggle. Baggo wondered what was so funny but he found himself joining in.

'He has a pretty twisted view of life. Apparently, not so long ago he was talking to a tree surgeon and said something like, "You cut trees down to size and I cut people down to size." And he does. So is he a warm suspect, then?' she asked gleefully.

'Not really. We've had some bizarre leads, and we are even investigating am extreme Catholic sect called *Vita Dei* in Glasgow. They're taking a great interest in the assisted suicide case that's on at the moment and it's just possible one of their crazier members killed Knox. He might have mistaken him for the QC defending in the assisted suicide case. So we're still looking in all directions.' Aware that he'd said more than he should have, he added, 'But keep all that to yourself, and if the evidence in the fraud trial gives you any ideas …'

'I know,' she said indignantly. 'I can keep a secret. Now, must dash.' She got up to go. Baggo opened the pub door with a flourish and waved her through ahead of him.

'Nice arse,' a cockney voice said.

15

Kenny Cuthbert was on his feet when di Falco arrived at Glasgow High Court. He was arguing that the right to control the length of one's own life was a basic human right, but was facing hostile comments and questions from the bench. The *Vita Dei* group were where they had been the previous day. Di Falco squeezed onto a bench beside Dolan, who was once more reading his Bible. It was the passage in 1Samuel describing David's victory over Goliath. As the afternoon wore on di Falco noticed that, although his lips moved as he read, he never turned a page.

When the court rose, Father Neil greeted di Falco warmly. 'A good day for us, I think, Billy,' he said outside. 'I believe their lordships may be coming to understand that human duties are at least as important as human rights.'

Di Falco agreed with him then explained how a mix-up of his shifts in the hotel had enabled him to come to the court unexpectedly. He accepted an invitation to join the group for prayers and tea.

Again di Falco had a rickety chair in the same upstairs room in the Gallowgate. This time, Father Neil's short sermon dealt with Christian duty. He argued that duties were imposed by God and so were far more important than rights, which were of man's devising. Di Falco was impressed by the way he picked up on the themes that had dominated the day's proceedings in court and gave them his own, very Catholic treatment.

After the sermon came a prayer, Christian duty the issue that was being addressed. Di Falco's attention wandered as he planned how he would tackle Dolan. Then something Neil said made him think.

'... and we pray for those who confuse duties imposed by human society with those fundamental duties that God has laid upon us. Sometimes man-made duties conflict with God's duties. Sometimes, faithful to man-made duties, a sinner can bear false witness before God and His church. Oh Lord, we have one such person here, in this very room. That person is preparing to persecute Your followers in the name of his man-made duty. Oh Lord, help that sinner confess and repent. Help that sinner to speak out now and renounce the works of the devil. *Vita Dei, Vita Dei, Vita Dei!*'

As he ended, the rest joined in the chant. Di Falco looked up from the floor and saw that everyone was staring at him. He felt very scared.

Slowly, he got up and went to stand beside Neil, the semi-circle of acolytes in front of him, their expressions hostile. 'The Father is right to some extent,' he began. He feared his voice sounded quavery and weak. 'I am a police officer, but I have no intention of persecuting anyone or renouncing the works of the devil because I do not do the devil's work. I am concerned about a number of letters, anonymous letters, that were sent from Glasgow to Mr Cuthbert. Does anyone know anything about them?' He searched the faces in front of him then turned to look directly at Father Neil who stared back, cold-eyed and unforgiving.

'No one here needs to confess to you,' Neil said.

No one moved and no one spoke. The only noise came from rush hour traffic on the Gallowgate. Di Falco tried to out-stare Neil but gave up. Moving slowly, as if from a dangerous animal, he walked to the door and left the room.

Continuing to tread steadily, he went down the stairs, aware of footsteps close behind. He was about to open the front door and reach the sanctuary of the street when someone whispered in his ear. 'Where the fuck do ye think you're going?'

It was Dolan. Di Falco felt something hard and sharp prick his right side and he was pushed into the main hall, which was deserted. Dolan shut the door behind them. He had a six-inch, serrated blade in his right hand.

'You're no' here about these poxy letters, are you?' Dolan hissed.

'Yes, actually, I am.' Di Falco tried to sound brave.

'Don't give me that shite. They wernae even threatening. You're here tae pin that lawyer murder on me as I've got a record.'

'I don't pin crimes on people.'

'Haw, that's whit they all say. You'll no' go after the guy whose wife was a right fucking Jezebel because he's one of yours. Ye see my record and it's easy. Just like the retired polis in the paper said.' Shaking with rage, he pushed the point of the knife under di Falco's chin.

'I promise I'm not here to fit you up,' then, with a silent prayer, he added, 'But I would like to question you.'

'I'll tell you once and that's all: I didnae kill that man. And I'm no' answering yer fucking questions.' He pressed the knife deeper, breaking the skin. 'And if you bear fucking false witness against me, I've got friends who'll make you wish yer mother had remained a fucking virgin. Remember that.' He took a step back, hid the knife under his shirt and went to the door. 'And remember, Father Anthony in St Andrews told Father Neil a lot about you. I know where you live. And where your family live.'

Di Falco lost no time in leaving the building. He forced himself to walk at a normal pace to the station. His chin had stopped bleeding but he was still shaking when he boarded the train to Fife.

* * *

Before seeing Baggo entering The Verdict, Osborne had passed an uneventful day. His hangover was far from the worst he had experienced, but it still made him ponder whether he should give up drink completely. The sight of a bottle of beer in the fridge made up his mind and he succeeded in finding the opener as Bothwell phoned from the lobby. Osborne had forgotten about their ten am meeting. He decided to give his hangover the fry-up treatment, pulled on some clothes and went down full of bravado to cover for his lack of ideas.

In the breakfast area Bothwell sipped a coffee while Osborne, in default mode, told him how he cleaned up the East End, omitting incriminating details.

'These posh hotels don't do a fry-up like a proper greasy spoon caf,' he complained after Bothwell had asked how he'd persuaded a particular villain to confess. A mouthful of black pudding gave him thinking time. 'Guilt's a burden,' he said, not mentioning the accused's broken arm. 'Sometimes it wells up inside the worst villains. They need to confess and they can't hold it in. The jury could see that and he went down.' No thanks to the ivory-tower, do-gooder on the bench, he thought to himself.

'So what do we put in the paper tomorrow?' Bothwell asked.

'Dunno yet, Pizza. Phone me later. I'm going to take a gander at this trial. Sniffing about, listening to your gut. That's what good detective work is all about.'

Soon afterwards, blinking in the sunlight, Osborne crossed the Lawnmarket to the High Court building and found the fraud trial that Knox had been prosecuting when he was killed. A tall, unhappy-looking man, clearly one of the accused, was giving evidence, denying that he had known from the start that the project was one massive scam. He was the sort of white-collar criminal Osborne detested, with his posh voice and fancy suit. He didn't like the prosecuting lawyer either. He was smooth, smug and artificially courteous.

Osborne had never before been in a Scottish court. The lawyers sat round a big table in the well of the court. The judge wore white robes with large red crosses. It reminded Osborne of the Ku Klux Klan costume without the hood. He could tell this judge was the real thing. On the few occasions when he did intervene, he did so intelligently and with quiet authority. At one point he scanned round the public benches, his searching eyes fastening on Osborne, who felt quite uncomfortable as the big man with hooded eyes and tiny glasses stared at him.

An hour of that was quite enough. Osborne crossed the Lawnmarket again, this time to visit the scene of the crime. While the court he had left was modern with artificial lighting and pine panels, Parliament House oozed history. Despite himself, he was impressed by Parliament Hall where the archery had taken place. There was a dark, high, wooden roof, a huge stained glass window and a highly-polished wooden floor on which lawyers in earnest discussion walked up and down. The corridors near the hall were flanked by rows of wooden boxes, each bearing the name of an advocate. Some boxes were overflowing with papers. Others were empty. Directed to Court Three, Osborne entered a strangely intimate courtroom, all old wood and red drapes. Two judges, a diminutive woman and an old man, were hearing criminal appeals against sentence. They were the sort of judges Osborne could respect, showing no compunction about rejecting eloquent pleas for mercy.

He was beginning to enjoy himself when the court

rose for lunch. Not hungry after his breakfast, he strolled down the Royal Mile, mingling with tourists from many nations. Venturing into a tartan shop, he could hardly believe how much money a tall Scandinavian youth was prepared to pay for a kilt, his puny white legs sticking out under folds of garish tartan to the apparent delight of his girlfriend.

For some reason the youth reminded Osborne of Pizza. He had no idea what he should say to him when he phoned. He decided to return to the G and V and read up about the case. The newspaper clippings failed to capture the real flavour and he felt little wiser. Looking out of his window, he saw Baggo entering The Verdict. Osborne decided to follow him and left the papers strewn round the bed. Casually and quietly, he walked into the pub and looked round. Baggo's back was to him. He got a pint of lager and sat in the booth behind him, hoping to overhear what was being said.

By the time Baggo and the girl left, Osborne was smiling. He could see she had a nice arse and said so, quite loudly. Baggo nearly jumped out of his skin.

The horror on Baggo's face turned to fury. He followed the girl out and Osborne could hear his raised voice in the street. The door swung open again and Baggo came back in. He sat opposite Osborne and glared. 'What the hell are you doing?' he asked.

Over the years Osborne had developed a variety of techniques for dealing with angry people, frequently colleagues. 'Why, Baggo, what's wrong? Can I get you a drink?' he asked, beaming serenely.

'Have you been listening to what we were saying?'

'Well I wasn't going to stuff cotton wool in my ears, was I?'

'You mustn't tell that shitty little reporter.'

'Or?' He put an edge into his voice.

'Or you'll make life even more difficult for us than it already is.'

'So you're asking?' Osborne's lips continued to smile but his eyes bored into Baggo's.

'Yes. I'm asking. But if they publish something that hinders our investigation we'll prosecute Bothwell. And we'd prosecute you, too. Do not think that we wouldn't.'

'Bollocks. The crown lawyers would throw it out. At least they always did when I tried that trick.' Baggo's face fell. Osborne could see he had won. 'Pint?'

'IPA.' A whisper.

'Fucking stupid name for beer.' As Osborne waited to gain the surly and slow-moving barman's attention, he remembered how things used to be. When he had run Wimbledon CID, he could tell Baggo to jump and he'd ask how high. Although their circumstances had changed, vestiges of their former relationship remained. At length the beers were poured. Osborne carried them to the table, brown IPA for Baggo, lager for himself. 'Down the hatch,' he said, slurping his drink, then asked, 'How's it going?'

Baggo ignored his pint. 'What that rag has been saying about Inspector Fortune should never have been written. She has been conducting this inquiry as well as possible in difficult circumstances. We are following the evidence and it will eventually lead us to the truth, so please do not make things any more difficult than you have already.' Still not touching his beer, he sat back and scowled across the table.

Osborne shook his head. There was no one nearby but he still spoke quietly. 'Did you learn nothing from me? I had you down as a likely lad. You talk about evidence. What is that? A collection of facts, half-truths and downright, fucking lies that you haven't seen through. Evidence can lead you so badly off course you need to call the fucking mountain rescue boys. What I did, and it fucking well worked, was identify a criminal and then look for the evidence that would persuade a court to find them guilty. I heard you talking about some religious nutter who might have thought Knox was someone else. Does he have a record? Well, does he?'

Baggo searched for the answer in his beer and took a first swallow. 'What if he does?'

'What if he does? It makes it much more fucking likely that he's your man. Your first time is the most difficult, whether we're talking shagging or murder. You should be going after him.'

'We are. Please do not put anything about this in the paper, but we have an officer undercover who has infiltrated the sect. If anything were to appear in the paper it would put him in great danger.'

Osborne silently clapped his hands. 'Right you are, Baggo. I'm glad you told me that. The more you tell me the more careful I'll be when I'm talking to Pizza.'

'Pizza?'

'The reporter. Have you seen the state of his face?'

'Oh, I get it. Acne.' Baggo caught himself smiling and checked himself.

'And this judge who fancies the rich widow. All my days in the Met and I never arrested a judge, worse luck. That would be a trophy for you, Baggo. What are you going to do about him?'

'I don't know, honestly.'

'Hunt him down at home. Take him by surprise. Stay on the offensive.'

'When?'

'Now, of course. He who hesitates is fucking lost.'

'What are you going to say in tomorrow's paper?'

'As you've told me something, I think I'll be nice. And I'll make the point that masterminds ain't wot they used to be. In the East End a mastermind who got caught had no right to call himself a fucking mastermind. Yet here we have your John Burns sitting in jail, ready to go down for how long? Six? Eight? Ten, even? I know the do-gooders on the Parole Board will have him out as soon after half time as they can, but even so it's a stretch. And will that four and a half million really be sitting waiting for him to pick up when he gets out? That makes me think, Baggo, and it should make you think too.'

Baggo said nothing but took another sip of beer.

'Now I'm not going to say anything about this little chat if you don't,' Osborne said. 'But it would be in both our interests to stay in touch. Allow me to put my number into your mobile. Put yours into mine.' He slid his phone across the table. Reluctantly, Baggo did as he was told. Osborne's grin revealed broken and stained teeth. 'And you may call me Noel. Now, must go.' He drained his glass and left the pub.

Angry and confused, Baggo replayed the previous half-hour, asking himself what he should have said and done. His most basic mistake was to be so anxious to impress Melanie that he had allowed his tongue to run away. Depressed, his drink unfinished, he left five minutes after Osborne.

16

After leaving Osborne, Baggo visited a golf driving range beside the Braid Hills and spent three quarters of an hour venting his frustration on a large bucket of balls. By the end his drives were no straighter but he felt better. He realised he was hungry and found a fish and chip shop. With a mouth-watering aroma filling the hired car, he drove to the road up Salisbury Crags where he parked in a lay-by and sat munching his fish supper covered with tangy, brown sauce. In front of him, the blue waters of the Forth stretched across to the purple shadows of Fife. But he was in no mood to admire the view. After the last greasy chip had slipped down his throat, he drove back to India Street and rang Lord Hutton's doorbell.

'Well, what is it?' the judge demanded. He was still wearing his suit trousers. His shirt, its collar removed, was open at the neck and sweat stains darkened the fabric under the arms. Baggo caught a whiff of gin.

'Detective Sergeant Chandavarkar, Lord Hutton.' Sounding as respectful as he could, Baggo produced his warrant. 'I regret having to disturb you at home but I need to ask you a few questions. It won't take long.'

Hutton inspected the warrant. 'The Serious Fraud

Office? You're a long way from home aren't you?'

'I was seconded to help in the fraud case Mr Knox was prosecuting and now I am helping to solve his murder, my lord.'

Hutton looked at him with what seemed lofty contempt. Baggo had already decided this would not be a doorway he would barge into if entry was refused. To his surprise the door opened fully. 'Come in,' Hutton said, turning away.

The smell of gin became stronger as Baggo shut the front door and followed the judge into his lair. They went downstairs into the basement then along a corridor to the back of the house and into the kitchen. It was a large room, facing west, and had French doors leading to a sunken patio from which the last rays of the sun had gone. An Aga took up most of one wall. In the centre of the room a rustic-style table had a single setting. Cardboard files, an open bottle of red wine, a nearly-empty bottle of gin and glasses formed a semi-circular barrier round the judge's place, outside which lay a phone and a laptop.

Hutton picked up a tumbler containing clear liquid and a slice of lemon, and drained it. As he did so the unmistakable ping of a microwave sounded.

'I put this on before you rang,' he said, as using a stained oven glove, he removed a plastic dish, peeled off the cover and heaped the food, which looked and smelled like paella, onto an Old Chelsea plate. 'Take a seat,' he said as he sat down, 'and have some wine. 2007 St Emilion. Drinking nicely now.' He poured generous measures into two wine glasses. 'And don't give me any of that "I'm on duty" crap,' he added sternly.

Baggo hesitated then did as he was told. He would get more out of the judge if he kept him mellow. He sniffed the wine. It had a fine bouquet. Then he took a sip and swirled it round his mouth. 'Lovely,' he said.

'So you have a palate?' Hutton said, the surprise in his voice audible.

'My father appreciated fine wine and taught me a bit.'

'Good, good,' Hutton said through a mouthful of paella. 'I taught myself.' He took another mouthful of wine and refilled his glass. 'My wife is away at the moment. She likes the country at this time of year. So I'm left here with my work and a cellar full of excellent wine. I try to get through both.' He smiled then pointed to the cardboard files. 'Criminal appeals. We sift them to see if any are worth a full hearing in court. Any real chance and we give them a shot, but most of them simply want to get interim liberation so they're out during the nice weather. It's the same at Christmas. That means we have a hell of a lot of reading to do. But why are you here? What do you want to know?'

'We have just learned that you were present at the function on Friday night when Mr Knox was killed, and I wonder if you can help us?'

'If I can I will.'

'Do you remember seeing Mr Knox after dinner?'

'Yes.'

'What was he doing?'

'Talking.'

'With whom?'

'A lady, not his wife. She was most attractive and wore a long black dress.'

'How would you describe the way they were talking?'

'Intimate, confidential.'

'Did you see either of them later?'

Hutton put a forkful of food into his mouth and chewed it carefully. Appearing to make up his mind, he drank some wine and sat back in his chair. 'I was involved in the archery match and went to collect my equipment from the judges' retiring room. On my way back to Parliament Hall, Knox said something to me in passing. He appeared to be a bit drunk and what he said was indistinct but it was a barbed remark about hitting the right target. I thought no more of it at the time.'

'But was that not rather cheeky of him, my lord?'

'Of course it was, but he was no respecter of persons. Neither am I, frankly, and that was the bit about Farquhar that I liked. It was certainly not worth making a fuss about. To do so would have made me appear petty and foolish.'

'What about after the archery?'

Hutton's small mouth twisted into a smile. 'I am of course aware of what is being said about Knox's death. Indeed there can be few who are not. After the archery contest was over I went for a drink and, as I was passing the end of the corridor leading to Court Three and other places, I saw the woman with whom Knox had been speaking after dinner coming towards me from the direction of Court Three. She had an air of excitement about her, that is all I say. She went past me, perhaps to the Ladies. I watched for a very short while, no more than half a minute, to see if anyone should follow her but no one did, and I got my drink. At the time it crossed my mind that illicit sexual activity might have been involved, but I thought little more about it until I heard that Knox had been murdered. By the way, you will probably find my fingerprints are identified among those gathered from Court Three as I sat there last week. Now, I want to know, how is your investigation proceeding?' He poured more wine into his own glass and topped up Baggo's.

Baggo, who had been taking careful notes, would not normally tell a witness how an inquiry was going, but this man was a judge. 'We have a number of leads, my lord, but it has proved difficult to narrow the field. We are following the evidence and expect to make progress.'

'Do you think it was that policeman, the woman's husband?'

'We can't entirely eliminate him, my lord.'

Hutton looked unimpressed. 'In other words, you haven't got a clue yet. But tell me, and forgive me for being personal, are you made to feel an outsider in the police, institutional racism and all that?'

'No, no, not really,' Baggo stuttered.

'So you are, but you have found ways of coping.' It was a statement. 'I hope you don't mind me asking, but I know how you must feel.' He swallowed more wine and emptied the bottle into his glass, filling it to the brim. Baggo knew this was no way to appreciate what was a very fine wine. He anticipated some indiscretion.

'In Glasgow when you're asked what school you went to, they want to know your religion. When they ask you that in Edinburgh, it's your social class they're trying to find out. I say I was educated at Merchiston. I see that means nothing to you, but Merchiston Castle is an expensive boys' school, close to Firhill, which is the comprehensive I actually attended. When I wis a laddie I didnae speak wi' plooms in ma mooth like I dae the noo. I changed it as I would never have progressed in my profession.' His accent switched to broad Scots from anglified and back again. 'I've always been an outsider in the law. Don't play bloody golf, for one thing. Thank goodness for the Judicial Appointments Board or I'd never have made the bench. I know I'm not popular, but frankly I don't give a damn. I do my job and I do it well. I work in a law court not a polite drawing room.'

'You must have made your parents very proud.'

Hutton nearly choked on his wine. 'Proud? My father was ashamed of me, particularly after I changed my accent. I was a traitor to my class, an English stooge. When I was called to the bar he refused to come to the ceremony.'

'He must have been a hard man.'

Hutton stared at Baggo. 'Hard isn't the word for it. He was like granite. When I was thirteen a group of boys from the school chased me. They hated swots and I was one. They caught me in the street in front of my house and began to beat me up. I shouted for my father and he came to the door. The boys stopped hitting me but then he said, "Fight yer ain battles or ye'r nae son o' mine." He went back in and closed the door. They carried on beating me up and left me bleeding in the street.' Trembling at the recollection, Hutton took a deep draught of wine.

'I was lucky. My father always looked out for me,' Baggo said, amazed and somehow privileged to have the judge open up in this way.

'I vowed that if ever I had a child I would do anything to protect them. And I meant it.'

'And do you, have a child, I mean?'

Suddenly abrupt, Hutton said, 'No. My wife and I are childless.'

They sat in silence, Baggo sipping his wine, Hutton swallowing his. Hutton changed the subject. 'Don't you get infuriated by the stupidity that criminals show? Do you ever long for a worthy opponent?'

'I am quite lazy, my lord. The stupider the criminals the better, as far as I am concerned. Of course, before I retire I would like to defeat at least one criminal mastermind so that I can boast to any grandchildren I might have, but the rest of the time I am happy with those who make mistakes.'

Baggo couldn't decide if the judge was playing a clever game, using unusual confidences to deflect him from asking awkward questions, or he was a lonely drunk, pathetically grateful for a stranger's ear, revealing things he would never have told someone he knew better.

'Is there anyone who is likely to remember you when you bought your drink after the archery, my lord?' he asked.

The judge saw that he was being asked for an alibi and

the atmosphere suddenly became frosty. 'No,' he said.

'And can you tell me what you did during the early part of yesterday evening?'

'I can't think why you're asking me that, but I went for a long walk, by myself, up the Pentlands, parking in the Flotterstone car park.'

Baggo sensed that it was time to go. He decided to try a technique that had worked on the television for Colombo. Finishing his wine, he thanked Hutton very much and told him he had to be on his way. He said he would see himself out but Hutton rose from his chair and, staggering slightly, led him upstairs and into the hall.

'One last thing, my lord,' Baggo said at the front door, 'you appear to be very friendly with Mrs Knox. Is there anything we should know about your relationship so that we can handle the matter discreetly?'

Hutton's whole body twitched. His gimlet eyes boring into Baggo's, he spoke slowly and calmly. 'That is a grossly impertinent remark which I am reluctant to dignify with a reply. But I will say one word: no.' He slammed the front door, pushing Baggo out onto the doorstep.

Baggo went to his car which still smelt of fish and chips. As he reversed out of his parking space he saw the judge's white face glowering out of a ground floor window. On his way to his B and B, driving along Mayfield Road, Baggo was stopped by Edinburgh police and breathalysed. He was relieved to pass. The judge cast a long shadow.

17

Refreshed by her best night's sleep for some days, Flick set off for the Thursday morning briefing in Cupar with new confidence. The previous evening, she had discussed developments with Fergus and she had allowed him to talk her into having a glass of wine. He agreed with her that the Traynors' story had the ring of truth. Moreover, the only way Lynda could have known where the bows and arrows were, was if she had emerged into the corridor as they were being stowed. If she was the killer, she must have gone to the judges' retiring room and picked up an arrow before returning to Court Three to stab Knox. If she had done that, someone would have been bound to see her. She had no motive for killing her lover and it seemed safe to eliminate her. The difficulty in taking an arrow from the retiring room unobserved also made the Chief Superintendent an unlikely killer, but he could not be entirely ruled out. He had, after all, lied about his knowledge of his wife's affair with Knox, and Flick was sure he was responsible for the bruise on her face.

Still unsettled by his visit to *Vita Dei*, di Falco had phoned to report Dolan's threats and his knowledge of the contents of the letters to Cuthbert.

Flick had said, 'If he mistook Knox for Cuthbert, without his wig, and saw him going off to have sex with Mrs T, might he have imposed his own punishment? Remember, no one notices waiters, so he might have picked up an arrow, hidden it in his uniform, and gone to Court Three and back without anyone thinking anything of it. And they had white gloves, so no fingerprints.' Fergus had agreed.

Baggo also had phoned to tell her about his meeting with Hutton, but neither Flick nor Fergus could see any motive for a High Court judge to murder a leading QC, even if he was a bit soft on his wife. Whatever she might say, Eloise Knox had a strong financial motive for ending her unhappy marriage through homicide, and she could not prove that she merely drifted about in the fresh air before the dancing began. However, it would have been difficult for her or the judge to pick up an arrow from the retiring room without being seen.

They had gone on to discuss the possible links to the fraud case. Flick said, 'The trial is going smoothly and as it nears its end, two people who have no connection we know of, but who have a link with the case, are brutally murdered. If it's a coincidence, it's a very odd one.'

Fergus said, 'My gut tells me it's too much of a coincidence, but I have no idea how it all ties in. And it's bizarre having two of the accused at the same function as the prosecutor.'

'There would be the same problem for them as the Traynors, picking up the arrow from the retiring room without someone seeing them. I think we need to look at the waiters, especially the pair with records: Dolan, who's violent and fanatical enough to kill both Knox and Walker, and Thomson, who happens to be the son of one of the accused, though they say they don't get on.'

Fergus poured himself more wine. 'That's another coincidence. You're getting there, my love. Slowly but surely.'

'And to hell with Inspector No.'

As she drove past productive fields, rich and yellow with oil seed rape, Flick mulled over what had been said and began to sort out the priorities of the day and the tasks she would allocate.

When she arrived at the office she found an autopsy report and an update from the Glasgow lab. Tam Walker had been struck on the back of the head with the African stone statue and then asphyxiated using a cushion. The pathologist gave the time of death at between six and seven pm on Tuesday evening. Walker had consumed beans on toast and lager about two hours before the fatal attack. His killer had been careful. The forensic scientists had found nothing that would aid the inquiry.

Looking at the whiteboard, Flick was pleased to see more green evidence than red questions. She drew a blank square beside Eloise Knox. If Chief Superintendent Traynor merited whiteboard anonymity, so did Lord Hutton.

The briefing started at nine am, Baggo being the last to arrive after driving from Edinburgh. More in command than she had been the previous day, Flick summarised the situation as she saw it then added, 'If we are looking at a murderer who is connected in some way to the fraud, we may well be looking at someone involved in the scam who has managed to stay under our radar. If so, that person has felt it necessary to kill two people in the last week. We might solve both murders by looking again at the fraud.'

'I agree,' Baggo said. 'The crown junior, Melanie Arbuthnot, told me that at the end of the court day last Friday, Knox said something about having to re-think things. He had been taking Burns through a lot of e-mails that he had sent but pretended not to understand. Maybe he really didn't understand them. It could be that Burns has been set up to be the fall guy. After all, barring a mad jury, he is bound to serve some serious time.'

Flick said, 'Why don't you get a look at these e-mails? Perhaps you'll find something we've missed.'

'I was planning to, Inspector ma'am. I might even find the missing millions, but that may be pie in the sky.'

Wallace held up a copy of that day's *Good News*. 'There are a couple of things of interest here,' he said. 'First, a quote from Osborne: "I am sure Inspector Fortune is handling a most difficult case as well as possible. I trained her well."'

Flick raised an eyebrow. 'He wants something,' she said. 'But he's not getting it. What's the other thing?'

'This is more serious,' Wallace said. 'Pete Bothwell writes: "The *Good News* reward of a massive twenty thousand pounds may be claimed later today. This newspaper has been approached by someone who says they can provide evidence against the savage killer of

Farquhar Knox. Don't fail to read tomorrow's paper to learn more." What should we do, ma'am?'

'I don't plan to read about it in the paper. We must find out who he's meeting and see what they have to say.'

Baggo said, 'The e-mails will still be there tomorrow. The paper is based in Edinburgh. Billy knows Bothwell by sight. I would like a shot at him, ma'am.'

Flick thought for a moment. By rights she had already given Baggo one important task and Wallace was her sergeant, ranking equally with Baggo. She should give Bothwell to him, but dealing with the press often required flexibility and inventiveness.

'Sergeant Chandavarkar and DC di Falco are to find Bothwell and learn all they can. Keep closely in touch with me,' she warned.

'What do you want me to do, ma'am?' Wallace asked. Flick sensed he had taken offence.

'Please take acting DC McKellar and interview or re-interview people who were at the function on Friday, concentrating on whether they saw the Smails, Maltravers, Mrs Knox or Lord Hutton between the end of the archery and the start of the dancing. Did they see any waiter behaving oddly then? Also, did they see Knox talk to anyone, apart from Lynda Traynor, at any time during the evening? We know he said something cheeky to Hutton before the archery. See if anyone remembers that. I shall remain here. DC Gilsland and I will be busy researching a variety of things on the internet.'

'Thanks, Lance,' she said to Wallace as they left the room.

'Ma'am,' he grunted.

Back at her desk she sat thinking how she might have handled it better.

* * *

Good News occupied a large steel and glass cube in the Newcraighall estate on the east of Edinburgh. What the building lacked in imaginative design it made up for with brashness. The paper's name was plastered along the top of each of its four walls. Lit up at night, those letters whose neon still functioned could often be seen from aircraft coming in to land. The letters with non-functioning neon revealed the state of the paper's finances more eloquently than any set of accounts.

It was well after mid-morning when Baggo parked outside the offices. A pretty girl in the shabby reception area greeted them with what seemed like genuine friendliness. Yes, she said, Pete Bothwell was in. Baggo told her that they were there to see him about the Knox case. He gave their names but did not say they were police. She lifted the phone but got no answer. She dialled another number and asked for Pete. Whatever was said made her giggle.

'He's avoiding me again,' she told the officers. 'Don't worry, though. I'll find him. Take a seat over there. There's a coffee machine in the corner.'

The coffee tasted like the residue from a chemical experiment and the magazines were old. More than half an hour passed without any sign of Bothwell. It was time for a different approach. 'We are police officers on a major investigation and we need to see Mr Bothwell now,' Baggo told the girl. 'If you don't find him within ten minutes I shall have to see the editor.'

Her face wrinkled with concern, the girl phoned different numbers, asking for Pete. Baggo stood over her. 'I just can't find him,' she said, anxiety making her voice shrill.

'I trust you are not giving us the run-around,' Baggo said quietly, 'or you could be in serious trouble.'

'No, honestly, no,' she stammered.

'Well I need to see the editor now. I can't afford to waste more time.'

'But Mr Waddell doesn't see people without an appointment.'

'He'd better start or he will be prosecuted for obstructing the police.' Baggo turned to di Falco and told him to stay there and make sure Bothwell didn't slip out of the building. Then he stood over the girl. 'Now,' he said, 'take me.'

Throwing her head back in a huffy gesture, she led him through a door leading to an open-plan office. At the far end was a door with EDITOR written on it. Tentatively the girl knocked on it. She was answered with a bellow of 'Fuck off'. Baggo opened the door and stepped into a cluttered, dusty room. A small, bespectacled man with rabbit's front teeth sat behind a large, pine desk. His pink shirt was crumpled and sweat-stained. A smell like the stench of prisons hit Baggo's nose. The man looked up from the computer in front of him. 'I thought I told you to fuck off,' he said.

'I am a police officer and I need to speak to Pete Bothwell urgently,' Baggo said, producing his warrant.

The girl slipped out, closing the door behind her.

'Why do you need to speak to Pete?' The editor's eyes shifted round the room as his tone became almost casual.

'We have reason to believe that he might be able to lead us to a crucial witness in an on-going murder inquiry. Please help us find him.'

'I don't keep tabs on my journalists.'

'I know you'll be looking to Bothwell for a story to put in tomorrow's paper, and I'm sure you'll be able to find him if you want to. You don't want to be charged with obstructing the police, do you?'

'No. Look, there's no need to take that sort of approach.'

'Well find him. Now.'

All bravado gone, the editor shrugged and lifted his phone. 'Alfie, where's Pete? Yes, now.' He listened, smiled then got up. 'Follow me,' he said.

Baggo followed as the editor went through the open-plan office and into the male toilets. One cubicle was occupied.

'Pete, you daft wanker, come out of there,' the editor shouted.

Slowly the bolt was withdrawn and an apprehensive-looking young man emerged. Baggo saw why Inspector No called him Pizza.

The editor grasped the front of Bothwell's shirt, making up with aggression for his lack of height. 'This is a police officer. We don't fucking mess with them. Right?' He turned and left.

'Right, Mr Bothwell, we need to find somewhere we can have a word in confidence,' Baggo said.

Pausing to pick up di Falco at reception, and to give the girl a stern look, Baggo went with a cowed Bothwell to a disused office. He told him to sit on a chair facing a desk. He and di Falco sat on the edge of the desk. It was designed to be intimidating and, from the expression on Bothwell's face, it was.

Quoting that day's paper on the subject of the reward being claimed, Baggo put his face close to Bothwell's. 'Three questions. Who? Where? When?'

'Journalists don't reveal their sources,' Bothwell's voice caught.

'This isn't a source. It's someone claiming a reward and they'll have to come out in the open.'

'Right now they're just a source.'

'This is a murder investigation. If you obstruct us we will prosecute you.'

'If this works as it should, I'll get my story, my source will come forward and get the reward and you'll have your witness. Without the reward this witness would not have come forward at all. I'm helping you, if only you'd realise it.' As he spoke he gained confidence, lacing the last words with contempt.

'We have to know now …' Baggo was interrupted by his mobile. It was Inspector No. He listened then said, 'Right, we'll be there.' He said to di Falco, 'Don't let him move.' Then he went out to the car to phone Flick without being overheard.

18

That day Osborne had wakened early, sunlight streaming through half-pulled curtains. His encounter with Baggo had stimulated him, got the juices flowing. He wanted to solve Knox's murder from the sidelines, show the politically correct bureaucrats infesting the top ranks of today's police force that old-fashioned methods really were the best. And more of this consultancy work would spin out his pension wonderfully.

To keep Baggo on side he had told Pizza, through gritted teeth, that Fortune was doing a difficult job very well. He needed to know what was really happening in the investigation in order to keep *Good News* at least apparently ahead of the game. The previous evening, Pizza had sounded strange on the phone and had then admitted he had been contacted by someone who wanted to claim the reward. The mystery caller had insisted that neither Osborne nor the police should be involved, and Pizza could not be persuaded to ignore that condition. It had been very frustrating.

As he devoured another fry-up he wondered how he should pass the day. Listening to lawyers in the fraud trial would drive him to drink, but there was not much else he could do. Unless …

After a couple of hours Googling the Catholic Church he changed into a purple shirt and dark jacket and trousers and took a train to Glasgow. It was not a long walk from the station to the High Court and cheery Glaswegians were happy to direct him. By mid-morning he found himself at the back of the public benches, watching the legal debate in the assisted suicide trial.

It was easy to spot *Vita Dei*. Dark-clothed, with tense body language, some paid close attention to the case while others bent their heads in prayer. Osborne looked carefully at them. There was a young man with sharp features whose lips moved as he read the book on his knee, presumably The Bible. His swollen, red knuckles showed Osborne he was a fighter. This would be the suspect. As he watched he was aware of another man turning to look at him. This man wore a dog collar and had an inquiring expression. Osborne smiled at him then pretended to listen to the lawyer's argument.

When the court rose for lunch, Osborne waited behind with *Vita Dei*. After the other spectators had filed out, the police waved the priest and his flock to follow. Osborne went with them. Out in the street he approached the priest, who appeared to be the leader.

'Are you *Vita Dei*?' he asked.

'Why yes,' the priest replied pleasantly. 'How do you know about us?'

'Good news spreads as well as bad news,' Osborne replied.

The priest looked him up and down. There was

intelligence and scepticism in his eyes. He was not someone to underestimate.

'And we are good news, I hope?'

'Oh yes. We must take a stand against suicide.'

'Which we do. Will you join us for lunch, my friend? Nothing too fancy, but in the church hall the blessed Marjorie will have soup and sandwiches and perhaps even a chocolate cake. I'm Father Neil.' The Irish brogue came across clearly.

'Er, thank you, Father. That would be wonderful.' Osborne shook his hand warmly, wishing only that there might be something alcoholic. He felt the need for Dutch courage. 'I'm Noel,' he added.

The priest's smile revealed shining teeth. 'So you share your birthday? What a blessing!'

'Share my … oh yes, of course. Jesus.' He felt he had recovered in the nick of time. As a child, a Christmas Day birthday had meant fewer presents. Definitely not a blessing.

On the way to the church hall Osborne told Father Neil that he was a retired publican from the East End, currently visiting Scotland on holiday. Remembering the Catholic view of divorce, he said his wife was dead, silently wishing he could have persuaded her to commit suicide. He said he had seen newspaper reports of the assisted suicide case and felt so strongly that, when a priest in Edinburgh's St Mary's Cathedral told him about *Vita Dei,* he wanted to come through to back them up. He hinted that he might be able to give some money.

By the time they reached the upstairs room in the hall,

Neil was friendly and relaxed. 'Would you like to become one of us?' he whispered.

'Very much,' Osborne replied. He looked at the others, trying to identify the undercover police officer, but no one stood out. Whoever it was, they knew what they were doing. He couldn't see the suspect, the young man with the fighter's knuckles. He guessed he was helping in the kitchen.

Two young men carried in a big pot of soup and set it down on a trestle table beside a dozen or so mugs which a woman proceeded to fill. She had curly red hair and had she made more of an effort Osborne might have fancied her. Mentally undressing her, she was not unlike Maria, but she had a pure, bovine, trusting expression that did nothing for him. The soup was good, though, full of vegetables and barley.

If he kept eating he didn't have to talk, so he helped himself to several egg sandwiches. He thought he was doing well, considering that until his Googling that morning he had known very little about the Catholic Church.

He was still eating when Father Neil stood facing the group and clapped his hands together for attention.

'We have been joined today by Noel,' he began. 'As well as sharing our Saviour's birthday, he wishes to share His suffering. He wishes to become one of our number. Do we welcome him in the time-honoured way?'

Osborne swallowed the last of his sandwich and saw that everyone was smiling and chanting, 'Yes, yes. *Vita Dei. Vita Dei.*'

'Thank you,' he said. 'I'm honoured.'

Neil approached Osborne and took his hands. 'Come before our congregation and kneel, facing me.'

They were an odd bunch, so this sort of nonsense was predictable. Osborne complied.

'Now take off your jacket and shirt.'

This was more bizarre than he had expected, but he was too far committed to back out. Slowly, he removed his jacket and shirt, placing them carefully on the floor beside him. Feeling foolish now, he knelt before Neil, his back to the rest, naked from the waist up, wondering what on earth might happen next.

'Let us pray,' Neil said. 'Almighty God, our Father and Redeemer, forgive our sins and may we humbly do thy will on earth as it pleases you. Our lives have been given to us by you, not to be shortened to avoid suffering. Lord, we remember the suffering of Our Lord Jesus on the cross. We remember these words of Padre Pio: "Anyone who wants to be a true Christian must mortify his flesh for no other reason than devotion to Jesus, who, for love of us, mortified His entire body on the cross." Lord, thy servant, Noel, wishes to share the suffering of the saints in the presence of this, Your congregation. Grant him his wish, we pray, and give him thy peace.'

As the others chanted *Vita Dei* again, Neil took from one of the group a cat-o'-nine-tails and handed it to Osborne, who stared at it, horrified. Made of leather, its thongs were knotted at the ends. Osborne wanted nothing to do with it.

'What, how …?'

Swiftly, Neil took it and, with a practised move, flicked it over one shoulder then the other so the thongs struck his own shoulder blades. Then he handed it back to Osborne. 'Or do you want one of us to do it for you?' he asked.

'No,' Osborne said, unable to keep the panic out of his voice.

Part of him wanted to pick up his clothes and flee, but he did not know if he would be stopped. Another part of him thought that, once initiated, he would be well placed to observe this bunch of maniacs at close quarters. Perhaps the youth with the knuckles really had been ordered to kill the defence lawyer in the suicide case and had murdered the wrong man. He decided to go through with the self-flagellation.

The first flick, over his left shoulder, felt like being stung simultaneously by a small swarm of bees. The second, to the right, was not so sore. He gritted his teeth and after about ten on each side, applied as gently as he thought he could get away with, he stopped. By now the repeated blows had made his back very sore.

'Ah, Noel, you are entitled to suffer more than that. Do you want one of us to take over?' Neil's voice was as smooth as honey.

'No,' Osborne said, his voice catching. He closed his eyes and kept going, trying to think of anything except the agony stretching across his back from armpit to armpit. His knees also ached. After a time he could take no more, whatever the consequences. He collapsed on the floor in front of him, the cat underneath him.

Neil began another prayer. 'Oh Lord, forgive thy servant Noel his sins. May he cease to tread the paths of duplicity and subterfuge and may he come to realise the error of his ways.'

Osborne turned and stood up. The members of the group were laughing at him.

Neil said, 'I don't know what paper you're from, but you're obviously a journalist and I doubt if you've ever sat through a mass in your life. I look forward to reading your report on today's activities. Just remember, none of us has laid a finger on you. There is no law which says that very religious people are not allowed to have a sense of humour.'

With difficulty Osborne stopped himself from punching that mocking, shiny face. Tears of rage, pain and embarrassment stinging his eyes, he picked up his shirt and jacket and left the room. He turned and snarled, 'You'll regret this,' then slammed the door. On the landing, he reached behind to feel the hot, painful weals then gingerly pulled on his shirt and jacket and made his way downstairs, already asking himself how he might get his revenge. Before going out on the street, he paused to wipe his face and collect himself. To his left was an open door. Inside the door was a pair of shoes, the toes pointing up. The wearer was the youth with the fighter's knuckles. He lay on his back, the brown handle of a knife sticking out of his front. It had been inserted beneath his ribcage, pointing up and to his left so it found his heart. Wet blood stained his white shirt with rivulets running down both sides. Osborne did not need a doctor to tell him that the youth was dead.

Now terrified, he rushed out into the Gallowgate breathing deeply and closed the door of the centre behind him. He told himself to think rationally. The local police would have to be involved, but it was Baggo that Osborne phoned on his mobile.

* * *

Baggo returned to the room where di Falco and Bothwell were waiting, puzzled expressions on their faces. Standing over Bothwell, his voice shaking, he said, 'This is now very serious. People are being killed. You must answer my questions or I will arrest you.'

Bothwell said nothing but his eyes were wide with fright.

Baggo said, 'Is your reward-seeker male with a Glasgow accent?'

Bothwell nodded.

'Do you know his name?'

He shook his head.

'Do you know if he is connected to a religious sect?'

Bothwell started as if given an electric shock. 'Well, on the phone he said something about the forces of Satan bearing false witness against him.'

Baggo and di Falco exchanged glances then nodded. Baggo said, 'Well you can stop protecting your source as your friend Mr Osborne has just found him dead. I need you to tell me everything you know. Now.'

Shaking, Bothwell remained silent as he tried to cope with a situation that was as far from his comfort zone as he could imagine. 'I got a call yesterday evening,' he said quietly. 'It was a mobile number which I can give you. The caller was a male, probably young, with a very strong Glasgow accent. He asked me lots of questions about the reward then said he wanted to speak to me face to face. I agreed to meet him and he said he'd be on Glasgow Green near the People's Palace at five-thirty today. I had to be alone and if the police or Osborne were there it would be all off. It was then that he talked about the forces of Satan bearing false witness. That's it, honestly.'

'And he gave no name?'

'No.'

'Why did you put that bit in today's paper? Didn't you realise it could put whoever it was in danger?'

'The boss insisted.' He nodded towards the door. 'Since we've been featuring the Knox murder our circulation has gone up dramatically. We had to keep the pot boiling, he said.'

Baggo nodded grimly. He had been surprised how aware everyone was of what *Good News* had to say about the investigation. 'You may have kept the pot boiling, but you signed one man's death warrant. You will hear more from us. Charges will be brought. And if anyone else tries to claim the reward, you must tell us immediately, and I mean immediately. Most importantly, you must print nothing more about this inquiry without police permission. Oh, and just make sure you remain available,' he commanded. Turning to di Falco, he said, 'We have to go to Glasgow.'

* * *

A small crowd had gathered round the entrance to the church hall in the Gallowgate. Baggo and Di Falco ducked under the blue and white crime scene tape and looked for the senior officer. A young female officer in uniform pointed them towards a big man in plain clothes standing in bright sunlight beside the outer door. He was running a hand through his hair in an harassed manner.

'Are you forensics or photographers?' the man barked at them, screwing up his eyes.

'We are police officers like yourself,' Baggo said, smiling broadly and producing his warrant. 'Detective Sergeant Chandavarkar and Detective Constable di Falco. We are investigating two murders which may be connected to this one. And you are?'

'How did you hear about this?' he demanded, ignoring the question.

'The fellow who found the body phoned me.'

'Why the fuck did he phone you?' There was sweat running down the man's highly-coloured face. He did not look like someone who enjoyed hot weather.

'It's a long story, which I can tell you. But we would like to see the body.'

The man's eyebrows shot up and he gasped. Then his eyes narrowed and he put his face up to Baggo's. His breath reeked of bad teeth. 'I don't know if you are taking the fucking piss but you'd better stop now. This is a Glasgow crime scene and I'm not going to let people I don't know trample all over it just because they've had a phone call. If we let anyone who'd had a fucking phone call turn up and look at crime scenes we'd be in the

National Trust for Scotland, and we don't do fucking cream teas either. So go away.'

'We could probably help you, but have it your own way. For the record, you are?'

The big man glared at him. 'Detective Sergeant Kelly. Now fuck off.'

'The inspector will be here in half an hour,' Baggo said to di Falco as they returned to the car which fortunately was in a shady spot. 'We might as well wait for her.'

* * *

Her Sat-Nav working well, Flick arrived at the Gallowgate, her pregnancy sapping her energy in the heat but her mind buzzing with questions. She was greeted by Baggo and di Falco and thought she detected an unusual sheepishness about Baggo. Having been told of Kelly's attitude, she marched up to him. Harassed and over-heated, he was barely courteous even after realising she out-ranked him. It was only after calling the DCC on her mobile and handing the phone to him that he became chastened and she got the cooperation she wanted.

Inside the church hall, SOCOs and a photographer were busy. A pathologist had come and gone, provisionally confirming the knife wound as the cause of death and the time at about one pm. The dead man had been Johnny Dolan and none of the Glasgow officers would be mourning his passing. The *Vita Dei* group had told the police that Dolan had been with them when they came together to the hall at one, but no one could actually remember him upstairs. One young man thought he heard a voice calling 'Johnny' as they came in off the street, but he could not remember if it was male or female and had thought nothing of it. Neither of the youths who carried the soup pot upstairs nor the red-haired woman had noticed the open door where the body lay. Their route from the kitchen to the stairs did not take them past it. The body had been discovered by an English tourist who was now in custody.

'In custody?' Flick and Baggo asked in unison.

'A constable was trying to get him to stay with the people who'd been upstairs,' Kelly explained. 'He wouldn't go where he was told and when the constable put a hand on his shoulder he lashed out. So he was arrested.'

'Where is he?' Flick asked, trying not to smile.

'What is it to you?' Kelly asked sharply and immediately regretted it as Flick's face clouded. 'I mean, he's at our London Road office, ma'am. I think there may be mental health issues. He swears he's a retired cop who cleaned up the East End of London.'

Flick turned away to conceal her amusement. Inspector No could stew in his own juice as far as she was concerned. While di Falco looked gleeful, Baggo stroked his chin thoughtfully.

'Exactly how might this murder tie in with your investigation, ma'am?' Kelly asked.

Flick told him about the fraud trial, Knox's murder and Tam Walker's murder. Dolan had been working as a waiter when Knox died and had been a member of a group that had sent unpleasant letters to a QC who could have been mistaken for Knox.

'And that newspaper …' di Falco began.

'Hasn't made our lives any easier,' Baggo interrupted, shooting him a warning glance.

'What newspaper?' Kelly snapped.

'*Good News*,' Flick said. 'They were offering a reward for information on the Knox murder. It may have been Dolan who was about to claim it.'

'It almost certainly was,' Baggo said, seeing no point in keeping anything back. 'We squeezed that out of Bothwell before we came here.'

'But how did the killer know that?' Kelly asked.

'Because the stupid newspaper editor insisted on alerting their readers in advance,' Baggo said. 'Now we'll never know what Dolan would have said.'

In the cool atmosphere of the church hall, Kelly was becoming less hostile by the minute. 'So how can we best cooperate, ma'am? I don't think we should concentrate only on your angle. There are a hell of a lot of people in Glasgow who would have stuck a knife in Johnny Dolan. I can reel off half a dozen names right now.'

Flick smiled. 'Perhaps you might follow your lines and we follow ours, sharing information as we go? I'd like copies of the pathology and lab reports and if there are any fingerprints you can't trace, maybe we can.'

'Certainly, ma'am. We're not short of cases here, you know. And I'm sorry about being awkward earlier.' A few words with the DCC and getting out of the sun's warmth had brought about a personality change in Kelly.

Flick and Baggo made their way towards their cars, di Falco following soon afterwards. Flick took Baggo's arm.

'My car. Now,' she said. He threw his keys to di Falco and, full of foreboding, sat in her passenger seat.

'It was you, wasn't it?' she said, her voice shaking with fury.

'It was me?' he said plaintively.

'You know damn fine,' she shouted. A well-upholstered Glasgow woman, laden with plastic shopping bags on both sides, turned to stare. 'Bloody No. How did he come to be here? How did he know your mobile number? How much have you told him?'

'Flick, listen …'

'Don't Flick me.'

'All right, ma'am. I made a mistake. I was in a pub talking to the crown junior in the fraud trial. She has been most helpful to us and will continue to be. I told her about *Vita Dei* but I didn't realise that bloody No had sneaked into the pub and was sitting behind me listening in. When I saw him I told him what he had said about you was a disgrace and that's why he was nice about you in today's paper. I also said we had an officer undercover in *Vita Dei* and I did not want his cover blown. I had not heard that Billy was no longer under cover. No has obviously decided to have a go at *Vita Dei* himself and it has all gone pear-shaped for him. As usual.'

Flick sat in the driver's seat, her hands rubbing the sides of her belly in circular movements. It felt as if the baby was learning the Highland Fling. 'Is that all he overheard?' she asked.

He was tempted to say yes, but honesty was the best policy with Flick. 'I did say a little about Lord Hutton.'

She buried her head in her hands. 'No!' she shouted.

'It was his idea that I should visit him last night,' he went on, 'and I think I learned something.'

Her eyes filled with tears of rage. 'How could you? I don't believe it.'

'How can I make it better?'

'You can't. I feel betrayed, I really do. Tell di Falco to get into my car and you can, you can … fuck off wherever you want to go but don't get in the way of my inquiry.'

He got out. 'Sorry,' he said but she stared straight ahead.

'Watch your step today,' Baggo said to di Falco as he told him to join Flick. 'And it's not all down to hormones,' he added ruefully.

* * *

The temptation to leave No in custody was strong but Baggo recognised that he might yet prove useful. And to make him useful, first he would have to be made grateful. That was not proving easy.

If the cells area of London Road Police Office had air conditioning it was not obvious. The smell of sweaty, stressed male bodies made the air heavy. Baggo remembered hot, sticky air from Mumbai, but it had not been as rancid as the stuff now invading his lungs. The sweaty, stressed male to whom he was speaking was suffering more than most as he had to work. Sergeant Smith, the custody sergeant was reluctant to let Baggo see Osborne. As far as he was concerned, the prisoner was going nowhere.

Both his voice and his colour rose as he spoke. 'Carstairs is where we keep the criminally insane in Scotland, and I'd say he was a candidate. He's been raving about conspiracies against him involving the Catholic Church and Wimbledon, all thought up by someone he calls "fucking Fortune". And he clocked one of our boys too.'

'I know it all sounds odd, but I've told you about him and about how he could help us if you release him. If you let me speak to him I'll find out more and I'll tell you. And I'll make sure he gets his newspaper to be nice to the Glasgow police.'

Either Baggo's persistence or the implied threat of bad publicity made Smith relent, and he led him down the cells corridor. From a cell at the far end emanated a barrage of foul abuse in a cockney accent. The parentage and sexual habits of Glaswegians were being slandered. From the other cells Baggo could hear low, dangerous rumbles. He thought that if he failed to get No out that afternoon the ex-inspector would be lucky to escape from the city alive.

No did not appreciate the precariousness of his situation. 'You took your bloody time. These clowns don't know their arses from their elbows. They've treated me like a fucking criminal. I'll have their guts for garters, just see if I don't.'

'Noel, listen …'

'I've only been in this blasted city for a few hours before I find a body. I tell them and they lock me up. I'm not staying here another minute, Baggo. They can find their own fucking bodies from now on.'

'And the first one will be yours unless you shut up. Now. Or I walk out and leave you here.'

The two men tried to out-stare each other. This time Baggo won. Speaking quietly as if to an over-excited child he said, 'Wimbledon CID is in the past. Now I am in charge and you must do as I say. You are in a very deep hole yet you continue to dig. If you are to get out of here you will have to apologise to a lot of people, including Sergeant Smith, the custody sergeant, who wishes to keep you here. Now what on earth happened? What made you lash out?' As he finished he could barely believe he had spoken to Inspector No in that way. A couple of years earlier he had been terrified of him.

The mirror image of that thought process went through Osborne's mind. He knew he had to do as Baggo said or his future would be bleak. He slumped onto the hard surface, equally uncomfortable for sitting or lying, his head in his hands.

'You must never tell anyone,' he said. 'I wanted to solve your case. I tried to join these Catholic maniacs and they put me through what they said was their initiation routine, but they were just taking the piss. I was in too far to back out so I whipped myself like they told me to. Yes, with a fucking cat-o'-nine-tails.'

Baggo tried to turn his spontaneous laugh into a cough.

'They're all fucking sado-masochists, Baggo. But they're not honest perverts like Miss Whiplash clients. They dress it up as fucking religion. After they'd had their fun at my expense I left. On my way out I found the body and phoned you. Then I dialled 999. These Glasgow goons wanted me to wait with the sado-masochists and one touched my sore back so I lashed out. Next thing I knew I was on the ground in cuffs, into the meat wagon and here I am in fucking Guantanamo Glasgow.'

Baggo turned away, his shoulders shaking. 'You are going to have to apologise if you are to get out,' he said after a pause.

'Apologise? For what?'

'For hitting an officer who was doing his duty, for repeated abusive rudeness to the Glasgow police, actually all of Glasgow if it comes to that. Think, Noel, just think of the alternative. Sergeant Smith would pack you off to the place they keep the criminally insane, you know. You have to start acting like a retired Detective Inspector. Now I'm going to call Smith and I'm going to talk to him. When we come back you are going to be as nice as ninepence. Very apologetic. Itching to give quotes praising the Glasgow police to *Good News*. Okay?'

'Okay.'

Baggo looked down on his old boss. Wet with sweat and dishevelled. Utterly despondent. He felt a little sorry for him, an emotion he'd thought he would never experience. 'Don't expect miracles,' he said.

* * *

He owes me big-time, Baggo thought as he steered his way through busy traffic to the M8. He had told Smith that Osborne had been in so many tight spots as he cleaned up the East End that finding the body had sparked off an episode of traumatic stress disorder. He had hit out not realising it was a policeman who had put his hand on his shoulder. It stemmed from an incident when "Coffin" Bob Trotter had caught up with him in a dark alley off Mile End Road. Baggo pleaded with the sergeant to be allowed to take the fine old crusader for justice away, so he could be properly looked after.

In the passenger seat beside him, No sat hunched and sulky. With Baggo glaring at him and the sergeant looking sceptical, he had grovelled as he'd never done before. He had guaranteed brilliant quotes in the paper. And yet it had been a close-run thing. He had even been made to sign a disclaimer agreeing that he had suffered no ill-treatment at the hands of the police and that he had refused medical attention.

Neither man wanted to be the first to speak. At Harthill Services Baggo stopped and got out of the car to phone Melanie. The court day was over and she sounded pleased to hear from him. She readily agreed to take home the file of e-mails that Knox had concentrated on the afternoon before he was killed, and to Baggo's delight, invited him to come to her flat at seven for dinner.

Osborne's resolve broke as they passed Livingston and Edinburgh spread out before them. 'What can I say?' he whispered.

'"Thank you" would be a good start.'

'Thank you, Baggo. I always knew you'd come through as a good 'un.'

A bit later Osborne showed what was really troubling

him. 'You won't tell anyone, will you? About the whipping?'

'Depends.'

'For God's sake, man. I couldn't hold my head up. Please. Remember all I taught you back in our Wimbledon days?'

'Still depends.'

'What do I have to do?'

'One, you come good on your promises to Sergeant Smith. We need to keep the Glasgow people sweet. Two, you praise Inspector Fortune to the skies. Three, you put what I tell you into *Good News.*'

'Of course, of course, no problem.'

Baggo glanced at him. 'Four.' He paused.

'Four?' The dismay was audible.

'Four, you do as I tell you, whatever that may be.'

'Come on, Baggo …'

'Or else …'

'Bastard.'

They drove in silence to the G and V. Osborne attracted some unfriendly stares from the receptionists as he made for the lift. They were not used to the Glasgow police checking up on their guests and they didn't like it one little bit. They particularly disliked their guests being called 'inmates'.

* * *

Flick watched Baggo walk to his car and speak with di Falco. She could see he had been upset by what she had said. That made her feel marginally better but anger still burned inside her. She was not yet ready to listen to the small voice at the back of her head that told her she was over-reacting. Di Falco approached, opened the passenger door and got in. Whatever Baggo had said made him tentative and he sat quietly while Flick marshalled her thoughts, a notebook and pen in her hand.

'Do you have the number of the person who called the paper yesterday?' she asked.

He sat up brightly. 'Yes, ma'am, and it was Dolan's. Before I left the scene I rang it and I could hear a phone in Dolan's back pocket. They hadn't moved him and it gave the SOCOs a fright.'

'Hm.' She rang Wallace who, with McKellar, was in Edinburgh talking to witnesses. He told her that the fraud trial had been going on all day with the usual break for lunch. No one involved in it could have stabbed Dolan in Glasgow at about one pm. She told him to check Lord Hutton's activities then to visit Eloise Knox and find out if she had an alibi, not only for that lunch time but also for Tuesday evening when Walker was killed. Lastly, he should do the same check on both Traynor and his wife.

'You drive,' she said to di Falco. 'I have more phone calls to make. And we're going to Dunfermline.'

As di Falco negotiated the mid-afternoon traffic out of Glasgow, Flick spoke to Spider Gilsland on her phone. Left behind in Cupar, he was collating new information from all sources as well as pursuing his own inquiries on his computer. First of all, McKellar had reported, the Dean's husband, who knew Lord Hutton slightly, remembered him queuing at the bar after the archery and before the dancing. They had not spoken but Hutton had appeared distracted and had failed to catch the barman's eye a couple of times. Bar service had been slow the Dean's husband had told McKellar.

Spider had done more research into the people working at the function, particularly the waiters. He had spoken on the phone to those who had recruited and organised the staff, pressing them as best he could. Then he had cast his net wider.

When he began to describe what he had found out about Gary Thomson, Flick could hear the excitement in his voice. 'I thought I'd start with his death by dangerous driving case, and it's quite a story. It all came out in the plea in mitigation. He had been adopted by the Thomsons and when Mrs Thomson's father died he drove up north to Inverness for the funeral like the rest of the family. It was before his finals and he drove from Dundee. The funeral went as well as could be expected but at the wake the lawyer told the relatives what the will said. It seems the old man was quite rich. Basically, the bulk of the estate was to be divided among the grandchildren, of whom there were five, including Gary. But the old man had been very specific: only blood relations were to benefit from his estate. Gary was to get nothing.

'Understandably, he was very upset. But stupidly he sank a dram, made a bit of a scene and left. He tried to drive down to Dundee but mistakenly thought a bit of the A9 was dual carriageway when it wasn't and he overtook a van on a bend. There was a Fiat coming in the opposite direction.

'It was a head-on crash. His injuries were minor but a young husband and wife who had been in the Fiat were killed. Their baby daughter survived but is now disabled. From what I could gather from the reports it could be lasting brain damage.

'Gary narrowly passed the breath test and went to trial claiming that his driving had been merely careless and not dangerous. Apparently quite a few have made the same mistake on that stretch of road. But the jury would have none of it and he finished up serving six years. He got parole after three and he's been out for eighteen months now. But wait for it, ma'am, the trial judge was Lord Hutton.'

'Him again,' Flick gasped. 'Did Knox have anything to do with the trial?'

'No, ma'am. But there's more. After the trial Hutton sentenced him to one year. He said the case was at the lower end of the spectrum of dangerous driving, and there was nothing wicked about what he did, so a long sentence was inappropriate. There was an almighty stushie – a fuss you'd say, ma'am. All the road safety people and the families of the dead couple were furious, the crown appealed and it was the Appeal Court that upped it to six years because of the particularly tragic consequences.

'After the accident Gary Thomson went to pieces. He dropped out of uni, where he was a bit of an IT wizard, and refused to have anything to do with his adoptive family. At the time of sentence he had traced his birth mother and his counsel said that gave him some security. But it's a sad story, ma'am.'

'Very. You've been busy, Spider. Well done. Can you find out more about his birth parents?'

'Not so far, ma'am. These things are very confidential. After an adoption order is made the process is sealed and kept in the sheriff court where it was made. His order was made twenty-six years ago in Dunfermline, but that is all I have been able to discover.'

'Well done anyway,' Flick said, anxious not to be seen as being grumpy after falling out with Baggo.

'Thank you, ma'am. And please tell Billy I've learned more at my computer screen than he has charging round the country.'

'Tell him yourself over a pint or two – after we've cracked this case. Keep going, Spider we're not there yet.'

'Hang on, ma'am, I have more. John Burns has a mother who is old and in a home, The Beeches, in Crieff. The fees are paid every month from a bank account in the Caymans. I am trying to get beyond their wall of secrecy but am not optimistic. I thought you might be interested, ma'am.'

'I certainly am. I might even buy you a pint myself. You're lagging behind Spider,' she said to di Falco so they both could hear.

As di Falco drove quickly and well to Dunfermline and found a parking space near Gary Thomson's flat, Flick's mind turned over the baffling quantity of data now available. She looked forward to kicking it about with Fergus that evening, but she knew he would tell her to mend her fences with Baggo sooner rather than later.

Out of breath after trailing up the two floors to

Thomson's flat, Flick was mildly surprised by the alacrity with which he answered his door, having been told on his intercom they were the police.

'Yes?' he said, barely opening the door.

'Detective Inspector Fortune and Detective Constable di Falco. May we come in?' Flick said as evenly as she could, scrabbling for her warrant.

'Suppose.' Ignoring the warrant, he shrugged and headed for his sitting room, letting the door swing behind him. Flick tried not to show any reaction to the messy squalor in which he lived. She thought he looked curious, as if his whole body had been put in a roller and elongated. The stained tee shirt and frayed jeans did not improve his appearance. All three remained standing, Flick not wanting to sit on anything in this flat.

'Can you tell us what you were doing at lunch time today?' she asked.

He showed no reaction. 'Why should I?'

'So we can eliminate you from an inquiry.'

'Or stick me in it.'

'Well, can you?'

'Yes. I was in bed. I did an early shift at Tesco then had a sleep. I'm only just up.' He pointed to his bare feet. 'I'll show you my bed if you like. It's probably still warm.'

'Is there anyone who can back you up?'

'Tesco will corroborate my shift, but I was the only person in my bed. Worse luck.'

His accent was broad, his delivery laconic. Knowing his story, Flick recognised someone embittered by life. Hope, ambition and happiness were for other people, not him. He had wiped out two innocent people and crippled a child in an accident. Could he have intentionally killed two or three more? Flick told di Falco to check his bedroom. Thomson went with him, leaving her in the sitting room. She looked at what was on the coffee table. Apart from food containers and IT magazines there was nothing of note.

Di Falco and Thomson returned. 'His bed was warm, ma'am,' di Falco said.

'What about Tuesday between five and eight in the evening? What were you doing then?' Flick asked.

'Tuesday? Let's think. One day blends into another for me. Yes, I remember, late shift at Tesco.'

'Thank you. We will check up, you know.'

'Oh, I know.'

Softening her tone and hoping to reassure the young man, Flick said, 'Mr Thomson, we're aware you were adopted. I wonder if you'd be prepared to tell us the identities of your birth parents? It would assist our inquiry and we won't tell anyone who doesn't need to know.'

At first he looked astonished then he pursed his lips in anger. 'None of your fucking business,' he said deliberately. 'Now if that is all, I'd like to go for a walk in the sunshine.'

Flick knew it would be counter-productive to push further. She thanked him and they left.

As di Falco drove back to Cupar she checked her phone and found a text from Wallace: 'Hutton in Appeal Court all day today.'

'Alibis are emerging like bulbs in springtime,' she muttered. 'Let's visit Tesco.'

The Dunfermline Tesco was not far out of their way as they drove to Cupar. While di Falco interviewed the store manager, Flick picked up a hand basket, intending to buy a few groceries.

Half an hour later she hefted a full trolley-load into the boot. When she climbed into the passenger seat, di Falco told her that Thomson's shifts had been as he said and that the manager regarded him as a good, reliable employee, too bright to stack shelves indefinitely.

As they approached Cupar, Flick's phone rang. It was Wallace. Eloise Knox had not been in when he and McKellar had first called about four pm. 'Her son,' Wallace spat out the words, 'said he was unaware of his mother's whereabouts and if we really had to trouble her we should return later. We went to the Traynors' house and saw both the Chief Superintendent and Mrs Traynor. Their son was at home too. It seems they've gone to ground. They alibi each other for Tuesday evening and today lunch time but no one can support them, except that they were in to receive a call from Glenalmond about eight pm on Tuesday. They said they've been staying at home, keeping their heads down.'

When the officers returned to India Street, Mrs Knox was back and told them she had been out to dinner with her solicitor on Tuesday. Their table at the Restaurant Martin Wishart had been booked for seven-thirty. McKellar had subsequently confirmed this with both the solicitor and the restaurant. But, she had told the officers, no one could vouch for her whereabouts at lunch time. She said she had driven to a long-time favourite spot in the Campsie Hills, just north of Glasgow, and gone for a long walk. 'So if she was spotted on the M8 today, she had an explanation, and we didn't say why we were asking,' Wallace added.

It sounded a bit suspicious to Flick. She congratulated Wallace and McKellar on good work. Before she rang off, a thought occurred to her. 'One thing, was Nicola Smail away from the fraud trial for longer than usual at lunch time?'

There was a silence at the other end of the line. 'Yes, she was away for a bit. Sorry, ma'am. We didn't think to mention that.'

'Well check it tomorrow,' she snapped, and immediately regretted her irascibility.

Back in the Incident Room, she brought her spreadsheet up to date. Surveying the new data, she told the baby, who was kicking wildly, 'Stay still, will you? Mummy needs to think.'

19

A hot shower to flush the stench of the cells from his pores and more after-shave than usual made Baggo feel good as he put on clean clothes for his date. A date it was, as he had in mind more than an evening looking at e-mails. Pausing to buy a bottle of vintage Bordeaux, as advocates seemed to like claret, he enjoyed a leisurely walk through streets cooling with an evening breeze and reached Melanie's door at five to seven.

It took time for her to buzz open the outer door and she came to the door of her flat with wet hair, wearing a man's silk dressing gown. More flustered than he had seen her, she grabbed his bottle and pushed him into the sitting room with instructions to pour himself a drink, all the time gabbling apologies and saying something about the bloody telephone.

It was a fine, big room with a high ceiling, more comfortable than stylish. The walls were adorned with an eclectic collection of paintings. Melanie appeared to like vivid colours and busy street scenes. To Baggo's eye most looked rather good. Beside the substantial wooden fireplace hung a painting of a woman's head with a fish lying across her crown. Baggo checked the signature and it was a Bellany. He hoped it was not one of Tam Walker's efforts. A tray of glasses and bottles sat on a table by the bay window. He mixed himself a generous gin and tonic and took a seat. He could hear the whir of a hair-dryer and wondered how long this lady would make him wait.

Just over five minutes later Melanie reappeared, her hair artfully loose, her make-up subtle. She wore a brightly-coloured, loose cotton dress that might have come from India. She poured herself a gin and tonic at least as strong as his, and without asking, took his glass and topped it up with more gin than tonic. 'Don't worry,' she said, 'I have the e-mails but let's enjoy dinner first. Any interesting developments?'

He told her about Dolan but restrained himself from describing No's humiliation. He did not mention his spat with Flick. Subconsciously influenced by the painting beside the fireplace, he told her about Tam Walker.

'Don't worry about that one,' she interjected, nodding towards it. 'It has excellent provenance.'

When he finished she screwed up her face. 'Do you really think that these murders in the West and Knox's killing are linked to the fraud? The connections are so tenuous.'

'But they're there, and that's why we need to look for something we've missed so far. But what about your day?'

'I've been listening to speeches. Yawn, yawn. I quite envied Smail's wife. She's sat through the whole thing but once Mark finished dealing with the case against her husband she upped and offed and didn't come back till nearly three when it was time for Smail's counsel to address the jury.'

'Really? When did she go?'

'I don't know. Some time before twelve. Why?'

'It would have been possible for her to have killed that guy in Glasgow.'

'Oh, yes. Hmm.' She drank her gin. 'I hope you won't need me as a witness. I think I'd be hopeless, too ready to admit I might be mistaken.' She took another sip. 'Today went well, you know. Mark was brilliant this morning, totally brilliant. He made it so simple. We had three defence speeches this afternoon, bricks without straw, I should say, but you never know with a jury. The trial should finish on Monday.'

'Gracious.' If he was going to make anything of their relationship he would have to move quickly.

Melanie moved the conversation to her holiday plans (Machu Pichu with an old friend from school) and then it was time to eat.

A low sun dazzled him as he entered the west-facing kitchen. She pulled down the blind and lit two candles. A CD of *Turandot* playing in the background, they sat opposite each other at a sturdy wooden table, eating a casserole of chicken thighs flavoured with apricots, turmeric and other spices she refused to divulge, served with quinoa. She had opened the wine to let it breathe and he could see that she loved and understood food. As he ate he was aware of her glancing at him, anxious that he should enjoy her dish. His grunts of appreciation and readiness for a second helping told her all she needed to know. When they were finished she produced a platter of exotic cheeses.

They talked easily about holidays, travel, childhood. He loved her infectious giggle, indeed everything about her. As she fiddled with the controls to repeat *Nessun Dorma*, he poured the last of the wine, wondering what to do next, tempted to forget about the e-mails.

'Now, coffee and work,' she said with a sigh. 'At the bar you get used to having nice evenings spoiled.'

Side by side on the sofa, they sipped dark, strong coffee and went through the ring binder containing copies of the e-mails with which Knox had tormented Burns during his last afternoon in court.

The e-mails had been sent during the early stages of the scam and at face value they showed Burns to be the driving force. Those from him displayed a detailed grasp of what was involved. In evidence he claimed that he had copied and pasted from other sources, including e-mails from his co-accused. He had been no more than a collator for them. None of the accused had done themselves any good by blaming the others, in Melanie's opinion. She thought they would all go down, with the possible exception of Maltravers, the planner, 'even if he is a sleazeball,' she added.

Aware of their thighs touching, Baggo was having difficulty concentrating and turned another page when he exclaimed, 'That's it!' He went back to the previous e-mail, which had been sent by Burns to Maltravers and read aloud from it: '"The soil type is Regosols, which you will know is well-drained and weakly developed. It is loose and very coarse and many golf courses on the East of Scotland are built on it, including Culrathie near

Montrose. Fescue grass would be ideal for us as it has been at Culrathie. The environmental lobby are notoriously difficult to predict, but they are likely to focus on the harmful effects of the necessary fertilisation on wild life. It may be that we might have to pay more in order to obtain eco-friendly fertiliser. I suggest that we retain meadow grass as our rough so we do not alter the natural environment too much. An undertaking to introduce Marran grass near the water might be environmentally popular. It is vital that our fairways should be of the highest standard and we should insist on Fescue for them.'"

'Fescue sounds like a Shakespearean character.' She stuck her hand out in a dramatic gesture. '"Forsooth, Master Fescue, art thou a fool?" "Nay my lord. I am a seed. Sow me well and I shall make the finest fairways in all Christendom."' She turned to him, grinning. 'Not bard but not bad?'

For the first time he appreciated how irritating Flick must find him. He knew he had hit on something important and was impatient to talk it through with her. 'On Friday, Knox said something to Rab Bertram, his ex-pupil,'

'Devil,' she interrupted.

'About revisiting the Culrathie inquiry when there had been all sorts of issues about soil and grass types and wildlife. They had to learn all about them.'

'So?'

'One, that evening it was still in the forefront of Knox's mind. And two, in that inquiry he was junior counsel and Hutton was his senior.'

She sat back, coming to grips with the implications. 'So Knox decimated Burns, who knew far less about soil and grasses than he did. Then it dawned on him that if Burns couldn't have written that e-mail, Hutton was one of those who could. The penny dropped for Knox on Friday afternoon?'

'Exactly. And Knox said something to Hutton after dinner but before the archery. Hutton said it was a cheeky remark about the archery, but maybe Knox told Hutton he'd rumbled him. Suddenly we have a High Court judge as a suspect.'

'And Hutton killed Knox before he could tell anyone? But why should Hutton write the e-mail?'

'Search me. Perhaps his was the brain behind the fraud.'

'That's ridiculous, isn't it? He's a High Court judge who reputedly made a fortune at the bar, enjoys a good salary and has a cracking pension to look forward to.'

'He's not happy. He's strived in his profession to reach the summit but now that he's there he hates the view. When I talked with him last night he seemed almost bored with the job.'

'But not bored enough to take up serious crime, surely? It's a nice thought, though, 'Orrible 'Utton banged up beside the poor buggers he's sent down.' Thoughtfully, she twisted a lock of hair round a finger then said, 'Of course it might be the other side of that coin. Perhaps, unknown to Burns, Knox was the hidden brains behind the fraud. He made sure he prosecuted it to control what came out, but on Friday he showed too much knowledge in cross-examining Burns. And it was for Burns that the penny dropped. He realised that the guy prosecuting him had actually set up the whole thing. Presumably because Knox had double-crossed him, Burns decided to have Knox killed. And he had the contacts to do it.'

'I hadn't thought of that,' Baggo admitted, 'but it is not very likely. One thing is for sure, you twist things beautifully. And you will do very well at the bar.'

She beamed. 'That's two things, but I'm not sure I like being called a twister.'

'It is a sincere compliment, believe me.' He took her hand and kissed it in a courtly manner.

'Then you are forgiven. Personally I think the two theories are equally unlikely. Come on, I fancy a drink. Do you? I have a nice Glenmorangie.'

'Why not? I'll quickly skim the rest of these e-mails, but I'm sure we've hit gold.'

He finished reading as she returned with the drams. He extracted the important e-mail from the binder and folded it carefully before putting it in his pocket. She fed the *Turandot* CD into the player in the sitting room and pressed some buttons. Then she sat down beside him on the sofa and put a hand on his knee.

'*Nessun Dorma* again?' he asked, his hopes of a sleepless night rising.

He did not return to his B and B until breakfast time.

* * *

The door leading to the kitchen closed as Baggo crept into

his B and B and upstairs to his room. He quickly showered and changed, and went down for breakfast as if it were an ordinary morning. But it was not. The last eight hours would be etched on his memory for life. Melanie the advocate had raised the bar for sexual ecstasy and as he dressed he giggled happily and shamelessly at the dreadful pun. During the walk back he had received a text from Flick: 'Hope you can make briefing @ 9. Many developments. F.' It seemed she was on her way to forgiving him and he wanted to reciprocate. He would need to hurry.

'Good morning, Detective Sergeant,' the landlord had a sarcastic note in his voice as he placed a plate of bacon and egg in front of him.

'Good morning. It is another lovely day, I see.'

'And this is a splendid time for a walk, before it gets hot.'

Baggo ignored this, bolted his breakfast and set off for Cupar.

Thanks to some fast driving on the M90, he was on time for the briefing. Flick nodded at him in a way that was neither friendly nor unfriendly and began to go through the information that had come to hand during the last twenty-four hours. Smiling at Baggo, Wallace pointed out that if Osborne had not been there to find Dolan's body, everyone might have assumed that it was just another Glasgow low-life meeting a violent end. Baggo then talked about the Burns/Maltravers e-mail.

When he finished, Wallace said, 'But you can't get away from the fact that the Dean's husband gives Hutton a virtual alibi for Knox's murder and he has an unshakable one for Dolan's as he couldn't have been sitting in the Appeal Court in Edinburgh and stabbing Dolan in Glasgow at the same time. He could have killed Walker, of course, but a judge doing that? Surely not.'

Flick said, 'It could have been a joint venture, Hutton with Eloise Knox. She has no alibi for her husband's death, or for Dolan's, and it could have been a woman's voice that called to Dolan.'

Baggo said, 'At least with a Hutton/Eloise conspiracy we have motives – her unhappy marriage and the insurance money. None of our other suspects has a decent motive that I can see.'

'Let's assume Dolan was killed because he had seen or heard something important regarding Knox's death,' Flick said. 'The killer must have read the paper and immediately identified Dolan as the informant. Gary Thomson is the only person connected with this business who knew Dolan. And don't forget that Hutton tried to give him that lenient sentence.'

Baggo said, 'Might Dolan have tried previously to blackmail the killer, whoever that was? Perhaps they met and couldn't agree or something went wrong, and so he decided to settle for the easier twenty thousand from the paper.'

'Our problem is we've theories galore but precious little evidence,' Flick sighed.

The phone rang and Wallace answered. 'It's for you,' he mouthed at Baggo.

It was Pete Bothwell. Sounding sheepish, he said that

Mona McBride had phoned him ten minutes earlier, looking for the reward. She said she had a painting in her flat that Tam had given her, telling her that if anything happened to him, she should show it to the police. 'Maybe you'll give me an exclusive on this,' he added hopefully.

'Maybe,' Baggo said. 'But don't dare put anything in the paper without my say-so. Thank you anyway,' he added, fancying that Flick had seemed impressed by his assertiveness.

When he told the rest what had been said, Flick announced that she would go through to Coatbridge immediately. 'We don't want anything to happen to this bit of evidence,' she said.

Baggo detected the hand of her husband, Fergus, in Flick's change of attitude towards him, but he wanted things to be right between them and he followed her into her office after the briefing.

'Again, I'm sorry about Osborne,' he said.

She sat in her chair, rubbing both sides of her stomach as she had the previous day. 'It was very careless, but I'm sorry I went off the deep end.'

'You did, but it is okay,' then he added, 'Flick.'

'I want you on the team and working,' she said, and added, 'I'd like you to come through to Coatbridge with me.'

'Delighted. But I have things to do in Edinburgh so we should take separate cars.'

'Right. It seems you may have *Good News* trained at last. They were very polite about me this morning.'

'I tried to turn the situation to my advantage,' he said with a grin.

'I won't ask how, but thanks. It hasn't been an easy time for us.' She patted her stomach and Baggo could swear he saw movement under her clothing.

* * *

Baggo and Flick drove separately then liaised at the McDonald's car park in Airdrie before going together in his hired car to see Mona. They did not have the local police with them and it would be unfortunate if two cars were to be vandalised outside the Whifflet flats while they were there.

There was, if anything, more glass littering the car park than there had been two days earlier. The stench of the lift that served as a urinal in their nostrils, they welcomed the overpowering musky scent with which Mona had liberally sprayed herself prior to their arrival.

This time she had squeezed herself into a black cocktail dress with dark tights and she tottered about in shiny black shoes with absurdly high heels. As far as Baggo was concerned, the effect was the opposite of what she intended as she reminded him of a human black pudding. Yet for all the caked make-up, theatrical dabbing of eyes and gushing grief, she seemed to have a warmth and generosity of spirit lacking in most of those who mocked her.

'I'd expected Mr Bothwell,' she said, after a lengthy speech about how wonderful Tam had been. 'I'll still get the reward, won't I?' She looked beseechingly from Flick to Baggo.

'That's up to the paper,' Flick said, 'but if it helps to identify the killer we'll back you up.'

'He painted it around Christmas,' Mona said, 'but it was just the day before he died that he told me to show it to you if anything happened to him.'

'Which one is it?' Flick asked, looking round the Picassos and Van Goghs vying for space on her living room walls with a huge flat-screen TV.

'Come with me,' she said, leading the way into her bedroom. Stretching the fabric of her dress to near bursting point, she reached under the bed and pulled out a TK Maxx polythene bag. Inside was a Bellany, perhaps half a metre by a third of a metre. Done in watercolour, it depicted a head with something across the crown. The head might have been male or female, age indeterminate, with a long, thin face, and a lower jaw so short that the chin began just under the bottom lip. The hair was dark brown with streaks of silver running through it. A misshapen, grey object with curls that looked like eyes, hanging down both sides, lay across the scalp. The eyes were looking out to sea and on the horizon was an island. There was a chest, out of proportion in terms of size, sitting on the island.

Flick and Baggo exchanged looks. 'We'd better take this,' she said.

Before leaving, they questioned Mona to see if she could help with any more information, but she could not. Thanking her and promising to help her claim her reward if the painting proved helpful, they left.

In the car, mercifully undamaged, as Flick checked her phone, Baggo took the painting out of the bag.

Flick exclaimed, 'Here we go again. Spider's been researching Tam Walker's trial, and guess who defence counsel was? Henry Hutton QC.'

'Surprise, surprise,' Baggo said. 'Now let us have a close look at this painting.' They both peered at it, searching for some hidden message.

'I think it just shows Lord Hutton and a treasure island,' she said. 'And that could be merely a cynic's view of defence counsel and the legal aid fund.'

'I agree it is a representation of Hutton. Whatever message it sends is there to be seen, but I do not think we are seeing all of it,' he said as she re-wrapped it.

As Baggo drove to McDonald's to pick up Flick's car, she frowned. 'So this could be evidence pointing to Hutton being involved in the fraud and probably the murders, but it will never stand up in court. We don't have anything against him except a whole lot of coincidences. And don't forget, he has alibis for two of the murders.'

'True,' he said, 'we are going to have to flush him out, but first we must understand the full message in the painting. Do you mind if I take it? There is someone I know who might help us and I will need to get back to Edinburgh. Oh, and I shall try to see Nicola Smail about her alibi for yesterday lunch time.'

Flick wished he would reveal more of his thoughts but she said, 'All right. Make sure and keep me informed.' Hoping she would not regret it, she placed the painting in the passenger footwell.

Aware of her hesitation, Baggo said, 'I will do the right thing by you, never fear.'

She said, 'I think we should probably pay an official visit to the judge tomorrow morning. I'd like you to come along.'

'Let us see what tomorrow brings,' he replied.

His Delphic remarks worried Flick. There were times she thought he had been too ready to take a leaf out of No's book.

For the rest of the day she fretted over the lack of a case to put before a jury, hoping against hope that one of her team would uncover a smoking gun. That evening she shared her frustration with her husband.

'It's the price of total integrity,' Fergus told her. 'If you can't find adequate evidence and won't make stuff up, from time to time criminals will go free.'

'What would Inspector No do in this situation?' she asked. 'Not that I am thinking of …'

'I didn't imagine otherwise,' he said, smiling. 'But even No would struggle to frame a High Court judge. With career criminals it was different. He'd look round for an unsolved crime and frame them for that.'

'In fairness to No, I never saw him invent a case against a completely innocent person. They'd always have done something, even if it wasn't what they went down for.'

'It's hard to think of a crime he could realistically pin on Hutton.'

'Baggo seemed to have an idea, but he wasn't keen to share it with me. He just said something about doing the right thing by me.'

'Well I don't think you've anything to worry about,' he

said. He put his hand on her stomach. 'It feels as if you have a loose maul developing in there,' he added proudly. 'Has it dropped a little?' he asked.

'A bit,' she admitted. She had felt some twinges that afternoon and was beginning to be concerned that the child might be early.

20

When Baggo arrived at the fraud trial, Lord Tulloch was charging the jury. As one pm approached, he told them that he would continue for about half an hour in the afternoon, then adjourn until Monday morning, when he would give them some brief final directions before asking them to consider their verdicts. It was essential that they should be in no hurry when they deliberated, so he was not going to put them out on a Friday afternoon.

When the court rose for lunch, Baggo sought out Melanie. She greeted him with a warm smile and squeezed his arm.

'Things are hotting up,' he whispered to her. 'I have to speak briefly with Mrs Smail, over there, then I need to pick your brains. I'll explain.'

Ignoring her puzzled exclamation, he went to where Nicola Smail stood in the foyer, waiting for her husband to finish talking to his counsel.

She looked at him coldly.

'May I ask what you did yesterday at lunch time?' he asked.

'Why?'

'A man was killed then and I believe you were away

from here for three hours or so.' As he spoke he searched for a reaction but saw none.

'Shopping. I went shopping.'

'Can you show me a till receipt that would show when and where you bought something?'

'I bought nothing except a sandwich and some juice to have in Princes Street Gardens and paid cash.'

'Did you know Johnny Dolan?'

'I don't think so. Who is he?'

Baggo was not going to play along. He wanted to surprise her, throw her off her stride. 'When did you last see your son, Mrs Smail?'

An expression of pure hatred on her face, she looked as if she might slap him. 'How dare you?' she said through gritted teeth.

'Well? You do have a son, do you not? He's about twenty-six and was adopted.'

The colour drained from her face and she glanced to where her husband was still talking to his counsel. 'Not so loud, please. He doesn't know we're in touch. And you're right. I did meet him yesterday at lunch time. He was up here on business. He's an accountant in London, but you obviously know that. And it has nothing to do with you.'

This time it was Baggo's turn to be surprised. He stuttered his thanks and went over to where Melanie stood waiting for him.

'Problem?' she asked.

'I tried to put a bit of the jig-saw in the wrong place. Now let's go and get something to eat.'

They found a place where they could get sandwiches and coffee. As they ate, Baggo described his morning. 'That painting contains a message and I am sure we have only understood part of it,' he said.

'What do you want me to do?' she asked.

'You have a lot of paintings. Do you know an artist who might be prepared to have a look at it and give us some ideas?'

She screwed up her face. 'Let's see. Yes, I'm sure Brenda would help if she's around.'

'Brenda?'

'Yes, Brenda Lenaghan. She's a successful professional artist and lives down the coast. She's a friend of the family, actually.'

'Would she see us this afternoon?'

'I'd have to phone first and I don't have her number to hand. Look, I'm going to have to get back to court. Why don't you wait till Tulloch adjourns for the weekend and give me a lift to my place? I'll ring her from there, and if she says yes we'll set off straight away.'

Baggo took her hand and kissed it. 'You are a star,' he told her.

* * *

'Ooh, how exciting!' Brenda Lenaghan trilled as Baggo sat on the edge of her sofa and explained his problem. 'I love mysteries. What a wonderful start to the weekend.'

Baggo had immediately taken to the artist, who welcomed them with tea and scones and whose neat, stylish appearance was not what he had expected. As she looked from him to Melanie, a twinkle in her eye, he could tell she had already worked out the nature of their relationship.

'How naughty!' she exclaimed when Baggo produced the painting. 'He was a jolly good craftsman, with an excellent technique,' she said after examining it closely. 'John Bellany would have known he hadn't painted it, but few others could say this was a fake.'

'What do you think he is trying to say?' Baggo asked.

'Well, it looks like a treasure island out to sea, but I'm sure you spotted that. The face is strange though, as if he is painting two people.'

'Two people?'

'Yes. It's the same face basically, long and quite thin, with that curiously short lower jaw, but the painting sends out conflicting signals about age.'

'Or gender?'

'I think age. Look at the silvery streaks in the hair and the knowing eyes. That points to old. But the skin is fresh and unlined, young looking. It's a male head judging from the Adam's apple. I think he's painting a father and son, and they're both interested in the treasure island. Might one of them be a lawyer? That thing on the crown might represent a legal wig.'

'We think so.' Baggo agreed then covered the object on the head with one hand and put his thumb and forefinger in the shape of a V where a beard would go. 'Gary Thomson,' he said under his breath. The two women looked mystified. 'If he is his son ...' he added, working out the implications.

'Have I been helpful?' Brenda asked.

'More than that, I think you may have cracked the case,' Baggo told her. 'Now I am afraid we must go. Please do not spill any beans about our visit.'

As she waved goodbye, Brenda wished them good luck. 'You make a lovely couple,' she added with a mischievous grin.

* * *

Melanie was gobsmacked when on the way back to Edinburgh, Baggo told her about Hutton's role at Thomson's trial. She could scarcely believe an intelligent judge like Hutton would expose himself to the trouble that would come his way, should it became known that Gary Thomson was his son. If he was, and if Knox had found out, it would have been a motive for murder.

'I should really tell Flick,' Baggo was saying, 'the trouble is, she will probably want to interview Hutton and Gary Thomson under caution tomorrow morning. And they will both shut their mouths like clams. We will be left with a lot of circumstantial evidence but not nearly enough to convince a jury. Tell me, if we could nail down only one of them, which one should it be?'

'Hutton, obviously. He must have been the main mover and we can't have a criminal sitting as a High Court judge.'

'Right. I agree. But how do we expose him?'

Squinting into the late afternoon sun, she gazed over fertile fields towards the distant Pentland Hills. 'Everyone has a weakness, an Achilles heel. I can hardly believe he tried to give his son a lenient sentence. If that got out it would be a resignation matter. He shouldn't have gone within a mile of the case.'

'But how do we use it, preferably netting Gary Thomson as well? We'd need DNA evidence to prove the relationship.'

She put her hand on his knee. 'Remember what they say about politics being the art of the possible? Well, so is law and maybe policing is as well. Use one to catch the other.'

He put his hand on hers and squeezed. 'Thanks for that,' he said, and spent the remainder of the journey driving on automatic pilot, deep in thought. She chatted about the traffic, East Lothian villages and the countryside. He appeared not to hear so she too fell silent.

As he patiently negotiated the traffic on the city by-pass, his mouth started to twitch. Still in a cocoon of concentration, he slowly nodded his head. By the time they returned to her flat he was in a state of high excitement. 'I have had a brainwave,' he said, pulling her back as she made to get out of the car. 'Listen and tell me if you see a flaw in my plan which I must execute instantly. There is no time to lose.'

Twenty minutes later she climbed out, frowning. 'Good luck,' she said huffily and went to her front door without a backward glance.

She had listened carefully and approved his plan, adding some refinements. When he phoned Flick she had enabled him to allay the inspector's fears that entrapment was involved: 'We are not getting him to commit a crime – if he does, it will be totally his choice,' she had scribbled on a note as Baggo initially struggled to respond. Flick's ultimate agreement to the proposal was to a large extent due to her. When Baggo phoned the man he called Inspector No, she got out of the car to insist to a hovering traffic warden that they were engaged on urgent police business. Yet he refused point blank to let her come with him. Deflated and offended, wishing him luck was all she could bring herself to do.

* * *

It was five past seven that evening when Osborne stood on the doorstep of Lord Hutton's house in India Street. He was very nervous. Judges were a species he loathed. The crap they spouted from the tops of their ivory towers made him want to vomit. They were also scary. He had not spoken to one outside a court, but he could not forget the day at the Bailey when he had been caught out in a porky pie and the judge had looked over his half-moon glasses. Speaking quietly he had said, 'I hope you realise, Detective Inspector, that perjury is a very serious crime, and anyone, even a police officer committing perjury, is likely to spend several years in prison. Do you understand that?' Then the old bastard had smiled. 'Yes,' he had replied, his mouth dry. 'I shall take a careful note of the rest of your evidence,' the judge had said, raising his eyebrows at the jury. His mind frozen, terrified to commit himself to anything, defence counsel had him on the ropes. He was stammering, avoiding the questions and all the time visualising the gates of Wormwood Scrubs, when the crown barrister threw in the towel and another villain had gone free. That had been nearly twenty years ago but the details were still horribly vivid in his mind.

This judge he was about to doorstep was supposedly a hard man. Osborne tried to tell himself he'd be powerless off the bench, but he didn't believe it.

He turned to check that Pizza, whose real name he had forgotten, and the photographer were standing behind him. They were, but did not give him any confidence. Pizza looked terrified, and spottier than ever. The photographer, called Bill, was overweight and in the warm weather had BO that a skunk would be proud of.

'Ready?' he asked.

The other two nodded so he rang the bell.

After a nerve-jangling wait the judge answered the door. Tall, severe, frightening. 'Yes?' he said abruptly.

As the camera flashed Osborne spoke. 'Lord Hutton, we're from *Good News* and we …'

Hutton's face withdrew and the door swung. After many years of making unwelcome calls, Osborne instinctively jammed his left foot in the gap. The last time he had done that he had worn heavy shoes but the flimsy slip-ons he had bought in Spain were less robust. 'Ouch,' he exclaimed as the judge slammed the stout wooden door against him.

Remembering his script, Osborne spoke loudly. 'Is Gary Thomson your son, Lord Hutton? Is that why you gave him only one year for killing two people? Were you and Gary Thomson involved in the Nicklaus golf course fraud? Did Farquhar Knox find out? Did you or Gary Thomson kill Knox to keep him quiet? Did you or he kill Tam Walker?'

'We have information and the public has a right to know,' Pizza squeaked behind him.

'Give us your side of it,' Osborne urged. 'Come clean to us and we'll be fair to you.'

They could hear scrabbling behind the door. Then Osborne felt an intense pain in the toes of his left foot as, using all his strength, Hutton brought a metal-tipped walking stick down on it. The intruding foot was pulled back immediately and the door was firmly closed. Job done, Osborne limped away with his companions.

* * *

Observing from his car, parked further up India Street, Baggo phoned Osborne to check that the message had been delivered and to repeat that nothing was to appear in the paper without police permission. Then he rang Flick to report. She had been held up by road works near the bridge but reckoned she would be with him in about twenty minutes. A quarter of an hour later she phoned back, excitement in her voice. Gary Thomson was working a shift at Tesco and had received a call. Looking worried and thoughtful, according to McKellar who was watching him, he had continued to work normally but with his shift finishing at eight he would soon be off. Baggo reported no sign of movement from the judge.

Soon after, Flick and di Falco joined him in his car to wait. It was nearly nine o' clock when Wallace phoned Flick. He and McKellar had followed Gary Thomson to his flat, where he had picked up some things and headed for the bus station. The officers had detained him in respect of Knox's murder and were taking him to Cupar for interview. The bag he was carrying had contained some clothes, his passport and five thousand pounds in cash.

'Right,' said Flick. 'Are we ready?'

'Showtime!' Baggo said, wishing he was as confident as he sounded.

Baggo and di Falco behind her, Flick rang the judge's doorbell. He took time to answer, and when he did the door opened a crack, allowing no room for a foot. 'What is it?' he barked.

'Lord Hutton, it's Detective Inspector Fortune with two colleagues. I'm sorry to trouble you at this time but there are some questions we must ask you.'

There was no response and the door did not move. Di Falco got ready to put his shoulder to it and the officers exchanged glances.

Before any action was taken, Hutton held the door open. 'You'd better come in,' he said grudgingly. As they passed him they could smell alcohol. The judge led the way to the kitchen and sat at the large, wooden table. At one end were dirty plates, the remains of a Chinese carry-out and an open laptop. Nearer the judge's seat were a phone, legal papers, a red-backed notebook and loose sheets of scrawled notes. Conveniently near his right hand sat a dictating machine and a wine bottle Baggo recognised from his previous visit. Hutton poured more wine into his own glass and looked at the officers who stood irresolutely at the opposite end of the table. He did not offer them any.

'You have interrupted my train of thought. I must finish this judgment then you can ask your questions,' he said. With them standing watching, he picked up the dictaphone and for nearly ten minutes spoke into it, pausing from time to time to consult the material in front of him. The officers could not help being impressed by the flow of logical, grammatical, erudite language in which Hutton explained his decision, apparently unaffected by the drink he had consumed. The theory on which they were working seemed increasingly unlikely as the judgment rolled off his tongue.

At length the machine clicked and he put it down. He took a large mouthful of wine. 'Well?'

Flick took a deep breath. 'Does the name Gary Thomson mean anything to you, Lord Hutton?'

A flicker of his eyes said it did. He screwed up his face, apparently in thought. 'I don't think so.'

'You tried him and gave him one year for causing the deaths of two people by dangerous driving. The Appeal Court increased it to six years.'

'Oh yes.' He nodded as if it had just come back to him.

'Is he your son?'

Hutton looked genuinely taken aback. 'How is that any business of yours, Inspector?'

'I am investigating two murders and a fraud, and my

suspicions are beginning to crystallise. I should tell you that Gary Thomson has been detained. He was found with his passport and a large sum of money, doubtless trying to leave the country. He has questions to answer about the murder of Mr Knox and the fraud.'

A muscle under Hutton's left eye twitched. 'Why on earth should he kill Knox?'

Flick leaned forward and put her hands on the table. 'Did Mr Knox have something on you?'

'Such as?'

'Such as Gary's parentage, which puts a totally different slant on the lenient sentence.'

Baggo intervened. 'Or that you and your son, assuming he is, were the controlling forces in the Nicklaus golf course fraud?'

Hutton looked at Flick coldly. 'Do you have a scrap of evidence to support these ludicrous suggestions, Inspector?'

Before Flick could reply Baggo cut in. 'We have evidence that clearly links you to the fraud and two murders, Farquhar Knox and Tam Walker, an old client of yours, I believe. It also links Gary Thomson with Knox's murder and the fraud. There is evidence that you are Gary's father and that can be tested using DNA. I can see both of you going down for life.'

Hutton sat back and curled his lip contemptuously. 'If I am a suspect you should have cautioned me.' There was no fear in his expression or voice.

Baggo said, 'You haven't told us anything yet.'

Simultaneously Flick delivered a full caution which

had the effect of intensifying the contempt on the judge's face.

Baggo sat on one of the wooden kitchen chairs and, now on the same level, fixed his eyes on Hutton. He said, 'Unless Gary thinks up a better story, people will believe he got that five thousand in cash from you. They may well believe that he was blackmailing you and that he killed Knox. Tam Walker was probably killed to protect both of you. It would be a short step from there to convict Gary of fraud. We know he's clever and good with IT.'

The officers watched in silence as the judge poured more wine and drank it. 'So the purpose of your visit …?'

Flick spoke solemnly. 'Lord Hutton, I am detaining you under the Criminal Justice Act …'

'I know, I know. But excuse me as I need a pee. One of the problems of getting old.' He sounded almost apologetic as he slowly walked out of the room. Flick told di Falco to follow him, 'tactfully,' she whispered, as she sat down.

'He knows he'll have to confess his own guilt if he's to help his son,' Baggo said quietly.

'You laid it on a bit thick,' Flick said.

'We can tone it down when the tape's running,' he replied. She raised her eyes heavenwards and they waited in silence.

'He's taking his time,' she remarked.

Baggo shrugged, not showing his growing concern.

They heard a rattle then di Falco asking Hutton if he was alright. They dashed out of the kitchen and found di Falco putting his shoulder to a door leading from the hallway. It was locked and required prolonged kicking before the wood splintered. A chair had been jammed against the door from the inside but it was not that which grabbed their attention. The judge was hanging by a leather belt from a water pipe leading to the cistern, his feet on either side of the toilet bowl. His head lolled to his right, eyes staring. They knew before they touched him that he was dead.

'Cut him down!' Flick yelled, and running into the kitchen, she seized a stout knife from a block. While Baggo and di Falco squeezed through the remains of the door and cut Hutton down, Flick phoned for paramedics, SOCOs and a photographer.

The room was small, containing only a toilet and basin, and there was barely enough space to lay the dead man on the floor. 'He must have dropped this,' di Falco said, pointing to a small cassette tape in front of the toilet.

'By accident or design?' Baggo said, picking it up. 'I think we should see if there is anything interesting on it.' He clambered back into the hallway and went to the judge's place at in the kitchen table.

'What are you doing?' Flick asked as he ejected the tape from the dictaphone and inserted the one from the bathroom floor. 'We should touch as little as possible till the photographer and SOCOs are finished.'

'We know what happened here,' Baggo said. 'I think he meant us to find this. Here goes.' He found the tape had been rewound to the start so pressed the play switch.

The recording was not of high quality but the dead man's voice came over strongly.

'I have just now been asked a number of questions by representatives of the press. It appears that certain facts which I would have preferred to remain hidden are likely to be made public. Further, I have committed some criminal acts and anticipate police attention in the near future. I have no intention of allowing myself to be pilloried, giving satisfaction to those who have been my enemies, and despatched in disgrace to one of these appalling institutions to which I have sent so many of my fellow citizens.

'Gary Thomson is my son. When I was a poor legal apprentice I had a brief affair with a typist. She became pregnant and I offered to marry her. The engagement didn't work out and we separated. By then an abortion was out of the question. I was never told anything about the baby nor was I ever asked for money. In those days the natural unmarried father had no rights when it came to adoption and I knew nothing about what happened to my child. My child ...' Emotion clouded his voice before he continued strongly once more. 'The upshot was that my son was adopted by the Thomsons. It was not a happy arrangement and Gary's relationship with his adoptive father was similar to the frankly abusive one I had endured with my father. I knew nothing of this. I had been shut out of my unborn child's life and did not even know its gender or whether it was alive or dead. I now wish I had made inquiries, but I didn't. I was busy making my way at the bar, but that is only an excuse.

'I first set eyes on him when he stood in the dock in front of me and it never occurred to me that we might be related until the sentencing diet. This was a particularly harrowing case. On the one hand you had a young family destroyed, with only a brain-damaged child surviving. On the other, you had a young man expecting to get a good degree in IT who made the same mistake a number of others have made on that wretchedly unsafe road. He was not drunk, not going at a ridiculous speed. He just made an error of judgement. There was nothing wicked about what he did. I'm sure the jury convicted him simply on the basis of the tragic consequences rather than looking at the quality of the driving, but I had to respect the verdict and send him to jail. I always intended to give him as short a sentence as I could, before I believed him to be my son.

'After the accident but before the case came to court, Gary, stung by his exclusion from his adoptive grandfather's estate, had done some research. He traced his natural mother and persuaded her to tell him who his father was. He resented me for, as he saw it deserting him, and did not contact me. When I was allocated his trial he should have objected, but he saw it as fate giving him the means of getting his own back and said nothing. Throughout the trial he had worn a beard but for the sentencing diet he shaved it off and I could see his chin was unusually shaped, like mine. The reports showed he had been adopted and when I saw his date of birth I was sure. I should have explained the situation to counsel but I didn't. I went ahead and gave him one year, which was far too little for the relatives of the deceased. When I sentenced him, he silently mouthed "Thanks, Dad".

As the officers exchanged glances, the doorbell rang. 'You see to it. You know what needs to be done,' Flick told di Falco. Disappointment on his face, he went to deal with the various professionals summoned to a high profile sudden death.

Baggo shut the kitchen door then restarted the tape.

'That began my disenchantment with the law. They say when you get a bad press that it will be a seven day wonder, but the vilification I was subjected to left scars. I was "out of touch", "unfeeling" and "callous". When you see your photograph on the front page of a tabloid with the heading "unfit for purpose" it erodes your confidence, makes you hate your job. And all that was without my relationship with Gary being known. We're not allowed to comment on our cases so I couldn't fight back. Not that they'd have been interested in my reasoning.

'When you reach your goal in life but become dissatisfied, your compass, whatever has held you on a steady path, wobbles. I found myself using pretentious language to sentence pathetic drug mules to many years in jail when few big fish were caught. The criminals I dealt with were squalid and stupid. I never had a criminal mastermind in the dock in front of me. My son was guilty of an error of judgement that any motorist might make, yet finished up with a longer sentence than many a knife-wielding thug. Of course he didn't serve the full six years. No one does. The politicians encourage judges to impose crushing sentences but once they're in power they let everyone out early in order to save money. And that goes for the evil and dangerous ones as well as those who should never have been in jail in the first place. My job was a disappointment, my wife and I had drifted apart and I felt in some way responsible for what happened to my son. After Gary's appeal, I expected the truth to come out, but it didn't. I became used to living with danger and the adrenaline that comes with it. I wanted to rebel. I formed a bizarre respect for criminal masterminds, those who planned crimes and got away with them. In the end I needed to prove to myself, if no one else, that I too could do that.

'I thought up the Nicklaus golf course fraud and what started as a weekend pastime became an obsession. I had to put it into practice. After Gary's release I had made contact with him. It was difficult for a time but we established a rapport. I needed someone clever with IT for my scheme and was happy to find a way of giving him money and encouraging him back to doing what he was good at. He did not know that it was a criminal enterprise. I told him it was an entrepreneurial sideline which, as a judge, I shouldn't have been involved in. Of course when the fraud became known he understood. He has been guilty of no crime relating to it because he lacked guilty knowledge when he did what he did. His computing skill enabled me to pull the strings of the fraud without anyone suspecting my identity.

'The people I used …' the first side of the tape stopped. Impatiently Baggo turned it and played the second side.

'The people I used were people who deserved their comeuppance. Smail is a stupid snob. He had prevented me from joining the Archers although I had taught myself to shoot as well as most of them. Thomson had been an abusive father to my son. Maltravers, I'm sure though I can't prove it, obtains planning permissions with the aid of brown envelopes, and has been doing so for years. Burns is a crook whom I tried a few years ago. It was a nasty timeshare fraud, most victims being elderly or gullible, but there was simply not enough evidence and I had to rule that he had no case to answer.

'For the fraud, I sent the instructions to Burns, using pay-as-you-go mobiles and untraceable e-mails and let greed do the rest. The one person who knew what was going on was Tam Walker, who produced brilliant artwork and forged Nicklaus's signature. He knew to keep his mouth shut as he would have incriminated himself if he had informed on me. But when that newspaper offered a reward for information regarding Knox's murder, he guessed that I had done it and calculated that he could claim the reward without putting himself in danger. I had paid him well for his work but he tried to get more, threatening to contact the newspaper. I drove through to talk to him. I left my car a distance from the flats and wore an old jacket so I would not be recognised. I tried to persuade him to be sensible but he would not listen. There was a primitive statue to hand, and when he was stupid enough to turn his back on me I killed him.

'I killed Knox too. Before the archery he came up to me. He had been drinking and made it clear that because of a mention of Culrathie in an e-mail, he had worked out that I had been behind the scheme. He was not the sort to back off something like that and I knew I had to act.

After the archery I saw Mrs Traynor leaving Court Three by the judge's door. I recognised her as the woman Knox had been speaking intimately to after dinner. I had not known Gary would be there as a waiter, but I saw him and asked if he had seen a man coming down the corridor from Court Three and he said no. I went to the retiring room, picked up an arrow and went along various back corridors to Court Three. Parliament House is a rabbit warren and only judges and a few others would have known the route I took. I found him sitting back, self-satisfied no doubt, and I just thrust the arrow in. I used a handkerchief to prevent my fingerprints from getting on the shaft. I returned to the party and trying to act normally, I queued up for a drink.

'My son is entirely innocent of both these murders and he lacked the knowledge to be guilty of participation in the fraud. We met occasionally and in secret. Once his period of licence expired he intended to go abroad and I planned to resign early and follow him. The money from the fraud has been tucked away and I do not intend to reveal more.

'My only son has not deserved the ill fortune that has dogged him thus far in life. I hope that no over-zealous prosecutor will attempt to make him pay for my misdeeds.'

Flick and Baggo sat in silence, thinking. Di Falco opened the door. 'Can they take the body away?' he asked.

Flick answered, 'Yes. To Dundee. Dr MacGregor will be performing the post mortem.'

His valedictory message ringing in their ears, they

stood respectfully as the judge left his home for the last time. As the body was carried from the front door to the ambulance, a press camera flashed several times. Minutes later Baggo's mobile rang. It was Pete Bothwell.

21

'Well, what happened?' The DCC scowled from Flick to Baggo and back again. It was another lovely morning, another cancelled golf game. On the desk in front of him sat the cassette tape and that day's *Good News*. The headline screamed, WE EXPOSED HIM. Underneath it read, TOP JUDGE ADMITS MURDER THEN HANGS HIMSELF.

Flick said, 'Lord Hutton's name kept on coming up in the inquiry and a painting by one of the victims pointed to both him and another person, whom we believe to be his son.'

'Gary Thomson?' the DCC asked.

'Yes, sir. The trouble was the judge was very clever and there was really no hard evidence against him. We felt we had to flush him out, as you might say.'

'In the police force we try to bring criminals to justice, not drive them to suicide, Detective Inspector.'

'I know that, sir. It's just unfortunate the way things happened.'

The DCC snorted.

Baggo spoke. 'The idea was mine, sir, and DI Fortune took some persuading to authorise what happened. The problem was that we had overwhelming suspicion but no worthwhile evidence. Had we simply taken Hutton and Thomson in for questioning they would both have clammed up and we would have got nowhere. The *Good News* reporter Bothwell and ex-Inspector Osborne owed me a favour so I persuaded them to challenge Hutton.'

'You mean you told them about your suspicions and asked them to put the questions?' The DCC sounded aghast.

'Yes, sir. As a result we admittedly have a dead body, but a dead body that was guilty and made a confession. But for what we did, he would still be sitting as a judge in the High Court.'

'In the paper Bothwell claims to have found evidence to back up their questions.'

'Yes, sir. I allowed them a scoop on the condition that they took the credit for the investigation, rather than saying that we set the whole thing up. They were happy to do that.'

The DCC looked at Baggo. Slowly a smile spread across his face. 'But who did kill Knox, Detective Sergeant?'

'I don't know, sir. Either it happened exactly as Lord Hutton described on the tape or his son did it on his instruction. It is interesting that as yet we do not have independent evidence that Lord Hutton spoke to his son just before the murder. He obviously assumed we had, or would get it, and he gave an innocent explanation for their exchange.'

'So the murderer might go free?'

Baggo said, 'If Gary Thomson did it he did so because his father told him to. Anyway, Hutton did not try to deal with the Dolan murder in Glasgow and I hope we might build a case against him for that.'

'Why did you think getting the press involved would be more productive than questioning Hutton yourself?'

Baggo spoke slowly, choosing his words. 'With the press asking the questions they did, he would have known the truth about Gary would be bound to come out and suspicion would settle on both of them. One evening during the investigation, I visited him in the evening and he was drunk. Sometimes drunks open up to whoever is around, and he told me a lot about himself. He had suffered from having an abusive father and he saw it as a father's duty to protect his children. He was clearly bored with his job and was dismissive about the intelligence of criminals. I believed that he would take the blame for the various crimes to exculpate his son. I did not expect him to do it quite in this way.'

The DCC raised his eyebrows. 'Is there any chance of recovering the money from the fraud?' he asked.

'Perhaps some of it,' Baggo said. 'We're going through Lord Hutton's papers, mobile and computer, and if we find out who he dealt with in the Caymans, we might be able to put them under pressure. He would have needed someone local to split up the money and send it in different directions. It's called "layering". We do a lot of this work in the SFO.'

The DCC leaned back in his chair and smiled. 'It's a bloody mess, but overall, a not bad bloody mess. We have an identifiable perpetrator and Traynor's in the clear, but this must have been dreadfully embarrassing for him. If we can recover some money as well, it will be an excellent result. *Good News* will be horribly smug, but we can't have everything.'

At that moment, Flick felt a sudden, painful twinge. 'Excuse me, sir,' she said, 'I think I'm going to have a baby.'

22

'This has been a wonderful day,' Baggo said as he sipped his wine and waited for Fergus to bring in the lasagne. 'Ganesh was with me. I have broken ninety on the Old Course and I can die happy.' His good round of golf had completed a most satisfying period. He was making real progress in tracing the money that had gone initially to the Caymans, and his affair with Melanie continued to be magical for both of them.

On the sofa, three-week-old Verity Catriona Maxwell sucked hard at Flick's breast, causing her mother to wince. 'So what news?' she asked. She had been surprised by how she had taken to motherhood but had found it frustrating to be out of the loop. Inviting Baggo to St Andrews for golf with Fergus and an evening meal had been an obvious step.

'Burns sang like a canary. You know that after Hutton's confession became known, he pled guilty during Lord Tulloch's charge on the basis that he was not the ringleader. There was a great fuss and the lawyers got their knickers in a twist but his plea was accepted. He promised to tell the full story and I think he has. So he'll expect leniency. He got all his instructions from untraceable e-mail accounts and pay-as-you-go mobiles with voice distorters. He had no idea who was pulling the strings. All the time Hutton kept coming up with the goods, and kept paying his mother's care costs, so he just did as he was told. He was unable or unwilling to finger Gary Thomson. As you'll know, the other three were convicted by the jury and they all come up for sentence next week.'

'Are you getting anywhere with the money in the Caymans?'

'We should recover some serious amounts, but it will take a while.'

'And has the fuss died down about that mercy killing case?'

'I think so. As you know, the judges decided assisting suicide was criminal in Scotland, but when Nugent pled guilty, the judge taking the case admonished him, earning blood-curdling threats against him and Nugent. Nothing's happened so far and that has to be good.

'Oh, by the way, we heard from the Glasgow police that a CCTV camera picked up Gary Thomson, quite identifiably, hanging around outside the High Court at lunch time on the day Dolan was killed. You see the right-to-lifers leave and Gary follows them. He appears to have something under his jacket. A couple of the *Vita Dei* people have identified him as loitering around the High Court that day, but that was just from a photograph. The theory is, that after his early shift in Tesco, he stole a car, drove to Glasgow, killed Dolan, returned to Dunfermline, dumped the car and went to bed, pretending to you and

Billy di Falco that he'd been there all day. But that's just speculation, of course.'

'Will we convict him?' Flick asked.

'I think we should get him for Dolan's murder, even if he gets off the fraud. It was a good result, whatever, and like politics, policing is the art of the possible.'

ACKNOWLEDGEMENTS

All characters are fictitious and any resemblance to living persons is coincidental. With one exception. Brenda Lenaghan is a genuine artist, whose work we are proud to have on our walls. She is also great fun. Another supporter has been my devil-master, Bill Reid. I thank him for the idea of bringing a genuine legal issue, the criminality of assisting suicide in Scotland, into the plot.

I am very grateful to the people at Matador and above all to Annie, my wife, for her unfailing support, encouragement and correction of errors.

After a legal career that included sitting as a judge in High Court murder trials, Ian Simpson has been writing crime fiction. In 2008 he was shortlisted for the Debut Dagger by the Crime Writers' Association. He was brought up in St Andrews. This is his third published book.